A DANGEROUS ATTRACTION?

Renee laughed softly. "I was seriously considering Chicago already, but any incentives you can bring to my attention are appreciated."

Evan stepped even closer and whispered, "Here's one more."

His fingers slid down the strands of her hair as he drew her face to his.

A dizzying current raced through her. She was lost in the smoldering, steamy embrace and the touch of his lips ignited wild sensations, making her limbs quiver.

His lips were soft but demanding, and she met their request with her own. As they melted into one, she knew he could feel her arousal. Wanting, wanting, wanting . . . it was all raised a level as she heard Evan moan and felt his tongue touch her lips.

This was all going too fast. She used the last bit of reserve she had left to push away.

"Was I too fresh?" Evan's voice broke. "I just meant to give you a good night kiss."

She'd never been kissed like that before . . . the speed with which it took her body over with desire was almost frightening. . . .

SUDDEN LOVE

ANGELA WINTERS

ARABESQUE

BET
BOOKS

BET Publications, LLC
www.msbet.com
www.arabesquebooks.com

ARABESQUE BOOKS are published by

BET Publications, LLC
c/o BET BOOKS
One BET Plaza
1900 W Place NE
Washington, D.C. 20018-1211

First Printing: June, 1999
10 9 8 7 6 5 4 3 2 1

Printed in the United States of America

This book is dedicated to the members of my immediate and extended family, and all those people who have known me since I was a child. The pride and happiness you've all shown at my success as a writer is priceless and means so much to me.

ONE

"You've got mail."

"Not now." Heavy into her typing, Renee Shepherd was reluctant to open her e-mail again. She'd just spent an hour and a half going through her messages, trying to answer each and every one. She wanted to ignore it, but the thought of letting it build up again was too distracting.

"Fine, fine, fine," she said out loud, even though she was alone in her apartment. She was always alone in her apartment.

Clicking the icon for her message box, she saw one message from a KKJLove@icom.com. The subject was QUESTION. She didn't recognize the sender's tag, but clicked on it anyway. Her e-mail address was printed in her last book, and readers regularly sent her e-mail, asking questions or commenting on something she had written.

To: RShepard
From: KKJLove
In the attachment to this message is
some information on a nutritionally re-

lated organization that I think might be fraudulent. I recently read a maga- zine in which you were quoted as an expert on health and nutrition and thought you might have contacts in the know. I already know you've writ- ten books about the issue this organi- zation claims to represent, so I'm asking what you might know. I know it's a long shot, but I'm desperate with nowhere to turn right now. Please respond A.S.A.P. I don't think I have much more time.

Renee read the message again. Fraud? What did this mean about not having much more time? Nowhere to turn? She was never sure if these messages were real or hoaxes. She'd gotten plenty of both, but this was a little different. Fraud wasn't anything she was familiar with. With a careless sigh, Renee downloaded the attachment, found it again and clicked the PRINT button. As the monitor on her printer blinked, the display read that twelve pages were coming. Twelve? She hadn't even finished packing for her trip. She clicked the reply icon and began typing.

Reply: KKJLove
I received your message. Unfortu- nately, I am on my way out of town. I have taken down your e-mail address and will contact you after I have a chance to look over your information. One piece of advice. If you really think fraud is at play, go to your superiors or call the authorities. As merely an expert on health and fitness,

my services would be very limited
here. Still, I'll see what I can do.

The papers were still printing as she sent the e-mail and began to compose a new one to Patricia Kelly. The flow for writing was gone, so Renee figured she might as well send a message to her best friend who was getting harder and harder to reach these days.

To: P&T
From: RShepherd
Where you been, girl? Forgot me al-
ready? Some best friend. Need an ear
to whine to. On my way to Chicago.
Write me back.

Renee had met Patricia Kelly five summers ago when Renee and her younger sister, Michelle, attended her self-defense class for women. It was one of Renee's only success-ful attempts to bond with Michelle. They'd had a great time. Even though Patricia's career as a systems engineer paid the bills, she taught the class three times a year at a local YWCA.

Both graduates of NYU, Patricia and Renee hit it off immediately. It was a surprise, being as opposite as they were in every way. Renee was tall at five foot nine, while Patricia barely made five foot three. Until her recent cut, Renee had always worn her jet black hair long and conser-vative with very little makeup and soft, basic clothes like sundresses. Patricia wore a lot of makeup, had short fash-ionable hairdos that changed every few months, and was a slave to attention-grabbing fashion. Renee was serious, life experiences having made her so, while Patricia couldn't be serious for five minutes if her life depended on it.

Romantically, Renee craved independence and control,

while Patricia always dreamed of the shelter of hopeless love and marriage with a man who would take care of her. Renee never tried to change Patricia, knowing her dream fit her needs. Patricia was unique and always would be. She wanted herself a husband from day one. That was her career goal and, despite her technical talents, she had quit her job without a second thought and became Mrs. Tony Robson last year. She'd gotten her dream.

Renee couldn't ignore the sudden feeling of doubt that final thought brought. Didn't they both have what they wanted? Renee wasn't sure how to phrase what it was she actually had? The rewards of independence or the consolation prizes of isolation?

Those were the questions that popped into her twenty-eight-year-old mind as she left her computer and strolled to her balcony, viewing New York City from her Central Park West apartment. It was spacious and warm, with soft tans and light, underwhelming pastels. Renee wasn't into the antique or ultra modern look. Her home was like a catalog cover for Pottery Barn.

Wasn't this the life so many women wanted? A single black woman making it on her own. It was a life where you made your own choices and determined your own financial destiny. Situations, challenges, and life in general were all clearer. Weren't they? Renee wasn't so sure anymore.

As she closed her dreamy, jet black eyes and felt the cool evening breeze touch her face, the doubt began to lift, but it didn't leave. It wasn't like the old neighborhood in Brooklyn. This breeze didn't tempt you with the smells of yams cooking or fried catfish. Instead, she smelled fresh paint coming from somewhere. That was it, but that was New York City.

Central Park was always beautiful to Renee on June evenings when the sun had begun to set and the sky was a purple and orange flame. The grass was a cool green and the trees were full of leaves. From her coveted, high-rise apartment, she'd spent many days sitting on her balcony watching the rollerbladers, joggers, and bikers poke out from the trees as they performed their daily ritual along the paths. She'd taken a thousand jogs there herself, but lately they'd been alone. She remembered them with more joy when she had been with a friend or a lover.

It was something she'd encouraged in her book, *The African-American's Guide to Fitness,* published a little over a year ago. She had devoted an entire chapter to the benefits of choosing an exercise partner, increasing the odds when it came to sticking with a fitness program. Her previous books, *Nutrition for the African-American* and *The Black Woman's Guide to Eating Right* also encouraged exercise as a necessary lifestyle component for today's black man and woman. All three books flew off the shelves, giving Renee a level of financial independence anyone would envy. It allowed her to travel and meet interesting people from all professions and walks of life. Most importantly, it allowed her to put her younger sister, Michelle, through college.

When their parents had died eight years ago in a tragic plane accident, Michelle was only thirteen and Renee twenty. It had been the longest summer of both of their young lives. Renee knew nothing would ever come close to such pain. The shock seemed as if it would last forever, and the hurt and loneliness even longer. Renee's foundation had been pulled out from beneath her, and she was expected to go on. At the time, she didn't believe she could, but after a summer, fall, and winter of uncertainty, she found the strength to return to college at New York University while Michelle moved into their grandmother's home in Brooklyn, only three blocks from where they had grown up. Half of the life insurance helped Renee finish undergraduate school and acquire her master's degree, while the rest went to help their retired grandmother support Michelle and save for her college.

When their grandmother passed three years later, Renee was Michelle's only family and means of support. The responsibility forced Renee to grow up fast. It was terribly difficult dealing with a teenager, especially one as wild and emotional as Michelle. Renee knew she could never replace a mother or a father, but she wanted the best for Michelle as she'd gotten herself. It wasn't easy with a meager income as a nutritionist and part-time fitness instructor, especially when the money left by their parents began to run out.

The idea to write a book came to her while she was dating a young pediatrician, Dale Talen. Dale, whom she met at a local community conference, expressed his constant concern for the unhealthy diets of so many of the black children he saw, especially those from economically depressed neighborhoods. He tried to counsel their parents, but it was difficult; there were so many and he was only one man. His commitment inspired Renee, who wondered how such an important message could be spread, not only in the boroughs of New York, but across the country. That's when she thought of writing a book. Parents would buy it and help their children. Doctors would buy it and counsel their patients. The press here and there would reach community leaders and politicians.

With her knowledge of nutrition, several months of research, interviews, and queries to publishers, Renee began a new career as an author. Impressed with her first attempt at writing, her publishing house signed her to a contract for two more books with a hefty advance. Renee quit her job to write full time. Her own future had become clearer. Michelle was going to be all right. She had choices she hadn't had before. They both did.

Renee had chosen to be independent. She loved

Michelle. She loved Patricia. She had a few friends she cared for, and there had been a couple of men she'd let in, but never too close. She wasn't ready for that type of commitment, although she wasn't sure why not. All the women she knew her age were either moving in with, getting engaged to, or marrying the love of their lives. Just like Patricia, whose love of her life, Tony Robson, had proposed last year. A quick wedding was followed by a military assignment to Japan.

"I've still got New York," Renee said to herself. She was one of a small but resurfacing group of people who openly, admittedly loved and adored their native city. Well, more often than not at least. New York could be hard on a person at times, and Renee had experienced many of those times, only they seemed to come more often lately. In the past, she'd always called Patricia and they would complain to each other. Only now Patricia was gone. Michelle was at school in Chicago and was coming home less and less often. There was no man in Renee's life now and there hadn't been for a while. New York didn't seem to make up for it all, as it had in the past.

Renee reached down and grabbed the letter she'd left on the balcony chair. Her lease would expire in two months and her landlord was sending her a second notice to renew or he was putting the apartment on the block. Earlier that day, she'd held it in one hand for an hour, a pen in the other. She came close to signing her name, only to pull back. She needed to think about it, and in doing so, her mind wandered as she got lost in the glowing sunset.

Renee knew she would be a fool to give up this apartment. There was probably a waiting list of unlimited numbers for a spacious two-bedroom apartment overlooking Central Park. She had waited a couple of years for an opening herself. There was an exercise room with a pool, a small convenience store, a deli, and a dry cleaner in the building. On a rainy or freezing day, she didn't even have to step outside. Who could ask for more?

"For Pete's sake," Renee said out loud, trying to convince herself as she turned to answer the ringing telephone. "I have underground parking. Everything a girl could ask for."

"Hello?" Renee took a seat in the comfortably worn leather swivel chair at her work desk.

"Hey, hon, it's me."

Renee recognized her agent, Karen Buckley's deep, raspy voice immediately. She sounded like a smoker, but had never touched a cigarette. "I just came from Prior Publishing and you're gonna love me."

"Tell me you sold my book." Renee crossed her fingers, biting her lower lip.

"Well, I went through the whole spiel again." Karen feigned a sigh. "You know, all about how after those high sales of your previous books, your contract with Becker Books was complete. I let them know Becker was very interested in a multibook deal, starting with *Soul Food Renewed,* just so they knew. A book of soul food recipe makeovers with lower fat and less sodium-filled alternatives will fly off the shelves. Prior was sniffing at my worm."

"Karen!" Renee was ready to spin in the air. She got so excited every time. "What happened?"

"Patience, love. You'd think you never sold a book before. You're supposed to act like this is old hat now. Really, it's fine. You're not interested in hearing about all my hard work getting your word out to our people, that's fine. Cut to the chase. Not only did I get your book sold, but for a five thousand dollar higher advance than Becker offered. Royalties are higher, too." Karen's jubilance was evident over the phone. She was in her usual chipper mood. "Higher by four percent. Plus, and there is a plus.

Plus, they want to discuss turning this into a very lucrative three-book deal. Now what d'ya say?"

"Karen, you're fantastic!" Renee let her pride and excitement show. Hearing your first book would be published was a unique feeling, comparable to none, but hearing it every time after that was still elation. Number four! If only her parents were here to see this, to know this.

"Now you know that's not what we rehearsed," Karen said. "What are you supposed to say?"

"I'm so sorry, I forgot." Renee stifled her laugh. "Thank you sooo much, Karen. You're the most beautiful and intelligent sister this side of Chi town. Was that right?"

Karen acted as if the words she had jokingly coached Renee to say came as a surprise. "Thanks a mill. So sweet of you. Just doing my job, but it's nice to be appreciated. They'll have the contract ready in two weeks. We'll set up an appointment to go over it with a fine-tooth comb then."

"I'm not sure I'll be here in two weeks," Renee said, glancing at the calendar above her computer.

"You're not still on that *I'm leaving this city* kick?" Karen sighed. "You can't leave New York, Renee. You've been here all your life. This is the place to be."

"It's not a kick," she corrected. "I'm seriously considering it. You're right. I've been here all my life and it's getting a little tired, but that's not what I meant just now. I'm just leaving for Chicago tomorrow. I'm going to visit Michelle."

"For two weeks? I thought she was in summer school?"

"She's only taking two classes so she can graduate at the end of the summer. She's got a part-time job, too. I'm sure I'm the last thing she's interested in, but I miss her, ya know?"

"How could I not?" Karen asked. "You remind me all the time. But two weeks sounds like a lengthy stay. The main reason I get along so well with my sister is that we spend as little time as possible with each other."

"I was planning on two weeks, but maybe . . ." Renee hesitated, knowing Karen was against her leaving New York. "Well, who knows?"

"I knew you were losing it last week when you went and cut all your hair off, but I'm really starting to worry about you, Renee. You're usually so sure. Every time I talk to you now, you sound so indecisive."

"I'm fine," Renee answered, uncomfortable at how obvious she must seem if Karen could tell so much from phone conversations. She didn't want to admit how detached she was beginning to feel. "Lay off my hair. You're always telling me I need some change, some excitement."

"Yeah, but six inches?" Karen asked. "I tripped when I saw you last week. Still no regrets?"

"None." Renee remembered her surprise when she first looked in the mirror at the salon.

Even though she'd wanted six inches, the finality of it all was more emotional than she'd expected. Then later, she was disappointed. The change, the risk, hadn't satisfied the need within her for more than ten minutes. She still felt in a rut.

"You have my sister's number," Renee said, returning her thoughts to the present. "Call me there if anything comes up."

"You gonna call her with the good news?" Karen asked.

"I thought about it for a second." Renee sighed. "I'll save it for tomorrow."

"The same old thing?"

Renee found Karen surprisingly intuitive. Or maybe she just told her so much. "Yeah. You know there's no telling how Michelle will react to my good news."

"I know. Sometimes she's happy for you. Other times . . ."

"Dead silence," Renee said. "Nothing. At least face to face, I figure I can see her expression and go from there."

"You'll work it out, hon. I'm sure you will. She's just a kid."

"I keep telling myself that." Renee's problem with that excuse was that Michelle was twenty-one now. The teenage mood swing excuse wasn't pulling the weight it used to.

"Hey, Renee?" Karen's voice came through after a short pause between the two.

"Yeah?"

"They were so impressed with you at Prior, honey." Her words were almost a whisper. "They really really want to meet with you. You're great girl."

"Thanks, Karen."

Renee replaced the receiver feeling better than she had a second ago. She knew when Karen used that tone, she truly meant every word she said. She was a well-respected agent in the business, representing a handful of big-time authors, and she knew a good book when she saw one. She was the one to first contact Renee after reading her first book. Agreeing to take Karen on as an agent had been one of the best career decisions she could have made. Karen knew everyone in the publishing and promotions business. She was tight with all the big players at the major chains, too: Barnes & Noble, Borders, Waldenbooks, all of them. Their partnership was a main ingredient in the success of Renee's second and third books. Karen expanded the black urban professional audience, a booming, well-paid target group.

Their partnership had also developed into a nice friendship. Karen was from the Midwest, thirty-eight, and married with two children. She and Renee had nothing in common outside of her writing career, but had found a way to get to know each other as women and form a friendship.

Renee reached for the printed out pages from KKJLove and folded them. Standing up, she glanced at the lease renewal from her landlord before heading for her bedroom to finish packing. Maybe it was time to move on. As an author, she knew she could live anywhere she wanted. Somewhere without snow, without traffic jams that lasted for hours every day. Maybe Miami or Phoenix. There are some black folks in Phoenix, she told herself. Some. Would Michelle like Phoenix? No, she'd like Miami better, Renee concluded. Only, Miami could get a young woman into a lot more trouble than Phoenix. Maybe Atlanta. No, they had traffic jams, too. Who knew? Renee was only happy to have an abundance of choices, even though she couldn't seem to make a single one.

Renee darted across her living room and placed both suitcases at her front door. They each weighed a ton. The doorman had just called for the second time to tell her the airport taxi was waiting.

"That snooze button got me in trouble again," she told him, as if he would care. He didn't.

"He says he's leaving in five minutes. No exceptions."

Everyone had their vice and being late was hers. And, of course, she had the nerve to be merciless with anyone who kept her waiting. Her flight left La Guardia in two hours. Grabbing her carry-on case, she looked around the apartment one last time. She would still forget something, she always did. Hopefully it wasn't anything too important.

Patricia!

Hoping for a reply message from her best friend, Renee clicked on the computer. Her laptop was already packed; or she would have tried in the cab. She knew she was pushing it, but she had already planned to tip the driver generously. She always did. Five minutes. She'd make it.

"You've got mail!"

"Yes!" Renee saw a message had been sent last night.

Only it wasn't from Patricia, she realized as soon as she opened it.

> To: RShepherd
> From: KKJLove
> PLEASE read materials I sent right away! I'm afraid someone knows what I suspect. Can't go to police because have no evidence. Can't go to boss because might be involved. Please hurry. I'm scared someone knows.

Renee paused and read the message again. Scared? What's this all about? Noticing the errors, Renee assumed this person was either tired or in a hurry when they had typed it. She felt sorry for them, but she was no detective. She would do what she could, which was read the information and tell the person what she thought, but that was it. Why would the person be scared? Of what, of whom? Was it that serious?

There was no time to reply as the telephone rang again. She knew it was the doorman.

During the flight to Chicago, Renee glanced through the materials KKJLove had sent her. It was all about BFK, Brain Food for Kids, a nonprofit organization based in Chicago, Illinois. BFK collected donations from the community and corporations through the persistent soliciting of mostly college kids. In turn, the money was used to buy and deliver healthy foods to impoverished families across the city's south and west sides. Renee had been sent a description of the organization, a couple of brochures copied on paper, and the latest quarterly financial reports. Renee made the connection, although weak. KKJLove must be familiar with her first book, discussing studies and reports on the relationship between children's diets and IQ levels and thought she knew of the organization. Only she hadn't even heard of BFK. She had a lot of catching up to do on her own industry. She did know a few doctors and professors in the Chicago area who had assisted her with information on those particular studies. She would refer KKJLove to them the first chance she got to reply, but there was only so much they could do. If the organization was fraudulent, although it seemed legit on paper, this KKJLove needed a watchdog group, a reporter, or a detective. Not another author, doctor, or college professor.

Renee returned the papers to her purse as the in-flight meal arrived. She knew she could hook her computer up, running on batteries, but the man next to her was doing the same and coach seats were too tight. She had no arm room. She wanted to relax and think of the fun things she could do with Michelle in Chicago. Shopping on Michigan Avenue, riding rollercoasters at Six Flags Great America, going to a Cubs game or one of the city's five-star steakhouse restaurants. Only she couldn't, because KKJLove's message stayed on her mind. Scared? That's what the message said. Was he or she scared of someone finding out what they suspected or of someone doing something to him or her as a result? Could it be that serious?

"Renee! Renee!"

Standing in the terminal lobby, Renee turned to find the face that fit the familiar voice. With a smile ear to ear, her eyes landed on little Michelle. Now a twenty-one-year-old who had blossomed into a beautiful young woman, she wasn't so little anymore. With long black hair like Renee's used to be and large black eyes, she looked so much like her older sister. She was tall and slender, also, but the physical was where the similarities ended.

Only thirteen at the time, Michelle had taken the death of their parents very hard. She fought the attempts of therapists, acting out her anger and pain, rebelling often. Renee remembered the arguments, confrontations, and cries into the night. It had torn her apart. She had tried her best to understand Michelle, but Renee had been young herself.

More accepting of the loss as she matured, Michelle Shepherd was still a little wild and rebellious, while Renee was always the responsible and stable one. She didn't have a problem with that. It had always been that way, and Renee assumed it always would.

Although she wasn't happy with it, Renee accepted Michelle's decision to leave New York for Chicago's Loyola University, majoring in liberal arts and sciences. She knew Michelle needed to get away from the city she had spent her entire young life in . . . the city that held so many years of parentless memories. Although Renee thought New York offered everything and anything one could want, Michelle could only think of what she didn't want. She'd felt confined and restricted. Renee understood that now more than ever. She wanted to believe that the move was best for both of them. They clashed so often. Living apart, they were both able to be their own person, while finding easy excuses to spend time together. Only, it was almost always Renee who initiated that time spent together, and those times were coming less frequently as Michelle became entrenched in her young adult life. Which only made right now more precious, Renee thought as she opened her arms for her baby sister.

"How's my little girl?"

"Stop that." Michelle wrinkled her nose and smiled a tender smile before stepping back to look at her older sister. Her long hair fell without order over her face. "Look at you."

"What?" Renee swung around for surveillance. She was dressed down in a Yankees baseball shirt and blue jeans.

"The hair." Michelle's mouth stayed open as she picked at her sister's short cut, ending just above her shoulders. "You really chopped it, girl."

"Thirty's a couple of years away." Renee picked up her carry-on. "I felt a more mature look was in order."

"You still look like a kid, Ms. Never-Wears-Nothing-But-Lipstick." Michelle snatched the carry-on from her sister and headed for the baggage claim.

"I spent a lot of money on this cut. You could at least say I look more mature, a little more sophisticated." Renee followed along, smiling just at the sight of the young woman she hadn't seen since Thanksgiving. Michelle had spent last Christmas in Europe with friends. It was a horribly lonely holiday for Renee. She had felt like she was invading Patricia's family gathering. "So how are your classes going?"

"Pretty good," Michelle answered with a shrug. She pulled the hanging clip to her denim short overalls back over her shoulder, only to have it fall to the side again. "I'll be able to graduate with the summer class. Don't worry."

"I wasn't worried." Renee noted the hint of cynicism in Michelle's voice. "Why would I be worried?"

"We both know I was supposed to graduate this spring with the rest of my class." Michelle's quick steps seemed a little harsher now that she was a foot or so in front of Renee. "I know you were disappointed. It's costing you a lot of money for the summer semester."

"I don't care about the money." Renee sighed, not wanting to bring up the *M* word. The result was always an argument. "The money has never been a problem. Not anymore at least."

"You finished undergraduate school in three and a half years, even after taking a semester off." Michelle's tone was edging on a confrontational remark.

"Michelle, please." Not the comparisons again. Michelle got into her moods when making comparisons was all she wanted to do. Renee had hoped for a few hours of peace beforehand.

"I know. I'm sorry." Michelle turned to her sister and smiled, her young face glowing with a natural beauty. "I actually have some great news."

"Good," Renee said, deciding to hold off on her news of the sale of her fourth book. Not the right time. Maybe later that evening, or tomorrow. Maybe next week. It would be nice for them to bask in Michelle's good news alone for a while. "What is it?"

"Let's wait until we get out of here," Michelle said as the two women boarded the tram that would take them from the terminal to the baggage claim.

It was a quick, efficient ride, and they soon had Renee's bags and were in the parking lot, Renee was hit with her first surprise when Michelle stopped behind a brand-new red convertible BMW and proceeded to open the trunk.

"What's this?" Renee asked. "A rental? Where's the Pontiac?"

"That old thing you bought me?" Michelle laughed with an indulgent smile as she loaded the suitcases. "It's still kicking, but I left it at home. This is part of what I needed to tell you. My great news."

"Let's have it." Renee kept her eyes on her sister as she positioned herself in the passenger seat. The car was no more than a year old, if that. There were still faint smells of new. "Let's start with who this car belongs to."

"It belongs to the man in my life." Michelle smiled with

pride as she backed out of her space without looking either way. "His name is Nick Hamilton and he works with me at Augusta."

"So Jason is out?" Renee asked, referring to Michelle's last boyfriend. Jason was the soccer player who never went to class. Before him, Keith was the biology major who had a bad habit of borrowing money that he never paid back. Now it was Nick Hamilton. Well at least Nick had a job.

"I already told you Jason was out." Michelle waved a dismissing hand. "I kicked him to the curb months ago."

"So Nick's a student?" Renee knew mostly students worked at the Augusta Foundation, an umbrella company for several local charities. They made phone calls to corporations and homes, asking for donations to the various causes. They also performed a lot of administrative paperwork, which was what Michelle did.

"No, he's the finance director." Michelle paused to pay the gatekeeper for parking. "Didn't think I could get that high did ya? Well I did, and he's twenty-eight and gorgeous. He's incredibly dynamic. He'll be very successful one day. One day soon."

"Why haven't I heard about him before?" Renee asked, thinking twenty-eight was pretty young for a director's role in any organization, even a small one.

"We've only known each other for three months," Michelle answered. "But three months was enough."

"Enough for what?" Renee wondered why her sister hadn't mentioned this *dynamic* guy in the dozens of phone conversations they'd had in the past three months. "Enough to know you love him?"

"Enough to know I want to spend the rest of my life with him." With a giggle, Michelle held out her hand to show a modest engagement ring. She twiddled her fingers with delight before returning her hand to the steering wheel. "We're engaged."

"Are you insane?" Renee roughly twisted in her seatbelt to face her sister. "Tell me you're kidding."

"I knew you'd be this way." Michelle shook her head as she made a left turn without using her signal. She didn't notice she almost caused an accident. Didn't seem to hear the angry horns around her. "This is why I didn't tell you about him."

"This is ridiculous!" Renee threw her arms in the air and let them fall to her lap. "I don't believe you. You still have school to finish. You have to think about graduate school. Married? You've only known him three months. How long have you been engaged?"

"Just this past weekend." Michelle was all smiles, seeming to ignore Renee's disapproving glare. "Don't worry. We're not going to elope and I'm not pregnant. We practice very safe sex."

"You what?" Renee was taken off guard at the idea of her baby sister having sex, but Michelle was almost twenty-two. She remembered being twenty-three herself, what some would consider a late bloomer. After her parents death, she'd been so reluctant to let anyone close. "Is he your . . ."

"My first?" Michelle laughed. "Close, but no. Nick was my second and he's fantastic. He knows how to—"

"I don't need to hear that part," Renee interrupted with vigor.

"Why not?" Michelle asked. "You're the one who taught me all about it. You should be proud. You told me I have to love the guy, practice safe sex all the time, and be responsible and willing to accept any consequences that . . ."

"Enough," Renee said, wondering if she'd been right to be so free with sexual advice. "I meant for you to be aware, not active. Let's get back to this engagement."

"We haven't set a date yet," Michelle continued like she was discussing her grocery list. Like Renee's mouth wasn't wide open. "I won't expect you to pay for the wedding. I know that's what you're thinking."

"Would you get off this money trip you're on?" Renee looked out her window at the road that was zooming by quicker than the speed limit allowed. She was trying to calm down. Yelling only made things worse with Michelle. "That has nothing to do with it."

"Are you sure?" Michelle asked as if she knew more about Renee's intentions than Renee did.

Renee held her frustration in check, focusing on the concrete expressway. She had to rationalize the situation and knew she couldn't do that if she was angry. It wasn't a disaster, she told herself. They were only engaged, not married. Not yet.

There was a long silence as neither woman seemed to know what to say. As Michelle sped across the interstate and headed for Lake Shore Drive, Renee wondered, as she had for years, why her sister viewed her the way she did. Money had been high on her list of concerns when they didn't have any, but they hadn't been in that situation for a while now. She couldn't help but wonder if she did place too much emphasis on money, but simply couldn't see it herself.

"You're gonna love him." Michelle finally spoke with a reassuring nod. "I'm taking you to Augusta right now to meet him."

"Michelle," Renee pleaded. "I'm in my traveling clothes. I look like a bum. I don't want to meet the people you work with like this. Your fiancé."

"You couldn't look like a bum if you tried," Michelle said. "You're what the brothers call a natural. Look, it's between here and home. We're going, and when you see him, you'll love him."

"You seem very sure of yourself." Focus on the positive, Renee told herself. Just chill out.

Michelle sighed breathlessly. "Renee, these past three months have been the best three months of my life."

"Tell me about them," Renee said, hoping she'd hear something to make her believe three months was enough time to know you want to marry someone. "Tell me about Nick."

"I met him when he started at Augusta six months ago." Michelle anxiously squirmed in her seat as she made a hard right. "He's from New York, too. From the Bronx though. I think it's crazy my soulmate lived in the same city as me for all those years, but you know how the boroughs are. They might as well be different states. He mostly ran with the Manhattan Wall Street crowd. He's very attractive. Tall, dark, and handsome. He's got this thing about him, you know. A cool aloofness that I love."

"That's attractive to you?" Renee figured Michelle had read too many of those old romance novels as a teenager. Older, wealthy man is terribly cruel to younger, helpless waif who can't help but fall deeply in love with him, torturing her soul because he's a complete jerk.

"Yeah, girl." She winked. "I love his control. He's got a very powerful personality. He didn't notice me for a couple of months, but I caught his eye and he liked me right way. Next thing I knew, we were spending every second together."

Renee wanted to know more, but it soon became obvious that was all Michelle had to say. "What is he like, though?"

"I told you." Michelle frowned as she swerved left, the new tires screeching.

"No," Renee said. "I mean his personality, his beliefs, how he treats you."

"He's a successful businessman." Michelle's irritation was evident in her tone. "He's not a bum."

"I didn't say that, but if you're going to marry someone . . ."

"Wait till you see the butt this boy has on him." Michelle pulled into Augusta's parking lot. "He works out almost every day. Look, just try to understand for my sake?"

"I want to." Renee shook her head, still uncertain. "I see you're happy and that's all I want, but. . ."

"Then fine, because I'm deliriously happy."

"It's only," Renee said, probably knowing she'd regret this, "you have that impulsive streak, and it gets you to do things you end up regretting soon afterward."

"Nothing so serious it couldn't be easily rectified." She parked over the line, making it impossible for someone to park in the space next to her. She didn't notice.

"That's not so with marriage." Renee saw Michelle's brows center in frustration. "Okay, I know your life is your own, but don't you feel like you have some more growing up to do before you commit yourself to something as serious as forever?"

"In case you hadn't noticed, sis"—Michelle slammed the driver's side door shut as they exited the car—"I'm an adult. I'm grown up."

That was a whole other argument that Renee didn't have the strength or desire to get into. So, she'd shut up for now.

She'd hoped Michelle would go to graduate school next year, although that was still a possibility. She'd also hoped Michelle would return to New York to start her career. Was that likely now? Think positively, she reminded herself, only hoping this Nick Hamilton was as fantastic as Michelle said. If so, then he would be supportive of Michelle's education.

"I'm anxious to meet this guy," Renee said, hoping to ease her sister's growing bad disposition.

* * *

The hallway was small, with beige-white walls and a blended blue and white speckled carpet. They could hear voices, but couldn't see anyone as they stepped onto the third floor.

"I guarantee you'll be impressed." Michelle's eyes lit up, her hair framing a hopeful face.

As Renee came face to face with someone, she was more than impressed with what she saw. The immediate attraction only made her hope this wasn't Nick Hamilton.

"Oh, hey, Mr. Brooks." Michelle's voice lifted to a high pitch as she greeted the man standing in front of them.

He responded, using her first name and flashing an electric smile for the young girl before turning to Renee.

His smile intensified for Renee and made the hair on her arms stand up. She eyed him back with a kind smile of her own. He was, by her quick judgment, the most handsome man she'd ever seen. A little over six feet, he had skin like smooth milk chocolate. His bald head was sexy, clean shaven and perfectly round. His thin-rimmed designer glasses were styled to fit exactly to the shape of his face and complimented his strong nose and piercing light brown eyes. In a denim button-down shirt, neatly tucked into khaki slacks, he looked like a male model, but with a little thicker build than most.

"This is my sister Renee from New York," Michelle said as the two stared at each other in silence. "Renee this is Evan Brooks. He runs things here."

"Hello, Mr. Brooks." Renee held out a long, soft hand she hoped wasn't shaking as she was all of the sudden very nervous. Maybe jet lag, she thought.

"Please call me Evan." He slipped his hand over hers

softly before gripping it firmly. "If I can call you Renee."

His hold was commanding, and Renee felt a quick jolt of power surge from her arm all the way to her face, flushing its cinnamon color with a flirtatious red. Something told her this was not jet lag.

TWO

Renee quickly withdrew her hand, hoping it would reverse the blush caused by his touch. She turned to her sister, who stood very amused, watching the two of them.

"Nice of you to grace our offices," Evan said as his eyes stayed with Renee.

"Michelle wanted to show me where . . . she works." Renee tried to hide the discomfort she felt from his eyes being directly on her by turning her face from his, but it turned back against her will, as if it had a mind of its own . . . as if her eyes were yelling, *we want to look at him!*

"I want her to meet Nick." Michelle's voice erupted with excitement as she mentioned her fiancé's name. "Tell her, Mr. Brooks. Nick is great, isn't he?"

Evan tilted his head with a laugh. "Well, he's definitely something." He blinked, the wide smile gone, but still pleasant. "How long are you planning to stay in Chicago, Renee?"

"I'm not sure." Was it possible that he was becoming

more attractive as the minutes went on? She liked his deep, cool voice and could tell he knew the effect he had on women. Smooth. He was used to this, even though he didn't seem to revel in it. "Possibly two weeks."

"Possibly more." Michelle wrapped an arm around her sister, claiming her proudly. "She's single you know."

"Michelle!" Renee's mouth flew open as she pulled her arm away. She could slap the girl clear across her face.

"That's very good to know." Evan's brows raised as he briefly glanced with amusement at Michelle.

"I'm sorry." Renee sighed, holding on to what little pride she had after practically being auctioned off. "Kids."

"Don't apologize," he returned, showing his bare ring finger. "I'm one of you, too. Michelle is deserting us, but we single folks got to stick together."

Renee laughed, forgetting momentarily how nervous this man made her feel. She was sure he'd taken a step closer to her just a moment or so ago. Or had she stepped closer to him? She couldn't think. She felt a little dizzy.

"You're a Yankees fan, I see." He lowered his eyes to her shirt, noticing the insignia.

"All my life." Renee tried to act as if his eyes' lazy linger didn't bother her, but it was hard. They made her more than usually conscious of a body she was normally proud enough of not to have to fuss over. Now, she wished even more that Michelle had let her change clothes and freshen up before coming here. Being tall and slim, she had a natural advantage in anything she wore, but that assurance wasn't enough for Renee right now.

"You a Mets fan, too?" he asked, pushing his glasses up his fine nose after they had slipped a bit.

She shook her head. "Only the Yankees."

He wiped imaginary sweat from his brow. "That's good. There's still a chance for us."

"Excuse me?" Renee asked, alarmed not so much at

what he'd just said, but by the quick rise in her temperature his words evoked.

"I'm a Cubs fan," he answered. "I could never date a Mets fan. We'd be lifelong rivals. Now, I like the White Sox, but not enough to hate their rivals, the Yankees."

"I wasn't aware we were dating," she said, finding his flirtation presumptuous at the least.

"Not yet." A cool, smooth smile formed at his lips as he raised a confident brow.

Renee raised a brow of her own, letting him know she wasn't so gullible. Although he looked like he was what Michelle would call *all that,* she wouldn't let him know she thought so.

"She's thinking of moving here." Michelle interrupted the charged banter between the two.

"Michelle." Renee stared sternly at her sister. "It's just a thought. Don't go telling people that."

"I hope I can help make it more than a thought," Evan said. "If you need any help, I mean with realtors, I can probably give you some names. I'm a pretty good tour guide myself."

"I'll keep that in mind." So, she had an excuse to contact him, if she chose to. She was tempted. She wasn't going to try and deny that for a second, but she quickly reminded herself she was here to see Michelle, not for a vacation romance.

Evan glanced at his watch and frowned. "I'm sorry, I have to go. We've got a serious issue to handle."

He stepped to the side of both women, pressing the elevator button. Even under the long sleeves of the cotton shirt, Renee could see his muscles.

"Is it about Kimmy?" Michelle asked with concern.

"Unfortunately." Evan's smile faded a little as he turned to Renee again. "I'm sure I'll see you again, Renee."

Renee said nothing, only smiled appreciatively. She was

flirting a bit, she knew, but he was the real culprit here. *I'm sure I'll see you again.* He was definitely a little cocky. Usually Renee was unimpressed, but as he flashed a last smile before the elevator doors closed in front of him, she felt her toes tingle. Life was made for exceptions.

"Wow." Renee exhaled in the comfort of her sister being the only one around to hear. "Is he always that . . . that . . ."

"Yeah." Michelle shrugged in response and headed down the hallway. "Come on."

"What's wrong?" Renee noticed her sudden mood change. Had she said the wrong thing again? There was no telling with Michelle.

"It's just sad." Michelle opened a hallway door and let Renee through before entering herself. "Kimmy. I mean, Kimberly Janis."

"Who is Kimberly Janis?" Renee stepped into a room full of chattering, racing college kids. A couple of kids stared, showing momentary interest in a new face before returning to their work.

"They found her late last night," Michelle said, her eyes to the ground. "Or early this morning, I guess. She jumped off the twentieth-floor balcony of her apartment."

"Was she a friend?" Renee winced at the tragic picture as it flashed in her mind. She could see Michelle was more affected than she wanted to show.

"Sort of." Michelle stopped with a heavy sigh. "She worked here and we talked sometimes. We went out for drinks after working late. She was kind of interesting, acted very individual, had a lot of stories to tell. Her mom was from Nigeria and Kimmy visited there a few times. She was only twenty-one like me. Just a student."

Somewhere, behind a cubicle, a student cheered, yelling that he'd just got a grand. His first thousand dollar donation.

"Maybe you should see a counselor about it." Renee touched Michelle's shoulder, squeezing gently. The pain of death was neverending. If she could wish for one thing besides having her parents back, she would wish for Michelle to never be hurt by an untimely death again. She knew that was impossible. "You know you can always talk to me."

"I'm fine," Michelle said. "It's just sad."

As Michelle looked past her, Renee noticed the somber frown quickly turn to a delighted smile as her sister's face lit up like a Christmas tree. Renee knew what the cause was before she even turned around.

"You must be Nick Hamilton," she said, holding her hand out to the young man who approached them with cool, confident strides.

Nick Hamilton was a handsome young man of normal height, his skin a coffee-colored brown. He had small brown eyes and a thin mustache above full lips. He had a very strict, businesslike haircut and a sharp, tailored suit to match. He looked clean-cut, but the expression on his face bothered Renee. It was overconfident, unlike Evan's tempered yet flirtatiously cocky expression. She couldn't explain it exactly, but she'd come across a lot of men in her work and life in general. Most were nice, but some were so full of themselves. It could've been a doctor who thought he was God's gift to the world of medicine or a Wharton MBA who could only talk about how successful he was. They had a standing expression, those men. Nick had that expression on his face now.

"And you're Renee, the famous author." Nick's voice was naturally raspy and his tone curt.

"To you," Renee responded, "I'm just Michelle's big sister."

"Isn't he fantastic?" Michelle wrapped her arms around

Nick and kissed his cheek. She looked at him like he was the grand prize at a competition. All hers.

Renee noticed Nick merely touched Michelle's side in response to her embrace. So, he wasn't one for public displays of affection. That surprised Renee, knowing Michelle was to the point of annoyance.

"You two are gonna love each other." Michelle's eyes switched from Nick to Renee and back. "You should have lunch while she's here. Just the two of you."

"We'll see," Nick responded, not seeming too anxious. "You know how important I am to Augusta. I don't have a lot of free time."

"I hear you head finance here," Renee said, trying to break the awkward silence that came after his quick dismissal of Michelle's suggestion.

"For now I do." Nick raised his chin, with a confident smirk. "I plan on moving into corporate finance in the securities market, but the foundation is a great stepping stone."

"I told you he was going to be very successful one day." Michelle nodded in agreement with herself. "Nick says he'll be the best thing that ever happened to stocks and bonds. *Black Enterprise* will want to put him on the cover every month."

"Well someone has to pay the bills." Nick gave Michelle a quick pinch in the rear before detaching himself from her affectionate grip.

Renee forced a curve of her lips as Michelle laughed away his chiding remarks. She knew she had only met him a few minutes ago, but was certain she didn't like him. Too condescending.

"Michelle," Renee said after passing Nick a sharp look. "I really need to get some rest. You know what flying does to me."

"And I've got to get back to work." Nick pecked Michelle on the cheek. "It was nice to meet you, Renee."

"Same here." Renee shook his hand as her lips formed a tired smile. Somehow, she knew he wouldn't expect more than that.

"Isn't he delicious?" Michelle kept her eyes on him as he walked away. "Look at that butt, girl. Didn't I tell you."

"You're not marrying a rear end," Renee said. "I hope you know that."

"Oh, hush." Michelle waved her sister's comment away with a swipe of her hand.

"That wasn't a very nice thing to say," Renee said. "Someone has to pay the bills."

"He's just joking." Michelle lightly socked her sister in her arm. "Loosen up. He always makes fun of my major. So did you, remember?"

"Well, I hope he was joking." Renee followed Michelle down the hall as they headed out the way they'd come in. She didn't remember ever making fun of Michelle's major. Had she? "He's not very affectionate is he?"

"Not everyone is big on hugs and kisses." Michelle shrugged. "He gets close when we're alone. He's not the PDA type."

"He just seemed a little cold," Renee added.

"Listen," Michelle said with an irritated tone in her voice as she stood in place. "He may not be a doctor, a lawyer, or a college professor, but I love him. Do you have to criticize everything about me?"

"I don't do that." It hadn't passed by Renee that Michelle had mentioned the occupation of her own past lovers. "He just seemed . . . well."

"Just because I'm not a famous author . . ." Michelle's tone was sarcastic, but in a whisper as people passed by. "It doesn't mean I'm . . ."

"What do I have to do with this?" Renee asked. "This is about you. Your choices and your decisions."

"Which never make the grade for you." Michelle paused from her snappy retort to greet an Afro-sporting coworker passing by. "I don't need your approval to be with Nick. All I want is for you to respect the fact that I love him. Cut me some slack, okay?"

They rode to Michelle's campus area apartment in silence. Renee was never sure how to handle these situations. Michelle was always on the defensive. Renee knew she was critical of Michelle, but only with the intention and purpose of helping her mature. She was trying to be like parents would be, questioning their children's choices just enough to make them develop a pattern of thinking before making the next one. She wanted Michelle to learn from her mistakes, to save her from repeating them. Especially with men. Wasn't that what big sisters were for?

In reality, she was very proud of her little sister and knew she would accomplish great things in the future. She just needed to focus. Renee wondered what she was doing so wrong to make Michelle react the way she did. Time and time again she assured her that no one was comparing them and that she had Michelle's best interest at heart whenever she criticized her. The situation was getting worse, and Renee knew she had to find a solution before it tore them apart. They were all the family each had left, and nothing was more important than that.

Back at the apartment, Renee settled into the sofa. Michelle's one-bedroom apartment was modest in size, but placed in a relatively safe area of the city. Most of the furniture was older and used, but still held up. Some Michelle had taken from home in New York, some pieces were left by the previous owner, and others Michelle had picked up at local garage sales. The combination gave the place a young, somewhat scattered but nicely intended look, like its owner. The living room sofa was the only new piece in the place. After almost breaking her back on the old one when she made her first visit, Renee bought Michelle a deluxe sofabed. Thinking back, she wondered if the act had insulted her sister. She was almost afraid to ask.

"Sorry, I was checking my messages." Michelle appeared from around the corner. "You settled in?"

"I'm getting there." Renee reached for her purse. "So what's next?"

"Why don't we have dinner?" Michelle sat across from her sister in an old but comfortable brown La-Z-boy. "I've got to go to a study session for my stats class, but we can meet somewhere."

"It's your city." Renee leaned back, feeling the jet lag. "Tell me where and I'll hop a cab."

"I've got to think." Michelle jumped from the sofa. "There's so many choices. I'll call you from my cell phone."

"Cell phone?" Renee didn't even have one of her own. "Where did you get a cell phone from?"

"Nick." She stuck her tongue out teasingly. "He didn't want me off on my own without security. See, he is a nice guy."

"Yeah." Renee thought it was more likely he didn't want her anywhere he couldn't reach her to keep tabs on her, but she'd give him a chance. One point for Hamilton. "He's paying for it, right?"

"He bought the phone. Isn't that enough?"

"Michelle." Renee took the point back. Minus one now. "Those monthly fees can be expensive."

"I have a job, silly." Michelle grabbed her purse. "See ya, love ya."

At least Michelle had a smile on her face, Renee thought as she watched her leave. Maybe she was just having a bad day earlier. Maybe Nick was having a bad day. Maybe, Renee thought, she was just overly critical after a long flight.

What she knew was that the girl was certain she was in love and she looked the part. It was clear from the look on her face. Not just bright and happy, but in love. Renee had seen it on Patricia's face when she was with Tony. She saw it now on Michelle's face. She couldn't remember ever seeing it on her own face, although she'd been in love before. Or so, she'd thought.

Shaking off the suddenly depressed mood that wanted to sweep over her, Renee focused on one of the positives that had emerged from today and that was meeting Evan Brooks. She wasn't going to get him off her mind, so why try? His *GQ* look and lazy smile was branded in her memory. Yeah, he was a little self-assuming, but not too much. She wondered what woman had that in-love look on her face because of him. She remembered he said he was single. A smile lit her own face.

On her way to the bedroom, Renee passed the mirror and stopped to take a look at herself. Michelle was right. She did look like a kid in her T-shirt and jeans. Overall, she was proud of her looks, born of genetics and a healthy lifestyle. Her jet black hair was shiny and strong, her cinnamon brown skin was soft, clear, and smooth. Large eyes, an average nose, and full curving lips. Regular exercise kept her figure firm and toned, her curves womanly and soft. Her tall frame helped her carry weight well and the daily approving eyes of men and the surveying eyes of women confirmed it. Renee had seen that approval in Evan Brooks' eyes today, but as flirtatious as he was, she wondered if he didn't look that way at every woman. He'd probably seen a million faces prettier than hers, with figures fitter than hers. Would he be interested in what was inside the package as much as he seemed to be interested in the package itself?

Renee laughed at herself for acting silly over a man she'd just met, and for less than five minutes at that. She walked over to the empty drawers Michelle had set aside for her. She tried to forget the spark she'd felt when he shook her hand, but she knew that wasn't going to be easy. Rarely did any man impress her with presumptuous comments and charming smiles she'd heard and seen a hundred times. So when one did, it was something to reckon with. Especially someone as sure of himself as Evan gave the appearance of being. Those were the seductive ones, the ones who made a woman forget her principles. She was careful to stay away from those. She knew she should stay away from Evan Brooks.

Placing some of her perfumes on top of the dresser, she noticed the pictures slid neatly inside the edges of the attached mirror. There was a picture of Michelle alone, smiling as brightly as sun is lit. There was a picture of Michelle and Nick with someone's dog in a park. Nick was barely smiling. There was a picture of Michelle and some girls in a bar, all young, beautiful women. Renee reached for the photo and turned it over to read the names. She knew Michelle always coded a picture on the back, just in case one day she couldn't remember.

April 98: Me, Rave Girl, Jackie Slick, and KKJLove. Rave Girl's 21st B-day!!!!!!!

"KKJLove?" Renee turned the picture over to look at the exquisite, dark-skinned girl on the left edge of the photo, trying to remember why that name was so familiar to her.

Then it hit her! She ran to her bag, lying open on Michelle's bed. She reached inside, rumbling through and pulling out a stack of folded papers. Unfolding them, her eyes went directly to the top left corner of the page. Sheet after sheet read KKJLove@icom.com.

Renee had heard of coincidences, but this was too much. Just then, her eyes caught the poster on the wall, next to the mirror. The screaming fuscia letters read: THE AUGUSTA FOUNDATION. Underneath the title were organizational chart blocks separating all six of the organization's charities and its executives. Brain Food for Kids was the second block to the left and Kimberly Keyana Janis's name was right inside the Finance Department block. Kimberly Janis was the woman who had committed suicide early that same morning!

Renee fell back on the bed as she made the connection, her mouth wide open. Kimberly Janis was KKJLove and she was dead. Could it be a coincidence? No, she decided that was impossible. Kimberly had written about knowing her from reading something, but Renee wondered if Kimberly was trying to avoid any connection with Michelle. But why? Renee didn't understand. Michelle knew Kimberly and had spent some time with her socially, even if only a little.

Remembering again that the last message had been sent late last night, Renee wondered what had happened between then and the early morning hours to make Kimberly want to kill herself? It couldn't be because she was so upset about a simple misrepresentation going on at a small charity. It had to be more. Maybe this was the last straw. Maybe the girl had problems and, as her illness reached its peak, she convinced herself someone was after her. If someone was bad off enough, imaginary fear could make them kill themselves. That didn't make sense to Renee. Her curiosity was piqued regardless now, because she felt somehow involved. She made the decision to ask Michelle more about Kimberly Janis at dinner.

After a long luxurious bath, Renee rested in the living room. As the answering machine picked up the phone call, she listened to Michelle repeat their plans for the evening.

"Hey, sis." Her voice came over scratchy on the cellular phone. "Where ya at? Probably passed out. You got some terrible jet lag. You should take some ginger. Anyway, we'll go to DiVinci's for dinner. Its on Halsted. Its not too formal, but it's nice. I have a change of clothes at Nick's. It's closer to me and easier than coming back home. I'll see ya at seven thirty. I made reservations."

"Sounds good," Renee answered as she returned her head to the soft pillow.

So, Michelle had a change of clothing at Nick's apartment. To Renee, even that seemed a bit fast for a three-month relationship. Just thinking of the engagement again made her eyes roll. Maybe if they were planning a long engagement, it would make her feel better. Only she knew Michelle, and even though she'd said from the onset that eloping wasn't in her plans, Michelle never waited a long time for anything she wanted. That was part of her problem.

With a sigh, Renee glanced up at the clock on the wall. Four thirty. "Plenty of time for a quick nap." Her eyes slowly shut.

"I said seven thirty." Michelle's hands were on the hips of her black velvet dress, making indentations in the smooth kente cloth strap around her waist. She waited for her sister to come up the stairs to the restaurant. "It's eight."

"I'm sorry. I'm sorry." Renee finally reached the doorway. "I fell asleep and it's only seven forty-five. Your cabbies drive slow."

"Only someone from New York would say that." Michelle looked Renee up and down, smiling her approval. "New dress?"

Renee nodded, taking a moment to straighten the spaghetti straps on her peach and white cotton sundress. She'd tried it on at Saks Fifth Avenue a couple of weeks ago and loved the way it draped her figure, flattering her every curve. It was fresh, soft, and sexy in an unassuming way. She had to have it.

"We already got a table," Michelle said, entering the restaurant.

"We?" Renee asked as she greeted the hostess. "We?"

"Oh, I forgot." Michelle turned to her sister. She held an index finger between her teeth and a childish grin on her face. "I told Nick he could join us."

"Michelle." Renee pursed her lips together to check herself. "I thought it was going to be just you and me."

"We have plenty of time for that," Michelle said as they reached Nick at the table. "You'll be here for a few weeks. Nick's very busy."

"It's nice to see you again, Renee." Nick nodded almost forcibly as he stood up while both women sat down.

"Hello, Nick." Renee decided then and there to wipe the slate clean with Nick. She wouldn't let the fact that she'd really wanted to be alone with Michelle cloud her judgment of him.

She glanced around the restaurant, noticing its pleasant, elegant design and intimate lighting. There was a nice mixture of folks patronizing the establishment, mostly couples, all well dressed. *Summer in Chicago is a glorious time,* their faces said.

"This place is a little pricey," Renee said, her eyes rolling down the menu. "Michelle, you don't spend your money at places like this, do you?"

"Can we not talk about money tonight?" Michelle asked in annoyance.

"I'm sorry." Renee wished she could take her words back. Maybe Michelle was right. Maybe she did place too much emphasis on money.

"Anyways," Michelle said, "the restaurant was Nick's idea. He went on and on about it. We had to come here."

"I have my reasons." Nick looked around the place, seeming preoccupied with other thoughts. "It's a nice place."

"How was your study session, Michelle?" Renee decided to generate a discussion as it seemed Nick was unconcerned with either of the women.

"I didn't go." Michelle pressed her lips together as she kept her blinking eyes on the menu. "What do you guys have a taste for?"

"Why not?" Renee asked.

"Nick got off work early." She shrugged casually, as she was so accustomed to doing. "So I hung out with him at his place."

"Afternoon appointment canceled," Nick said with a smile that quickly faded as he seemed to realize Renee didn't care about anything he had to say.

"Isn't statistics the class you're having the most trouble with?" Renee asked, trying to hide her disapproval. She was sure she knew what they were doing, hanging out. "That's the class you didn't pass last semester."

"Just rub it in, why don't you." Michelle rolled her eyes.

Renee sighed, lowering her menu to the table. She

couldn't seem to say anything right. "I'm just trying to understand why you would—"

"Please," Nick snapped at the women, standing from his seat. "No bickering. Not right now."

Renee stopped in the midst of her sentence. No he didn't, she said to herself. Who was this man to curtly silence her? He didn't know her like that. Not at all. To hell with clean slates, she was ready to give him a piece of her mind.

Before she could speak, she suddenly realized he was no longer interested in her, but someone approaching from behind.

Evan Brooks entered the dining room, a statement in itself as he wore a sharply tailored black suit. Turning around, Renee felt a rush of heat run through her at the sight of him. She hadn't forgotten how attractive he was from that morning, but in this suit, right now he was magnetic. She felt her pulse race as she took in a full view. Then as sudden as anything, her heart screeched to a halt when she saw he wasn't alone.

She was beautiful. Tall as a runway model and very trim, her caramel skin glowed and her reddish-mahogany tinted hair flowed down her shoulders. She wrapped her lanky, jeweled arms around Evan, and Renee felt a tinge of jealousy she knew was unwarranted. There was no reason for her to care, but she couldn't deny she wasn't happy at the sight of them exchanging pleasant glances.

Renee turned away, looking again at her menu. She couldn't concentrate enough to read a line straight through. She wanted to pretend she didn't care, but that was impossible. Especially as Nick waved for the two to come over. Renee felt her mind taken to distraction. Trouble.

"Hey, Evan!" Nick offered an eager smile and outstretched hand to his boss. "What a surprise seeing you here."

"Nick. Michelle." Evan shook the man's hand and smiled at Michelle. He turned to Renee and his smile widened. "I told you I'd see you again, Renee. Glad I was right?"

"Hello, Evan." Renee smiled before turning away to hide the flush she felt at her cheeks as his eyes momentarily lowered to take in a full view. She was bothered by this involuntary and seemingly instinctive response to him.

"Alicia." Evan wrapped a gentle arm around his companion. "This is Nick Hamilton and Michelle Shepherd. They work at Augusta. This here is Renee Shepherd, visiting from New York. Everyone, this is Alicia."

"Very nice to meet ya'll." Alicia spoke with a sweet southern accent as she smiled, showing her perfectly white teeth.

"Likewise," Renee said in unison with Nick and Michelle. She found some satisfaction in the belief that Alicia's blue sequined dress seemed overboard for the restaurant. So maybe she wasn't perfect.

Nick quickly dismissed the waiter who had come to take their order so he could go on about how much of a coincidence it was they ran into each other since he'd never dined here before. Renee knew this was no coincidence whatsoever. Michelle seemed annoyed as Renee studied her face, doing everything she could to keep from looking at Evan.

She could feel his eyes on her constantly, like lasers, heating her brow, making her wonder if she'd applied her makeup right. Were her thin straps sturdy? Too much cleavage? He was so aggressive with his attraction. She was surprised he was so deliberate with his gaze while in the company of another woman. She was more surprised that she wasn't as offended by that as she knew she should be.

"So, Renee." Evan's words stunned everyone because

they interrupted Nick in the middle of a sentence. "Enjoying Chicago so far?"

"I always enjoy this city." She lifted her head and smiled politely, thinking he was entirely too attractive for his own good. Probably never even had a pimple.

"Excuse me, sir." The hostess cordially tapped Evan's shoulder. "Your table is ready."

"You all have a nice dinner," Evan said to all before turning again to Renee. He paused and caught her eyes. "I'll see you again, Renee."

"Have a nice evening," was her only response as she turned to her drink, examining the glass like it was just as interesting as he was. He was very confident, wasn't he? It unnerved her. She didn't doubt she'd see him again, and that truth made her more nervous than she'd been in a very long time.

"Bull's-eye." Nick made a victorious fist as he smiled with pride and sat back down.

"That's what this was all about, wasn't it?" Michelle asked, now with a full scowl.

"What are you talking about?" Nick leaned back in his seat, satisfied as if he'd already eaten and was full.

"This was all about running into Evan Brooks." Michelle swung sideways in her chair, staring her fiancé down.

Renee was happy to see her sister realized what she herself had figured out the second Nick asked Evan over. She was also happy to see her show a little strength, having begun to believe that Nick was the only boss in this relationship.

"And done perfectly." Nick noticed Michelle's frown. "What difference does it make to you? I'm treating you to dinner at a nice restaurant. Just be quiet and order."

"Hey!" Renee wasn't about to sit by and allow anyone to talk to her sister that way.

Nick's eyes darted at Renee, making it obvious by his

expression that he wasn't used to anyone confronting him as she'd just done. She met him with a formidable gaze and he quickly turned his attention to his menu with a stubborn frown and mumbled an apology. The waiter's return gave everyone a chance to calm down, but as he left, Michelle continued.

"You thought you impressed him? That's what you thought, wasn't it?" She took a quick sip of her martini.

"How do you know I didn't?" he asked with a self-assuming, although annoyed expression.

"Because any idiot within three tables of here could see all he was interested in was my sister." Michelle rolled her eyes to finish telling him off.

"I don't know about that," Renee said, not for Nick's sake, but to divert the conversation from herself and Evan.

"Like you didn't notice," Michelle said, calling her bluff. "If he hadn't gone off to handle that horrible mess with Kimmy Janis this morning, you would've probably been sitting here with him instead of us."

"But someone else is here with him." Renee looked in Evan's direction. She had a clear view of his table and spotted him just as he caught her glance. A ripple of excitement shot through her, making her turn away quickly.

"So what?" Michelle asked. "You're up for a challenge, aren't you?"

"Speaking of Kimberly Janis," Renee said after rolling her eyes. "Did you know she sent me e-mail twice yesterday?"

"How did you know Kimberly?" Nick asked.

"I don't." Renee corrected herself. "I mean, I didn't."

"What did she e-mail you?" He placed his napkin on his lap as the waiter brought their salads.

"Some brochures on Brain Food for Kids." Renee thanked the waiter.

"Just brochures?" Ignoring his food, Nick leaned in

closer over the table, his eyes intently on Renee. Before she could respond, Michelle spoke up.

"She asked me about you just last week." Michelle paused like she was trying to remember. "I've talked about you before. Told her about your books. She kept asking about what you knew about stuff. Wow, that's pretty weird that she mailed you and didn't tell me."

"What stuff?" Nick asked again, passing Michelle an annoyed look for interrupting.

"Just for my insight on the charity." Renee assumed Nick's concern was genuine. He had worked with Kimberly. It made sense he cared. "I guess she thought I might have been familiar with it."

"What kind of insight?" Michelle asked.

"I'm not sure exactly, but it seems like she thought something illegal was going on." Renee took a bite of her salad, reminding herself how hungry she was. She hadn't eaten since the flight meal, which she barely picked at. "Maybe misrepresentation of purpose or illegal use of funds."

"She was acting very weird last week," Michelle said. "She seemed . . . I don't know. I guess, paranoid. That might explain a lot. I just never thought . . ."

"Did she say what she thought was going on?" Nick asked. "If there's something fishy, I need to know about it. I'm the finance director, and my reputation is on the line if someone's doing something. I can't have my name connected to negative things like this. Not at this point in my career."

"Not really." Renee should've guessed this was Nick's real concern. His own business reputation was at stake. Who cared about a young girl's suicide? "She was a little incoherent. Her typing seemed like she was rushed or uncertain."

Nick poked at his salad. "She was doing a lot of that

and more than just this past week. She'd behave paranoid like Michelle said one minute and depressed the next. I never really liked her. She had too much drama in her personal life. She was weird."

"Do you think it was a chemical imbalance or something like that?" Renee asked, still wondering why the young girl would go so far. "Emotionally, it doesn't make sense. I've read a little psychiatry and usually when someone first becomes depressed they attempt suicide with no intentions of following through. Especially women. It's a call for help."

"Maybe she wasn't taking her medication," Michelle said.

Renee knew Evan was looking at her. She was doing anything she could not to look at him. "What medication?"

"I don't know." Michelle shrugged. "Aren't depressed people supposed to be on Prozac or something like that? Maybe she hadn't been taking her pills recently. You know, Nick, like your aunt."

"Dammit Michelle." Nick slammed his fork down. "I told you I don't want people to know about that."

"This is my sister." Michelle sighed, turning to Renee. "He's embarrassed because his family isn't perfect. Whose is?"

Renee was confused. "What's the issue here?"

Michelle waited for Nick to speak, but he only frowned at her. She smacked her lips impatiently before speaking for him. "Nick has an aunt in New York. She's a manic depressive. She takes Prozac or some variation of it. It's not a big deal."

"I don't like to talk about it." Nick pouted as he sipped his drink.

This one's a charmer, was all Renee could think. Not only is he mean, but he's a pouting baby. She really needed to talk to Michelle, but how?

"The point is," Michelle continued, "she takes the medication and she's perfectly normal. Just like you and me. You were just visiting her last week, Nick. She's fine isn't she?"

"I wasn't visiting her." He picked up his glass, put it to his lips but didn't take a drink. "I was handling family business. She was there."

"But she's fine, right?" Michelle asked.

He shrugged. "Kimberly just transferred to Loyola from Penn State last year. Who knows how many times she's been depressed? No one even knows why she transferred. Every time I asked her, she brushed me off, like she was real uncomfortable talking about it."

"Let's drop it." Michelle's face held a disconcerted frown. "Let's talk about something positive."

"Yeah, let's," Nick agreed.

With a sigh, hoping for the best, Renee told them both of her new book deal. A pleasant surprise, Michelle was elated instead of envious and Nick found it within himself to appear a little impressed.

There were no more arguments that evening. Michelle had been busy planning activities for the two of them, and Renee was interested in every one. She did her best to participate in the conversation, but it took all her strength just to appear involved with Evan staring at her throughout the evening. His gaze was distracting and disturbing, but at the same time she found it stimulating and satisfying. No man had ever piqued her curiosity like this. Why was he different?

She waited at their table as Nick walked over to Evan to say good night. She managed a farewell nod as he looked one last time in her direction before heading for the door.

* * *

"Evan was on to you, girl." Michelle turned sideways in her seat to look at Renee. She smacked the dashboard to add emphasis.

They'd said their goodbyes to Nick and had been on their way for a little while.

"What do you mean?" Renee asked, knowing exactly what Michelle was talking about.

"Brother's got bank is all I know." She snapped her fingers. "His eyes were glued to you. Anyone could tell."

"Including his date," Renee added. "Which was kind of rude, don't you think?"

"She may have been his date, but if she was his woman, she would've cut him with her butter knife. You know a sister don't play that. It must've been a business dinner or something noncommittal."

"You've thought this through, haven't you?" Renee had to admit to herself how much she hoped Michelle was right. "Whatever the case, it's not polite. He's a bit aggressive."

"You know who he reminds me of with you?"

"Who?" Renee was used to Michelle not making sense when her thoughts got ahead of her words.

"Alex Cassidy," she said. "The lawyer. He was so fine. He seemed to have it together all right. Doesn't he remind you of Evan? They dress kind of biz casual. Preppie, confident, and determined."

"I hope to God he's nothing like Alex." Renee felt her stomach turn just thinking of her ex-lover. "He was a long time ago. I'm surprised you remembered him."

"He was nice to me." Michelle paused, before letting out a heavy sigh. "I guess I mean he seemed to only have eyes for you. He seemed to care about you a lot. Evan seems like he'd be that kind of guy."

Renee hadn't told Michelle the whole story about Alex Cassidy. He was a mistake from the beginning. Yes, he was a confident, determined, and successful lawyer on the outside, but he was possessive, jealous, and controlling inside. Michelle had confused Alex's need to control Renee's every move with care.

"That relationship was a growing experience," Renee said. "You live, you learn. The main thing is finding a guy that respects and cherishes your individuality and independence."

"Nick thinks that's a bunch of crap." Michelle pulled down the passenger side mirror and played with her face.

"What does he mean?" Renee wasn't at all surprised. "Men don't have to be that way or women don't really want that?"

"The second thing. There." She pointed to an available parking spot, which turned out to be a fire hydrant. "Damn."

"Michelle, please."

"Sorry." She giggled. "Parking is guerilla warfare around here. Gotta be tough."

"That's okay with you?" Renee asked. "That he thinks that way."

"He doesn't mean it." She rolled her eyes before pointing again. "There's one."

"Michelle, you know this big Pontiac ain't fittin' in there." Renee didn't even slow down. "Doesn't mean what? What did he say?"

"That women really do want a man to take over. I mean, not like caveman type, but that women don't want to be burdened with the big decisions in life."

"How can a marriage be a partnership if only one person is making all the big decisions?"

Michelle stared at her sister for a moment. "I guess . . . Well, he was just kidding. I think."

"You need to find out." Renee pulled into a space just one foot into the illegal area on the corner. She didn't care. She was tired.

"You need to call Evan Brooks," Michelle said, un-snapping her seatbelt. "He's after you."

"We'll see." Renee was used to catching the eye of attractive men and being tempted, although none quite as fine as Evan Brooks. The only difference was, in those cases she knew most of them were just interested in the wrapping. If she wasn't interested, she merely ignored their stares and they'd eventually turn away. It was different with Evan. She could tell he wasn't one to turn away easily. She wasn't sure just what he was interested in, but still she couldn't get him out of her thoughts and had to admit she wasn't trying hard to.

Falling into a comfortable sleep that night, Renee revisited his smile across the restaurant over and over again and laughed at herself, thinking a little crush never hurt anyone.

THREE

"Thanks," Renee accepted the Marshall Fields' bag handed to her by the saleslady. The bag held the hottest pair of emerald green suede pumps Renee had ever seen.

"You're welcome." She flicked back a straying strand of sandy blond hair, revealing inch-long black fingernails. "Special occasion? These ain't no everyday pumps."

"Yeah," Renee answered. "Only, I haven't been invited yet."

"Window shopping gone awry?" The sales woman laughed. "Happens a lot."

"I always come to Water Tower Place when I'm here. My plan was only to browse, but these shoes hooked me."

"They're absolutely gorgeous," she said. "You made a beautiful mistake. Don't be so hard on yourself. Where you from?"

"New York."

"Just think of Michigan Avenue like Madison Avenue.

I'm sure you can't make it down there without putting a serious hurt on your credit card.''

"That's why I stay away," Renee said as she turned and headed out.

Midday on her second day in Chicago was setting in as Renee returned to the hustle and bustle of Water Tower Place Mall. The streets outside were twice as busy as inside, and Renee felt right at home. Even the cab ride to Michigan Avenue was a near death experience. Just like home.

She enjoyed watching the suburbanites in their fold over socks and khaki shorts taking a day from the calm for a bit of excitement, clutching to each other for dear life as they crossed at the light. She observed the executives, too busy running quick errands on their lunch break to crack a smile and realize how beautiful a day it was. She'd been to Chicago just under ten times and found herself liking it more every time. Even in late January, when she thought she would freeze to death from the cold winter chill reaching right through her thick coat. The wind felt like a slap in the face, but it was part of a trade off for a glorious summer in a wonderful city. Renee could see herself living in Chicago, and with Michelle's new plans, she thought she might need to seriously consider it. Getting married. Married to Nick Hamilton. She rolled her eyes at the thought. Michelle couldn't even keep a plant alive for more than one week.

Heading up the escalator, around the center of the third floor and down the elevators to the main dining room of the Ritz Carlton Hotel, Renee decided to think it over during lunch. She knew her choice was indulgent, but decided she deserved it. It was her congratulatory gift to herself for another book sold. She laughed at her temporary lack of humility while alone in the elevator. She praised herself on rare occasions, but her confidence had grown with each book sold and with time. She considered herself a successful author and a successful woman and had just recently begun to realize that was okay. There was nothing snotty or haughty in that. It was a great accomplishment. She even began to see herself as a role model of sorts for all those young African-American girls out there wondering how far they could go with that urge to take a pen to paper.

"Michelle is right," Renee said to herself. "I just need to relax, chill out."

She asked the waiter for a copy of the *Chicago Sun Times* after he delivered her grilled calamari appetizer. She sipped a glass of chardonnay and gazed out the large windows overlooking downtown Chicago.

Renee knew she needed to treat herself more often. She'd always held back, just in case. Just in case Michelle needed something more. Just in case the books stopped selling. Illness, even worse. She just wanted to be prepared for it. But right now, today, it was time to let life be that just in case she was waiting for.

The idea of getting her Ph.D. came to mind again as it had occasionally in the past. If Michelle chose not to go to graduate school, Renee knew her money situation would loosen up, allowing her to continue her own education. She thought of the University of Chicago as a possibility. Northwestern University in Evanston. With this recent engagement, Renee had to face the strong possibility that Michelle was staying in Chicago. She'd been wanting a fresh look for a long time and would love to be near Michelle. They had these issues in their relationship that needed to be addressed. She wasn't certain she could solve the occasional spite that seemed to stem from her sister, but it was important she do something about the constant comparisons. Only, what was that something?

If Renee knew anything, it was that relationships weren't her strong point.

There was Dale, the doctor who introduced her to the idea that spawned her first book. She'd always be grateful to him for that and remembered the fun they'd had together when they found the time. Dale was the first man she made love to. She remembered it being an awkward situation, neither of them knowing much of what to do, but Dale was sweet and patient, two important characteristics for a successful doctor. Only the relationship didn't last as long as she'd thought or hoped it would. Dale was devoted to medicine and Renee became immersed in her writing and in looking after Michelle. They were both young, and as they found themselves, they went their separate ways. Renee had wanted to keep it together, but had no idea how.

Then came Alex Cassidy. She shuddered at the thought of that mistake. Never again.

She'd tried harder to hold on to what she had with John Bryant, a professor at Columbia University. Very attractive and young at heart, John was several years older than Renee and when she interviewed him for one of her books, she had no idea this was the man she would call her lover for two years. She enjoyed being with John and cared deeply for him. She respected his intelligence and learned from his worldliness. Their friends suggested they marry, but Renee wasn't ready for such a commitment. This became a problem for John. With a pained heart, Renee remembered the night when it all came to a tilt.

"You know I wasn't interested in marriage when we were first together," John said as they shared dinner at Morton's, famous for its steaks. "It's been a few years now, but my divorce was very ugly. It left a bad enough taste in my mouth to turn me off to the idea ever again."

"I know." She reached across the table, gently brushing his caramel-colored cheek. She loved the warmth of his soft beard. "I told you I understood."

"I'm asking you to understand again." He took her hand in his, squeezing tightly. His hazel eyes beamed into hers. "I've gotten over the past. I'm ready to move on."

"What about living together?" She didn't want another argument, but could see one coming.

"I suggested that a year ago." He waved the waiter away. "You didn't want it then."

"I didn't think it would be appropriate then. Michelle had just left for school. I was adjusting to adult life on my own. She'd need a place to come back to on breaks and holidays and I didn't think it was a good idea."

"And now?"

"Now, it's diffcrcnt." Rcnee knew it wasn't really different. She just didn't want to lose him. She loved John.

"Well," he said with a sigh, "now it's different for me. I love you, Renee. I want to get married. I want children, and I'm almost forty."

Renee's eyes lowered to the table, her hand slipping from his. Her heart told her this wasn't fair. Not to John. She loved him and she would find strength in that fact. Only, she knew she couldn't marry him. She wasn't ready to love to a degree where loss would devastate her again. And she knew in reflection that John's similarities to her father were too strong to trust that she wasn't looking for a replacement, although she kept telling herself she wasn't.

"I can't, John," she whispered. She felt the tears swelling in her throat. She knew this was it, and it hurt her more than she'd expected. It tore her apart. "I'm so sorry, but I can't."

There were other men, but Renee was never intimate with them. They were casual acquaintances; dates for special occasions and lonely Saturday nights. Besides Alex, she didn't have any regrets. She enjoyed the company of men, only sometimes she wondered if she'd ever love someone with a burning sun intensity. Would there ever be a man who made her toes twinkle just from the sound of his voice? One hadn't made his way to her yet.

As the waiter handed her the day's paper and her pasta dish, it struck Renee that she hadn't made love to a man in almost a year and a half. Did she miss it? The heat she felt come to her face told her, yes, she did miss it. Who wouldn't? She closed her eyes, trying to picture herself making love to a man. Her eyes flew open as Evan Brooks' image appeared in her picture.

Where did that come from? She was frightened, even though this was her own imagination. She wasn't ready to go there.

Turning her attention to the paper, she passed over the usual bad news: corrupt politicians, crime, road construction causing backups for miles. It reminded her of New York and the reasons she wanted to leave.

Just as she thought the paper wasn't such a good idea, Renee saw a picture that jogged her memory.

It was Kimberly Janis. Renee immediately recognized her radiant face and smile from the picture over Michelle's dresser. Next to the picture were a few words about her death. She seemed so cheerful as she stared at Renee and she couldn't help but dwell on the waste of this beautiful girl. She was immediately saddened and her heart went out to Kimberly's parents. The only thing possibly worse than a child losing her parents was for parents to lose their child. They were probably racking their brains, wondering what reasons would cause their baby girl to want to kill herself, wondering what they could have done. Wondering why, why, why.

Why Kimberly Janis would kill herself seemed to be the question Chris Jackson, the reporter covering her death, wanted an answer to as well.

Kimberly Janis (pictured left), a Loyola finance student, was found dead on the pavement outside her campus area apartment very early yesterday morning. Police report the recent transfer from Pennsylvania State University apparently committed suicide, jumping from her twentieth-floor balcony. She left no note, which would seem to be crucial in a conclusion of suicide.

Friends report Ms. Janis as well balanced, a young woman who did not take drugs and appeared to be very happy about her fresh start in Chicago, where she recently moved from University Park. This leads an inquisitive mind to wonder why, or maybe if, she would kill herself. Should the case close here?

Renee leaned back in the chair, her mind racing. Why would Chris Jackson suggest it wasn't suicide? Hadn't he talked to people at Augusta? Maybe he'd talked to people closer to Kimberly than Michelle and Nick. There was something wrong, Renee quickly summarized. Michelle had said Kimberly acted paranoid and Nick suggested she was depressed. Renee remembered the weirdly written message Kimberly had e-mailed her shortly before her death. What did it all mean? Did it mean anything?

It suddenly occurred to Renee that she had been one of the very last people to communicate with Kimberly. Probably the last. She wondered if researching BFK had been her last request to anyone? Renee felt a sense of obligation begin to form, and she didn't want to spend the day shopping anymore. She finished her lunch with haste, already knowing where her next destination would be.

Named after the city's first black mayor, the Harold Washington Library was enormous and beautifully decorated and offered the latest in information services. You could find a little something about everything there. After consulting with a librarian, Renee headed straight for the free-access computers.

The first article she found about BFK was a short excerpt on the fund-raiser's inception party held two years ago. The group's director, Alan Smith, had one arm wrapped around the current mayor and another around a corporate sponsor. The general overview. The next article went into more detail, also explaining Augusta's purpose, past successes, and accomplishments. Renee felt a spontaneous smile jump to her lips at seeing Evan Brooks's name in the column as the one who had spoken with the reporter. That was all the information on record at the library. Renee hadn't expected much more. BFK was a small, relatively new organization in a nonprofit ocean. An article in both of Chicago's two major papers was generous publicity.

She left the main library screen and clicked on the Internet access symbol. Finding a search engine, she typed in AUGUSTA FOUNDATION. Not to her surprise, Augusta had a website.

"Everyone and their grandma has a website," she said to herself. "Everyone but me."

The basic necessities—Augusta's website didn't hold much more than a mission statement, organization overview and brief description, and contact information for each of the charities. Clicking on BFK, she found the information was the same as in the paper. Nothing extraordinary, a good idea based on nutritional reports and studies. A small group, but growing faster than any other Augusta charity. A smiling picture of Alan Smith, director.

She clicked on the picture, and the next page formed a short bio. A graduate of Howard University, Alan Smith's last ten years had been spent with charitable organizations.

He was involved in several associations promoting social causes, particularly those concerning African-Americans.

"Nice guy." Renee shrugged, smiling as the elderly woman at the computer across from her rolled her eyes.

Her smile got even wider as she returned to the main page. Clicking on LEADERSHIP, she found Evan's picture, among others.

"You just can't look anything but fine, can you?" she asked the computer, this time forcing the elderly woman across from her to smack her lips in disgust.

Clicking on the picture, she saw that Evan's bio was much longer. Laughing at herself, because she knew this was silly, Renee printed the page out.

Evan was well educated and connected and well known in Chicago for being an eligible bachelor and a philanthropist. His father, Frank, was famous for having invented an adhesive substance that almost reformed the industrial engineering industry. He made millions, which Evan and his sibling inherited. Evan was well known for giving back to the community, carrying on a tradition his father had started. He helped build a children's center in the city, donated to several charities and colleges, and as executive director for the Augusta Foundation, planned several fund-raisers for the foundation's charities, which were attended by local sports and television celebrities as well as powerful politicians and businesspeople.

"Not only is he gorgeous," Renee whispered, hoping not to incur the old lady's wrath again, "but he's kind and giving, too?" She sighed, knowing now she only liked him more. With a sweet southern accent, she said, "I hope the beautiful Ms. Alicia knows what she has in him."

"Young lady," the older woman whispered with a sharp tongue, "this is a library, please."

Renee covered her mouth and winked as she grabbed her printouts and left. She felt so silly and it was coming from nowhere. All of the sudden. Her thoughts focused on Evan Brooks and she felt an overwhelming urge to laugh. She knew he was taken and she had no intention of changing that, but she couldn't erase him from her mind.

She decided she didn't need to try to as she went about her day. She had enough confidence in herself to know she would never go after another woman's man, no matter how attracted she was to him. She wasn't that kind of woman. So, she had her thoughts, knowing that's all there could be between them. No trouble in that.

"What were you up to today?" Michelle fell back on the sofa, across from her sister. Just home from a morning at classes and an afternoon at work, she looked as tired as a vibrant twenty-one-year-old could.

"A little shopping," Renee answered. "A little walking down Michigan Avenue."

"What'd ya get?" Michelle asked, heading straight for the bag as Renee pointed at it.

Renee turned Jeopardy off with the remote control. She wasn't scoring very well today anyway, her thoughts distracted by Evan Brooks and Kimberly Janis. "I read about Kimberly Janis today."

"Where?" Michelle was already trying the shoes on.

"In the *Sun Times.*"

"What did it say?"

"Not much." Renee shrugged. "Except that it seemed weird to the reporter that she'd commit suicide. He's saying those close to her thought she was perfectly normal. In fact, she was happy and optimistic."

"Well Alan seemed resolved to the fact that she killed herself." Michelle left the living room, in search of the closest mirror. "He's as close to her as anyone can get."

"Who's Alan?" Renee followed her sister into the hallway.

"Alan Smith."

After remembering where she had heard that name recently, Renee said, "Isn't he BFK's director?"

"Yeah," Michelle answered, after appearing to think it over a second. "He's also her boyfriend. Or he was."

"He thinks she killed herself?" Renee found it interesting that Kimberly dated the director of the organization she suspected of fraud. Why not go to him? Was she concerned her allegations would anger him and hurt their relationship? Did she suspect him?

"When he came to get the rest of her stuff out of her office today, he told me she'd been depressed lately. Didn't say it was chemical or like you suggested. Just maybe some stuff was getting her down." Michelle eyed the new shoes at several angles from the mirror in the hallway. "These are smokin'."

"Well, I suppose he should know." Renee stood behind Michelle in the mirror. "You look good. You can borrow them while I'm here, but I wear them out first. If I can find a use for them."

"You'll find a use for them while you're here." Michelle gave her sister a coy wink before heading back to the living room.

Renee was fondly reminded of earlier years when she had to chase her hyperactive little sister around the apartment just to have a conversation. She missed those times desperately. "Continue."

"On your date." Michelle returned the shoes to the box. "But you gotta find a dress to match these puppies."

"What date? With whom?"

"Basic black would do." Michelle continued speaking as if Renee never said a word. "With those long legs you'd look good in anything."

"I'm gonna pop you with one of those shoes if you don't tell me what you're talking about."

"From the beginning." Michelle sat down, crossing her arms and laying her hands on her lap like a school girl. "I get to my cubicle at work, okay? I'm like ten minutes late so I freak out when I see a note from Mr. Brooks to see him in his office. I've been late before, you know. Nothing like you, but a few minutes here and there."

"Okay, okay." Renee's curiosity was piqued at the sound of Evan's name.

"Turns out," Michelle continued, "I wasn't in trouble at all. As a matter of fact, he didn't ask me a single question about myself. They were all about you. How's your sister? She enjoying her stay? How long will she be here? Is she in a relationship? Is she really moving to Chicago? Did she say anything about me? On and on. He's usually Mr. Suave, but he was a little eager beaver today."

Renee listened as a thoughtful smile curved her lips. She was flattered by his interest, but knew something was still unanswered. "What about Alicia?"

"Good question," Michelle said, now leaning back casually on the sofa. "I told him you weren't seeing anyone seriously, but that you were actively dating. You know, to keep him on his toes. I asked him if he was seeing someone, but he shrugged the question away. I guess she's not that serious. Maybe she dumped him after seeing the way he was looking at you last night. I would've."

"I don't know, Michelle," Renee said cautiously. Something wasn't quite right.

"That bald head is a great look. Reminds me of Michael Jordan."

"So what else?" Renee couldn't help herself. She wanted to hear everything Evan Brooks said about her. She wanted to know his every facial expression when he asked this and that question, what inflection was in his tone when he asked how she was, if she was seeing anyone. She felt like a teenager hearing about a boy in her class who liked her, but wasn't ready to tell her so to her face. She hadn't felt this giddy in a million years.

"I answered his questions and gave him my phone number." Michelle reached for the remote and clicked the television on. "He's got the number in the employee files, but he didn't want to presume. So maybe he's not as presumptuous as you thought. *Jeopardy?* It figures with you."

"Did he *ask* for your number?" Renee asked with anxiety. "I don't want him to think I was trying to make you give it to him."

"He asked me into his office, remember? Look, it was obvious he liked you. He didn't need to ask. I would've offered. I'm surprised he hasn't called yet as pleased as he seemed when I gave it to him."

"I hope you didn't tell him I'd go out with him. I don't want to seem desperate."

Michelle's face held a calculating grin as she flicked the remote over and over again. "Maybe I can get a raise out of this."

"You're supposed to be marrying the director of finance," Renee said, laughing at her sister's motives. Youthful honesty. "Isn't he the man who handles raises?"

"What's that mean?" Michelle's expression turned serious, like she was offended. "Supposed to."

"I didn't mean anything by it," Renee responded, surprised by her sister's sudden turn. She should be used to it, but wasn't.

"I *am* marrying Nick." Her voice was strong, her stare obstinate.

"I know you are." Renee tried to smile, although the topic didn't make her happy. "You misunderstood me."

"I know you don't like him." Michelle lowered her head, focusing on her short blue denim skirt. "You hate him."

"I don't even know him well enough to hate him."
Renee leaned forward on the sofa, knowing she needed
to be honest despite the reaction she was sure to get. "It's
just that . . . Well, he seems sort of cold."

"I told you he isn't very affectionate in public," Michelle
said defensively.

"I know, but he also seems a little rude, condescending."
Renee sighed. "I don't know. Maybe last night wasn't a
good night for him. Do you think he really respects you
as an individual?"

"Respect is earned, Renee." She lifted her head, her
eyes focusing on the television.

"No, deep respect is earned. You're a woman. You
deserve respect from a man right off."

"Why don't you give him another chance?" Michelle
scooted up, pleading with her large eyes. "Why don't you
have lunch with him tomorrow?"

"Just the two of us?" Renee wasn't too comfortable with
that suggestion.

"Yes, a fresh start. You'll love him."

"I don't know." Renee was set to protest, but before
she could, Michelle had jumped from the sofa and was on
the phone, dialing. When she hung up, it was confirmed.
Tomorrow, Renee would go to Augusta and meet Nick for
lunch.

They were going to go to a nice Italian restaurant next
door that Michelle promised was the best around despite
its less than impressive decor. Renee was hesitant, but saw
the excitement in Michelle's eyes and knew she had to try.
Michelle was in love and forming a friendship with Nick
was possibly a way to bridge the gap in their relationship.
So lunch tomorrow it was. Renee thought, if nothing else,
maybe she could catch a glimpse of Evan on her visit to
the foundation.

Renee stayed up late that night, claiming she wasn't

tired. It wasn't the truth. She was exhausted really, but what if the phone rang? Who knew?

She couldn't deny it. As Renee stepped onto Augusta's third floor, she knew she was hoping to see Evan Brooks more than anything. She didn't know if it was a good or a bad thing for him to call, but she had been anticipating the sound of a telephone ring all night long last night. The telephone rang, but all the calls were for Michelle. Renee had forgotten how much young girls loved to talk on the phone at night.

Renee was more excited than she cared to admit to herself. Just in case she happened to run into him, she had dressed the part. A forest green satin tank that raised softly at her round breasts and slid into her thin white cotton mini, wrapping gently around her hips. With the usual lipstick, Renee added a touch of mascara to her already long lashes, making her large eyes stand out even more.

As she approached Nick's office, she'd already made the decision to relax and let go of her first impression of him. For Michelle's sake she would start over, hoping this lunch would ease some of the nagging objections she had to this engagement and this man.

"He's not in there."

Just as she was about to knock on Nick's door, Renee turned to face the short, middle-aged woman who stood behind her.

"Mr. Hamilton," the woman continued, "is in a meeting."

"Hello." Renee held a hand out to the redhead in a leopard print, very tight suit. "I'm Renee Shepherd. My sister is Michelle."

"Oh, yeah." The woman shook her hand with the vigor

of a strong man. "The little fiancé. Your lil' sis know what she's getting into? He's a holy terror sometimes. I'm sort of the floating secretary around here. I do my best not to float this way if you know what I mean."

"He's not harsh with Michelle is he?" Renee crossed her arms. "I mean, if you don't mind my asking."

"I understand." She winked. "Checking up on the guy. That's expected. From what I've seen, he's all right to her. You know. She'll train him. We all have to."

"I suppose." Renee smiled. "I'm having lunch with Nick. Will he be back soon?"

"I don't think so." She frowned, biting at the tip of her pencil. "He's in a meeting with Mr. Brooks in his office. It's down the hall to the right."

Renee took a deep breath as she walked down the corridor, running her fingers through her hair. She still wasn't used to it stopping way before it used to. A certain sense of security gone. She was amazed at how nervous and excited she was at the thought of seeing Evan and forced herself to settle down. Why would the mere thought of running into a man she didn't even know concern her so much? Renee had experienced sudden crushes before, but nothing like this. She felt an involuntary smile of anticipation fighting its way onto her face. Since when could a man she barely knew make her feel like a teenager? This was different, she told herself. Evan was different. That could be trouble.

The area outside Evan's office was empty, his secretary's desk unoccupied. His office door was closed. Renee glanced at her watch and saw it was ten after noon. They were supposed to meet at noon, so she decided to wait a few minutes more and took a seat against the wall. She situated herself, facing the left, her legs crossed, her head back just in case.

"You're crazy, girl," she told herself. "You have lost your mind."

She grabbed a magazine, but only glanced at the pictures as thoughts of Evan distracted her from reading the articles. She couldn't remember feeling so silly.

It was soon twelve thirty, and Renee was beginning to lose her patience. For once, she'd been somewhat on time, only to have to wait. She tried to be considerate, knowing emergencies can happen, knowing she'd been late herself on more than a few occasions. Evan's secretary was obviously out and Renee had no reason to expect her back soon, so she decided to leave a note on Nick's door to reschedule the lunch.

Just as she stepped behind the secretary's desk to find a pen and pad, Evan's office door flew open. Renee jumped and turned, coming face to face with Nick as he stood in the doorway, appearing less than happy.

"Nick," she said after taking a moment to catch her breath. "I-I was w-waiting for you. I was a-about to—"

"Forget it," he said, cutting her off in midsentence. His brows drew together in an angry frown. "I'm too busy. Tell Michelle not to schedule lunches for me anymore."

Astonished by his rudeness, Renee could only stare at Nick as he coldly walked by her. The nerve! Not only was he horribly rude in canceling their lunch so abruptly, but he gave her an order!

"I apologize for Nick's behavior." Evan Brooks appeared in the doorway, a half smile on his face. "That was very rude."

"Yes it was." Renee turned to Evan.

Seeing him, she immediately forgot about Nick and his abhorrent behavior. Evan was devastating in his apparently usual casual work clothes. The sandy brown button-down blended nicely with his dark skin. Khaki pants gave him an outdoor, rugged look that Renee found very sexy. She didn't miss his quick and approving examination of her. Nor did she miss the electricity that flowed through her in response to it. It seemed to Renee to be a response more powerful than herself that came whenever he looked at her.

"Please come in." Evan stepped aside.

"Really, I just came to . . ." Renee reluctantly stepped inside the modest but well-decorated office and suddenly realized there was someone else there. She knew she didn't know this man, but he looked oddly familiar.

Evan held out his hand to introduce them. "Renee, this is Alan Smith. He's a director of one of Augusta's charities. Alan, this is Renee Shepherd."

"Hello, Ms. Shepherd." Alan held his hand out to her. "It's nice to meet you."

"Same here." Renee shook his hand, noticing his loose grip. "You run BFK."

Alan Smith was a very average looking man, young, light in complexion with green eyes being the only detail that stood out. His half smile held a touch of sadness, matching the somber expression.

"I guess you should be leaving, Alan." Evan's voice was muddled as he turned to his desk and shuffled some papers together.

"Yes." Alan answered without looking in Evan's direction. "I guess I'll go."

"I'm very sorry about Kimberly," Renee said, calmly and tenderly making eye contact with the distraught-looking man. What death did to those left behind.

"How did you know her?" Alan's eyes widened. His voice was weak, defenseless.

"I didn't know her personally," Renee said. "My sister works here and she knew her casually. I only know her from . . . well, the computer."

"The computer?" Alan asked somberly, but more alert than before.

"I don't want to upset you if it's too difficult to talk about her." Renee briefly turned to Evan who appeared even more interested in what she had to say than Alan.

"You won't," Alan said. "Please tell me."

"Well, the night she ... passed, she sent me two e-mail messages over the Internet." Renee was sorry she'd brought the topic up, feeling suddenly uncomfortable as all eyes were on her. So intensely, at that.

"What did they say?" Evan asked.

Renee was confused by the concerned look he gave her, his eyes staring squarely at her through his thin glasses.

"Oh, nothing, really," Renee answered. "She was just a fan of my books."

"You're an author?" Alan asked.

"I've written some books on health and nutrition." Renee saw some apprehension leave both men's faces as the subject changed.

"I may have read your stuff. I've read so much. Who knows." Alan turned away from her abruptly and grabbed a sandal-brown suitcase from off a nearby chair. He faced her again. "Yeah. I think I remember you. Not sure. Either way, it was nice meeting you."

"The same." Renee smiled tenderly, noticing the coldness between Alan and Evan, who said nothing to each other as the younger man left.

"You enjoying your day, Renee?" Evan smiled with candor and no concern, as if the recent uncomfortable moment hadn't happened.

Renee nodded, lowering her eyes. The sight of him made her want to smile. She didn't want to make a fool of herself, although she was sure Evan was used to women smiling uncontrollably in his presence.

"Where were the two of you headed?"

"What?" Renee asked, second guessing everything she was about to say. "You mean Nick and me?"

"Yes." He let out a quick laugh.

"Just next door to that Italian place." She couldn't help but yell at herself on the inside. She was certain she sounded like an idiot. She could hardly look him in the eye for fear her attraction would be revealed. Renee hated feeling so vulnerable. Evan, on the other hand, seemed to have no problem showing an obvious attraction to her, which made her wonder how strong it was.

"We've got some problems in the financial department. Nothing to be concerned about." Evan leaned back on the front of his desk, folding his arms across his chest. "Nick gets very upset whenever there's the smallest glitch. He wants his reputation to be spotless."

"Obviously." It almost made her angry to see the ease with which he just stared at her while she was living in complete fear of a giggle uttering from her mouth.

"May I fill in?" he asked with a side smile.

Her instinct was to scream *yes, yes, yes,* but somewhere in the back of her head was a voice telling her this man made her entirely too uncomfortable for a friendly lunch.

"I have good manners and promise not to embarrass you in public." Evan jokingly pled his case as he seemed to notice her hesitation. "I don't eat with my hands. I won't belch, unless of course you find that entertaining. In that case . . ."

"Okay, okay." Renee tried to muster the most nonchalant smile she could. It wasn't his eating habits she was concerned about. "It's just that . . . I don't really know you."

"Well, I'd like to change that." A more serious look came to his face as the tone of his voice tendered. He stepped closer to her. "I think that's obvious."

Renee felt a strange inner excitement as she was flushed

by the suggestive tone of both his words and his action. She was starting to like this forwardness, much to her surprise.

"It's just next door, Renee," Evan added. "I promise you'll enjoy yourself. I can be pretty charming when I try."

"I'm sure you can," she responded, no longer able to resist the flirting smile he was giving her. Very persistent.

He had an undeniable energy and power that propelled her to him. Yes, she was sure she would enjoy lunch with him. She was only afraid she would enjoy it too much.

FOUR

Pomodoro's was just as Michelle described it. The menu was all Italian, but the atmosphere was more like an American fry-everything diner than a quaint ethnic restaurant. It was smoky, a little cramped, and very noisy. Renee figured they probably had the best Italian food in the entire city. That was how it went sometimes.

"I suppose I should thank Nick," Evan said loudly over the crowd noise after the waitress left with their order.

"Why's that?" Renee calmly placed two thin paper napkins across her lap. She couldn't believe that Nick would come here. Didn't seem his style.

"I was looking for an opportunity to ask you out." He laughed a bit. "Nick gave me an easy transition. I'll have to thank him."

"You don't seem to me to be the kind of man who needs to wait for an opportunity for much of anything." Her impression of him was of a man who was too self-assured and presumptuous. She was pleased by a hint of vulnerability and honest approach. "Do I scare you?"

"I guess scared isn't the right word." He concentrated on her for a moment before speaking again. "Underneath that baseball T, I could tell you were an intelligent woman with a lot of class. Those ordinary lines wouldn't work with you."

"Lines usually work for you?" This man didn't need lines. A simple hello would do for most women. It had for her. One hello and he hadn't been off her mind since.

"I've been developing them since the age of twelve." He sipped his drink, a long swallow. "But I'm a busy man. I don't get much of an opportunity to use them."

"I find that hard to believe. A man as good-looking as yourself must get plenty of opportunities."

"A misconception I've heard before." He raised a pointed finger. "I don't date much. I work late pretty much every day. Most of the evening and weekend events I attend are fund-raisers that my organization planned. Always working the room for Augusta. I don't get much time to meet and mingle for my own purposes. I don't do the blind date thing anymore. Too many disasters."

"That's unfortunate." Renee thought of the best way to bring up the next topic, and decided the direct approach was best. She had nothing to lose. "I suppose you just got lucky when you met Alicia."

"Alicia?" he asked.

"Yes." Renee did her best to appear as if she could be talking about the color of the sky right now. Uninvolved. In actuality, she was on the edge of her seat in anticipation of his response. "That was her name from the other night, wasn't it?"

"Oh, yeah." He nodded. "Alicia."

"Beautiful woman," Renee added, a little confused by his suddenly humorous smile.

"Yes." He paused. "A wonderful sister-in-law, too."

"Excuse me? Sister-in-law?"

"Alicia is married to my brother, Calvin," Evan explained. "She's a model and she's in town doing a shoot. You thought she was my girlfriend?"

"I didn't think anything really," Renee lied. She hoped desperately she was hiding the spurt of joy she felt at the sudden turn of events. The fact that he was available was as dangerous as it was exciting.

"Of course not," Evan said, rubbing a strong hand over his bald head as he winked at her, not underestimating her interest.

Renee couldn't help but stare. His shaved head added individuality and character to his practically flawless dark skin. With this new news, he somehow seemed even more attractive, if that was possible.

"How about yourself?" Evan asked. "Michelle told me you aren't currently involved."

"Not seriously." Renee's pride kept her from admitting she hadn't had a date in almost six months. "But, you know."

"So," he said with a wide smile. "Tell me about Renee Shepherd. The sister, the author, and especially the woman."

"Exactly what would you like to know?" Renee wished the tension she felt being so close to him, having his full attention, would ease soon. She was bound to say something silly. She felt her stomach fluttering with butterflies.

"Can I ask anything?" He leaned forward with a mischievous grin.

"You can ask." Renee made sure her tone was elusive.

"But will you answer?"

She gave a sideways smile. "No promises."

"You're comfortable with power." Evan leaned back in

his chair, assessing her confident expression. "You have this date pretty much under control."

"Date?" she asked in mild surprise, intrigued by his suggestion. "I thought this was just lunch."

"Yeah, you're right." He gave a matter-of-fact smile, keeping his eyes directly on her as the waiter brought their food. "Shall we start?"

"Be my guest." Renee tried to keep eye contact, but it was hard. He hid nothing and she was as intimidated by that as she was impressed. The food, smelling glorious was only a mild distraction as she dug in.

"What's your favorite color?" Evan smiled at Renee's surprise.

"Purple." She tried to suppress her laugh. So, he wanted to tease. Fine. She could play along.

"What kind of car do you drive?" he continued.

"Standard compact Honda." Wait until it was her turn.

"What's your favorite movie?" Evan still held a straight face, as serious as ever.

"*Mahogany* with Diana and Billy Dee."

"Your favorite book?" His eyes were clear and observant, like in a desert where one could see everything while only looking in one direction.

"*Beloved,* by Toni Morrison." Renee was drawn to the vitality and life he seemed to emit.

"How old are you?" Still a face of stone.

"Don't even try it," she said, catching herself before she answered.

"I almost got you there." He snapped his fingers.

"These are very important, personal questions you're asking." She leaned forward this time, mocking impatience. "How long is this going to continue?"

"Until I find out everything about you." He took a bite of lasagna.

"That's no fun," Renee said, twirling her angel hair pasta. "Wouldn't you prefer a little mystery?"

He eyed her with seduction as if studying every inch of her face. "You have a point. Why don't you tell me what you want me to know and let me figure out the rest."

"What makes you think I want you to know anything?" Renee met his suggestive glance with a coy rise of her finely styled eyebrows.

"I don't." He shrugged smoothly. "But I like to gamble. After all, this isn't a date. So what's the harm?"

Renee knew there was a lot a harm in letting this man know all about her. She stepped closer and closer into harm's way with every second she spent with him. Nevertheless, he was persistent and she finally gave in and told Evan about herself. Not everything, but enough for him to know what she was about and how she got to where she was. She told him about growing up in Brooklyn to working-class parents who gave her everything they could. She told him about college and then losing her parents. Not wanting to concentrate on somber times, she went into her introduction into the world of writing and her subsequent career.

Renee enjoyed his attentiveness. The past few times she'd been out with men on a first date, all she had wanted was to get through the evening without having to call the police. Now, she found herself wanting him to look at her and be pleased with what he saw. She wanted him to see that she enjoyed talking about her family and talking to him as he listened intently. He wasn't flinching, she could see. It wasn't his style to hide his feelings and he wasn't at all shy about the fact that he was interested in her. Renee only wished she could be the same.

It was his turn next, Renee insisted after finishing her own edited biography. Unlike her, there was no hesitation on Evan's part. Not only did he comply immediately, but told her almost everything about himself. She studied his face and expressions as he talked. She found it easy to get lost in his charm and candor, its casualness making her feel at ease. He was smooth, but not in a precontrived way. He didn't seem caught up in himself or his looks, only comfortable with everything he was.

Evan Brooks had been born on Chicago's North Side thirty-five years ago. His parents were both teachers, his father at the collegiate level and his mother at the high school level. He had a very normal childhood, besides the hard time he gave his parents in the awkward teenage years. He grew up a Chicago Cubs fan, skipping school to attend day games at Wrigley Field. He was a high school senior when his father, an engineering whiz, invented an adhesive that could dissolve itself over time if coated with a certain mixture of liquids, literally disappearing. It was a treasure for engineering and architectural firms who used it mostly for their models, allowing easy and quick modifications and the reuse of materials. The find made Frank Brooks a wealthy man. Renee was sorry to hear Frank had passed away five years ago and she felt a connection to Evan as a flicker of respectful grief flashed in his eyes, his smile fading for a moment.

Evan's mother remarried and was living in the U.S. Virgin Islands. His only sibling, a brother, Calvin, lived in Charleston, South Carolina, with his wife Alicia, whom Renee considered her new best friend now that she knew she wasn't Evan's girlfriend.

After graduating from Howard University, Evan worked in public relations and public affairs at the capitol in D.C. before returning home to Chicago. Back here, he went on to work for several local politicians, developing powerful contacts in the city. He had taken over the Augusta Foundation two years ago.

"What made you decide to go nonprofit?" Renee asked,

pushing her plate away now that she'd eaten enough. She was staying away from that garlic bread.

"It sounds a little sappy," Evan said, "but I found my life lacking that feeling of contribution. Being around politics is supposed to have the opposite effect. But trust me, with all the red tape, it doesn't."

"Doesn't sound sappy at all." Had she felt her heart flutter? "All the money and power in the world can't make up for the feeling helping others gives you. Changing lives."

"Same for you," Evan said. "Your books have helped a lot of people change their lives."

"I hope so." Renee smiled. "I just want our people to understand how important good health is. You know, how diet and exercise affects every aspect of our lives. Physically, emotionally, spiritually, secularly, and mentally."

"If my dad had read your book, maybe he would've cut down on all those porterhouses and picked his rear end off the sofa every now and then. He had a great mind, but the laziest body ever created."

"You've learned from him." Renee pointed to Evan's almost empty plate of vegetarian lasagna.

"I learned a lot from my father." An affectionate smile. "Good and bad."

"Were you two very close?" Renee hoped she wasn't getting too personal, but she wanted to know everything about this magnetic person sitting across from her. She loved to hear about the relationships between parents and their adult children, having been practically a kid when she'd lost both of hers. It helped her imagine what it would be like to have parents now.

"I suppose," Evan said. "He was a professor and the university took a lot of his time, but he always fit us in there somewhere. Well, not always, but he tried to be there, and I guess that's saying a lot."

"More than what most get." Renee lowered her head, not expecting the sudden memories of her own father that came to her. Always teasing and affectionate. Strong, yet utterly at the mercy of the three women he loved.

"You thinking about your dad?" Evan asked after a short silence.

"Yes." Renee was touched by the tenderness of his smile and the concern in his eyes.

"You were young when you lost your parents, but old enough to have a lifetime worth of memories."

She nodded. "And they're all good."

"You and Michelle must be very close." Evan took a moment to instruct the waiter to remove their plates. "Sisters usually are, but your loss must've brought you even closer."

Renee felt a bottomless contentment at the thought of her feelings for Michelle. "It's never easy, but she means everything to me."

"I get the impression she's almost like a daughter to you." Evan's expression was sincere, but cautious. "You've taken care of her like a mother, haven't you?"

"Pretty much," Renee agreed. "My grandmother helped for a little while there."

"Am I getting too personal?" Evan asked.

"A little," Renee said politely, protective of her relationship with Michelle, "but I know you don't mean to."

Evan accepted the check. "Let's change the subject then."

"Actually." Renee looked reluctantly at her watch. "It's after two o' clock. I don't want to keep you."

"You're not." His tone was certain. "My afternoon is pretty free and I'm enjoying myself. Come on, think of a topic, a place, a person."

"Okay." Renee was happier than she expected to be,

knowing he was as eager to stay as she was. "How about Kimberly Janis. You're handling her death with the press?"

"There really isn't anything to handle." A serious expression hit his face. "It was suicide. The press is only bothering us because she has no family in the area to bother. After a few days, they won't care too much. I'm sure they're asking the university a couple of questions. Everyone has agreed its an unfortunate suicide."

Renee noticed he made that point twice. "That *Sun Times* reporter, Chris Jackson, doesn't think so."

"I read his blurb in the paper yesterday." Evan handed the waitress the check and some cash. "I wouldn't pay too much attention to it. The media today tries to create the news instead of report it like they should."

"You know, I lied earlier today," Renee said, lowering her lashes a bit.

"About what?"

"About how I knew Kimberly." She sighed, happy to get the truth out in the open. She hated lying. "She didn't e-mail me a fan letter at all. She was actually very nervous and agitated about BFK."

"What about it?" Evan leaned forward.

"She thought there could be some corruption going on inside the organization." Renee wasn't sure this was the best way to approach the executive director about fraud in his organization, but she'd started and might as well get it all out. "She wanted me to give her some advice. I guess she thought, because I had written a book about nutrition and intelligence in children, I might be familiar with the group and know something about it, know someone to talk to."

"Did she name any names?" Evan asked. "Did she say exactly what she thought was being done?"

"I don't think she was sure about much." Renee noticed

Evan's ever increasing interest. "She seemed uncertain, nervous, and preoccupied. She sent . . ."

"How do you know her mood? Did you talk to her?"

"No." He didn't realize he'd just interrupted her. Why was he so anxious? "She sent the letters via e-mail, but her grammar was a little off, making it seem that way. You know, rushed."

"When did you speak . . . I mean communicate with her last?"

"Just before her death apparently." Renee shook her head at the thought. "That's why I cut the subject off at your office. I didn't want to upset Alan. He seemed hurt enough."

"They weren't together long. What was she worried about with BFK?" Evan posed the question mostly to himself as he drifted off into his own thoughts. "Can't be losing money. That group is pulling in record numbers. Maybe some other kind of misrepresentation."

Renee watched Evan as he went over thoughts in his mind. He seemed oddly preoccupied with her news. He was more interested in hearing about what she knew of Kimberly than when Renee had been talking about herself earlier. She figured he might have been close to Kimberly and had his own doubts about the cause of her death.

"We'd better get going," Evan finally said as he glanced at his watch. "The afternoon is calling."

As she grabbed her purse and slid out of the booth, Renee could swear she'd just heard him say his afternoon was free.

They returned to the office more than two hours after they'd left, but the time seemed much shorter to Renee. She hadn't enjoyed herself like that in a while, being entertained by a man and being so flattered that he was entertained by her company. She'd forgotten how fun such an old-fashioned way of dating was. No expectations, no blind date disasters. Just fun and a little bit, no a lot, of sexual tension thickening the air, making a game of it.

The fun stopped, the game intensified as Evan gently touched her arm with his strong hand. A sweet shudder heated her body as she felt her skin tingle underneath his fingers. She hadn't forgotten this feeling.

"Renee." Her name came as almost a whisper from his mouth.

She turned to him, her eyes hiding her fear as she looked into his. There was no one in the hallway, but she wouldn't have noticed if there had been. For that moment, she was mesmerized by his closeness and frightened to death by its effect on her. In that moment, without knowing anything else, she knew she could lose her heart to this man if given half a chance.

"I'd like to see you again." Evan spoke with quiet, but confident determination as he stepped closer to her. Only inches from her now, his eyes held all the seriousness of his intent.

"I don't know if I . . ." Renee's tongue felt like it weighed ten pounds. The words were hard coming. "I'll only be here for a couple of weeks."

"I know, but think about it," Evan urged. "I really want to see you."

"I'll think about it," Renee answered, not to his words, but the warmth of his touch on her arm as his fingers tipped her skin. It was a gentle touch, but the effect was burning through her skin. He was so persistent, determined, and centered. He got what he wanted almost always, she was certain of that.

When he finally removed his hand to grab a card from his pocket, she wanted to protest, but controlled herself. She'd have to be satisfied with the lingering feel of his hand on her. He pulled a pen from another pocket and jotted down some numbers on the back.

"This is my card," he said, handing it to her. "My home number is on the back. I'll wait for your call."

Renee didn't respond to his confident statement. She knew she wasn't expected to. She simply watched as his full lips formed that charming smile one last time and he turned to walk away. She felt herself exhale for the first time since he had touched her and realized how centered she'd been on that moment, on him. It took her a second to remember where she was and what she was doing there.

"You're in trouble, girl," she whispered.

As she turned and headed for Michelle's desk, Renee placed Evan's card neatly into her purse. She would definitely consider it. She wasn't going to kid herself; she already had. It was just a matter of how soon she could call without seeming too eager, yet time was not on her side. Maybe Evan was out in the open from the beginning, but Renee wasn't one to put all her cards on the table at once. At least not until she was more certain.

Renee knew Michelle started work at 2 P.M. most days and, as expected, she was in her cubicle shuffling papers and talking on the phone at the same time. Renee waved for her attention and waited for Michelle to finish her call.

"So how was lunch?" Michelle replaced the receiver on the phone and motioned for Renee to grab the empty chair at the next cubicle.

"My lunch was fantastic," Renee answered, sliding in, "but it wasn't with Nick."

"What?"

"I was here at noon, but Nick was in a meeting with Evan and Alan Smith. I waited outside Evan's office for Nick for a half hour. When he finally came out, he brushed me aside and practically ordered me to order you not to schedule lunches for him anymore."

Michelle blinked her embarrassment, but said nothing.

Renee continued. "I understand emergency meetings and whatever. I used to work at an office myself, but he was pretty rude to me."

"Nick gets that way when he's really rushed or bothered by something." Michelle lowered her eyes to hands laid on her lap. As if she had nothing more to say.

"That's all right with you?" Renee asked, not liking this reaction at all. Was Michelle resigned to this behavior by Nick? That wasn't okay.

"What kind of question is that?" Michelle threw the question at her sister. "Did you expect him to kiss up to you because you're some hotshot author?"

"Michelle, that was uncalled for," Renee said, a little shocked. "I expected him to be available for lunch when he agreed to be."

"I'm sorry," Michelle said in a calmer tone. "You just seem like you're above being stood up for a lunch. Happens to everyone. He tried. He wanted to have lunch with you. That should stand for something."

"It does." Renee paused with a sigh, wondering if she'd blown the situation out of proportion again. "I tried, too. I hope you recognize that."

"I do." Michelle's smile returned as she touched her sister's knee. She blinked and her eyes lit up with excitement. "You said your lunch was fantastic. Who did you have lunch with if it wasn't Nick?"

Renee's smile was uncontrollable. Just at the thought of him.

"I can see this is gonna be good." Michelle scooted her chair closer to Renee's.

"I had lunch with Evan," Renee whispered.

"Oooh. First-name basis. Tell me everything."

"There really isn't much to tell," Renee said. Not much aside from the fact that she had been in virtual euphoria for the last two hours. "It was just lunch. He was just standing in for Nick."

"Yeah, right," Michelle said, rolling her eyes. "Evan Brooks isn't a stand-in for anyone. Not even my Nick."

Renee agreed. Evan would never be a second choice. He was first choice all the way.

"When are you going out with him again?" Michelle asked.

"Slow your roll, girl," Renee said. "I don't know really. He'd like me to give him a call and I'm tempted. I plan on calling him, but I don't know if I'll be here much longer. What's the point of starting if I can't finish?"

"Oh, Renee." Michelle sighed. "Don't be so cautious all the time. Nothing's wrong with dating without strings attached. You never know. Evan Brooks could change your life like Nick has changed mine."

Renee was acutely aware of that fact and she wasn't so sure how she felt about it. "I'm thinking about it."

"I got an idea," Michelle said. "Why don't we go to Nick's office and reschedule a date?"

"I would really like to schedule a date with just you." Renee stood up reluctantly.

"Oh, no." Michelle sat right back down after pointing to the same redhead Renee had seen earlier outside Nick's office.

"What is it?" Renee whispered.

"She's part of *the man* around here," Michelle whispered back. "I gotta get back to work. You go see Nick yourself and let me know what you two decide. I'll be home around six thirty."

"All right." Renee hesitated, not looking forward to facing Nick alone after this afternoon. After a brief hesitation, she said goodbye and headed for the finance department.

* * *

Renee assumed it was fate that she and Nick wouldn't get together when she found his office empty. After waiting inside for a few moments, she left a note asking to get together at a time more convenient for him. Half of her wanted him to note the sarcasm, half didn't. She peeked at the open calendar on his desk. This afternoon was empty, making her wonder where he was.

It caught her eye that Nick had scheduled Alan Smith's visit to the office today, with the calendar noting that he was to get the rest of Kimberly Janis's things. Although she remembered Michelle telling her that Alan had done that yesterday, Renee was quickly distracted by thoughts of poor Kimberly and felt a sudden urge to see where Kimberly had worked.

Looking around, Renee searched for any clues as to where her office would've been. Not finding any, she finally asked a young man making copies in the corner office. He pointed her to an office a little farther down the hall. The door was slightly ajar and as she reached to open it a bit more, she heard a clicking sound, like fingers touching computer keys and knew someone was in there. Renee cautiously peeked inside. She wasn't sure what she was expecting to see, but was definitely surprised at what she did see.

Evan Brooks, oblivious to her presence, was at work on Kimberly's old computer. His face was barely a foot from the screen, his concentration deep. Even from her distance, she could see he was entering Kimberly's file manager, containing all her documents from every program. He was looking for something specific as he rolled past several files, stopping every now and then and peering closer. He'd open it, his shoulders lower; then, he'd close it and resume searching.

Renee felt uneasy watching him, backing away to get out of sight of the crack in the doorway. Intuition told her it was the wrong time to interrupt him with a hello or anything else. Puzzled as she walked away, she wondered what he'd been looking for and why she had such an uncomfortable feeling watching him look for it. Could it have been business? It seemed likely, but it made more sense to Renee that Evan would go to Nick to discuss financial matters, not search Kimberly's computer himself.

She remembered how interested Evan had seemed when she spoke of Kimberly to Alan in his office earlier and then later at lunch when she mentioned her own ties to Kimberly. She knew it shouldn't seem unusual for him to care about something so tragic happening to someone he knew, but something kept Renee from accepting that. Maybe it was her own curious spirit, she thought. Something could be going on, or she might simply be misinterpreting a situation that was none of her business in the first place. She was still trying to figure out why she cared so much about Kimberly Janis and her death. What kept that girl on her mind? Was there something she could have done?

All day long, Renee's thoughts focused to her lunch with Evan. Preparing dinner for herself and Michelle, she recalled his charming smile, smooth voice, and tempered confidence. She thought of his powerful shoulders, his eyes, searching and honest. She remembered his laugh, strong and sincere. Maybe Chicago would jump to the top of her list of places to move to. It had rush hour traffic and brutally cold winters, but it was beginning to make up for that with so much more.

The sound of the phone ringing broke her from her

trance. Picking up the receiver, she knew she was hoping it would be Evan on the other end.

"Hey, girlfriend. How's Chicago?"

"Hey, Karen." Renee recognized the familiar voice. "Everything is fine here. Well, sort of."

"Go ahead," Karen said, sounding motherly. "Tell me everything."

Renee explained the engagement bombshell Michelle had dropped on her as soon as she arrived. She told her about Nick's behavior and her not too favorable opinion of him, Kimberly Janis's suicide, her own preoccupation with it and the idea written by Chris Jackson that it wasn't a suicide at all. Karen was intrigued by it all, but mostly by Renee's account of meeting Evan and having lunch with him.

"Sounds like you've had a busy few days," Karen said after it was all out.

"You could say." Renee fell into the kitchen chair with a sigh.

"At least you met a great guy. So, when are you seeing him again?"

"I don't know." Renee's tone expressed her doubts. "He's interesting in so many ways, but if things start happening, what do I do when it's time to leave?"

"You won't," Karen said with finality.

"Aren't you the woman always telling me I need to stay in New York? I couldn't possibly be happy anywhere else, you said."

"If this guy is as great as I think he might be from listening to you, I would be doing you an injustice by not encouraging you to go for it. You need someone to knock you off your feet. You haven't had that happen in a while."

"I know." Renee smirked at her love life, or lack thereof. No one had ever knocked her off her feet. "Maybe I'm getting ahead of myself. I'm just contemplating a second date."

"Go for it anyway. It's been a while."

"Quit reminding me." Renee let out a laugh. "I was just thinking that same thing myself. Maybe I'll call him tomorrow and get together with him later in the week."

"Now you know you have to wait a few days," Karen said over the sound of her two-year-old, Michael, playing close by.

"Why?" Renee was admittedly anxious to see Evan again. A few days?

"So you don't seem too eager."

"I know you're right," Renee said after contemplation. "But three days? I'll only be here another week or so."

"Give him something to think about, girl." Her voice faded away as she yelled for Michael not to pour his bowl of grits into the VCR. "Sounds like he's in hot pursuit of you, so you won't lose him. Give him more time to pant."

"Fine," Renee agreed, "but then can I go out with him?"

"Yes," Karen said. "You have my permission. Only, make sure it isn't next Wednesday afternoon or next Friday night."

"Why not?"

"I heard a couple of things going on through the grapevine and hooked it up for you."

"Hold on." Renee jumped up and headed for the pad and pen magnetized to the wall. Karen doubled as a publicity agent when the mood hit her, knowing the end result was to her benefit as much as the author's. "Go ahead."

"I got you a book signing at Black America Booksellers on Michigan Avenue at two on Wednesday."

Renee got a kick out of book signings. "Meet the fans, give some advice, sell some books. All good. What's on Friday?"

"The Association of Minority Health Care Professionals is having their Midwest Chapter annual dinner. It's a small fund-raiser for minority medical school scholarships, but its also an excellent networking opportunity for you to meet potential collaborators and interview subjects for future books. I snagged you an invite."

"Karen." Renee wrote as fast as she could. "I don't know what I'd do without you. You're a genius."

"Tell me something I don't know. Give me your address in Chicago and I'll overnight everything to you."

She gave Karen the information before going on about upcoming book ideas. Karen updated her on continuing discussions with the new publishing company.

"They're gonna really push these books, babe," she said. "So they're counting on you to be game when it comes to traveling. I know you're not too crazy about that."

"I've changed." Renee reflected back. "Self-promotion was pretty hard in the beginning, but it's because I used to be such a private person."

"Well, you of all people know that's something authors give up to sell books." Karen laughed. "I remember that speech you gave in Baltimore six months ago. You were nervous as hell."

"That was a first for me." Renee remembered the thunderous applause she got afterward. "Now I look at every opportunity with excitement."

"You sound like a billboard." Karen's voice held hints of doubt. "You sure?"

"I just remember how blessed I am to be doing this for a living."

"You're lucky," Karen added. "Your work lets you live wherever you want."

Renee thought of how grateful she was to Karen after hanging up. She kept her eyes and ears open for her just as earnestly as she did for her million dollar fiction authors who made the bestseller's list year after year. She'd helped Renee build her confidence over the years and she would never forget that.

She was going to call on that confidence to ask Evan Brooks to next Friday's fund-rasier. Only, she wasn't waiting until next Friday to see him. She wanted to see him again now. Just a second off the phone and her thoughts returned to him. She went over in her mind how to approach him, feeling like a school girl again—shy and self-conscious. Then she decided she'd wait like Karen had told her. She'd spotted him as aggressive and very self-confident. He was a take-the-ball-and-run-with-it kind of guy, but she wasn't going to throw him the ball too soon. The next three days would be the longest three days of her life.

FIVE

As she pulled the Pontiac up to the front doors of Augusta, Renee's eyes danced with excitement and her stomach churned with nerves.

It was Friday, two days after her last meeting with Evan. She'd done what she was told, she didn't call him. It was hard, but Renee stood fast. She didn't want to believe one man could occupy her mind so much that she couldn't think of anything else, but that's how it had been.

So much so, that when Michelle made plans for Renee to pick her up from work to start a Friday night on the town, her heart jumped. Would she run into Evan? It was entirely possible, and Renee had made up her mind what she'd do if she did.

Of course, they had to be alone, but she intended to ask him to dinner. Two days was enough. Besides, whether or not she decided to move to Chicago in the future, her time now was running out.

D'Angelo was on the radio singing his Smokey Robinson

remake. A classic. The words were soothing, his voice sexy. Renee leaned back in her seat, closed her eyes. A smile formed on her lips as the breeze from outside traveled through the window and fanned her.

She sang along, "I can just lay there beside you and love you."

"You just made me week with those words."

Renee screamed as she jolted up, her eyes flying open. She looked up to find Evan leaning over the driver's side window. He had a suggestive smile, his eyes hidden by sporty sunglasses.

"I'm sorry," he said, laughing. "I didn't mean to frighten you. Well, actually I did, but . . ."

"Well, you got what you wanted." Renee found a smile to cover her embarrassment. The attraction hit immediately. She hated not being in control. "I guess you should know. I'm not one to let the fact that there's no one around keep me from saying anything out loud."

"That's an endearing quality." He leaned in closer, his forehead at the top of the open window. "At your age, I mean. When you get older, they'll put you somewhere for that."

"Something to think about." She wanted to look in his eyes, but then thought better of it. They were too mesmerizing. She was having enough trouble with the white polo shirt that fit him too well and had all the buttons undone, giving her a glimpse of his chest.

"How are you, Renee?" This time, Evan removed his glasses. His eyes showed honest interest as they caught hers. They held her even though she didn't want to be there.

"I'm fine, Evan." He pulled no punches. Those eyes showed everything. There was no misunderstanding his interest. Very forward. "Thanks for the roses you sent me today. Purple is my favorite."

"You're welcome." He smiled, but his eyes didn't move. "Your favorite color."

"And thank you for the lilies yesterday," she continued, feeling her throat start to dry up. Could she just grab him right now and throw caution to the wind? "They were lovely."

"You're welcome again." His eyes moved across her face.

Renee blinked twice, wondering if this was real. Her thoughts. She was afraid if he moved any closer, she'd kiss him and make a fool of herself. He was so smooth, so self-assured.

"I was hoping to hear from you," he said. "This weekend . . ."

"I was going to call you," Renee interrupted, mustering the courage to leap into this. "Michelle and I have plans . . ."

His eyes diverted from hers for half a second, but that was apparently enough. Renee realized, in that moment, she no longer had his full attention. She didn't have his attention at all. Turning to see what had won him over, she spotted a young woman standing in the doorway to Augusta.

Not a day over twenty, she held a natural, careless beauty. Tawny brown skin and auburn hair highlighted almond-shaped black eyes, a small nose, and tiny lips. She was very thin, her jean shorts barely holding up at the waist. She looked at Evan with uncertainty, what Renee sensed as apprehension. Whatever the case, Evan's head leaned away from Renee and focused on her. Renee tried to fight the tinge of jealousy that wanted to hit her, but realized it wasn't necessary when she looked again at Evan. It wasn't attraction in his eyes at all.

"Renee." After a long pause, he turned to her. "I have to go, but I hope we can talk again soon."

"I can call . . . you." His face was tight, but expressionless and Renee's curiosity was eating at her. She wouldn't ask. Couldn't. "I was going to . . ."

"That would be great." He'd leaned all the way off the car now. "I'll be looking forward to it." He quickly said goodbye before heading straight for the girl.

Evan passed Michelle after she pushed through the revolving door and dodged for the car. Focused on Evan, Renee missed the excitement on her face.

Michelle was already talking before she got into the car. "We have six o'clock reservations at the Shark Bar on Canal. Great soul food. Then we hit the flick."

Renee watched as Evan spoke to the young girl. She was upset, but talking. Nodding. She couldn't see Evan's face, his back turned to her, but he wasn't nodding.

"Then we go to Illusions, Dennis Rodman's club," Michelle continued, fixing her makeup in the mirror.

The young girl shrugged her shoulders and shook her head. Renee found it interesting that she wouldn't make eye contact with Evan. She was looking everywhere else but his face.

"Nick is gonna meet us at Illusions, if you don't mind."

Renee's eyes followed as the girl turned and started walking down the street. Evan called to her, but Renee saw she didn't respond. His profile showed a frustrated face as he started after her.

"Hey!" Michelle yelled. "I'm talking here."

Renee blinked and shook her head. "Oh, yeah, what?" The girl disappeared around the corner with Evan following.

Michelle turned around to see what was so interesting. "What? What? I don't see nothing."

"Anything." Renee sighed, a million thoughts in her head.

"What?" Michelle slid her seat belt on, looking at her sister with perplexity.

"You don't see *anything,*" Renee corrected again.

"Did you hear one word I said?"

"Yes." Renee blinked. Who was that girl? Why had she put Evan in a trance? "Well, no."

"Our plans." Michelle heaved an impatient sigh. "What are you looking at? There's nothing there. Did I miss something?"

"No." Renee pulled her seat belt on and started the car. "It was nothing."

"It wasn't *anything.*" Michelle flipped the mirror flap back down and checked her makeup again.

"Is this club okay?" Renee asked. "Dennis Rodman's name makes me think of . . . well, stuff I don't care to think of."

"You'll love it. It's a cool bar." Michelle turned her head, looking out the window There was a short silence. "You don't have a problem with transvestites, do you?"

Renee sighed and stepped on the gas.

After having more fun than she'd ever admit to anyone, Renee woke up earlier on Saturday than she'd expected. She hadn't gotten much sleep the night before. All she could think of was Evan Brooks and what she would say when she called him today. She'd waited three days like Karen told her to. Three excruciating days. As she had come to expect, that morning's dozen flowers arrived at ten, and this time they were azaleas.

Still, she was nervous. She knew there was no real reason to be. Despite yesterday's mysterious interruptions, from Evan's own behavior and words, she didn't see the chance of rejection. Nineties women asked men out all the time. Most men Renee knew found it refreshing. So, why was her stomach full of butterflies and an incessantly goofy smile on her face every time she thought of talking to him? She couldn't give even herself a reason, but she knew yesterday's perplexing encounter with the young woman outside Augusta wasn't romantic. Didn't look that way in the least. Intriguing, but not romantic.

"Did you dream about him again last night?" Michelle poured her sister a second cup of coffee before sitting across from her at the kitchen table.

"I should've never told you," Renee said, referring to the dream she'd had of Evan the night before last. "It was nothing."

"You dreamt about him." Michelle bit into a strawberry pop tart. "Damn, this is hot!"

"Michelle!" Renee hated cursing and Michelle knew that.

"Sorry." She sipped her orange juice. "How is it that this outside crust is lukewarm, but the fruit stuff inside is hot as hades? I don't get it."

"Did you read the ingredients on that box?" Renee pointed to the carton holding the treats.

"Don't start with me." Michelle stuck her tongue out. "This is fruit and carbs. Energy. Besides, I don't have a weight problem."

"It's not about weight," Renee said. "It's about health."

"Yadda, yadda, yadda." Michelle rolled her eyes. "Will you sign my book please?"

Renee ignored the snide remark. "Besides, the dream the other night meant nothing. He just walked past me on the street and said hello. That was it."

"Only naked," Michelle said. "Completely nude. In the buff. Butt . . ."

"Michelle!"

"Sorry." She fanned her face. "Got a little carried away there. So anyway, you dream about him last night?"

"No." Renee took a bite of her toast. Michelle burned everything. "What little dreaming I did was actually about Kimberly Janis."

"Why are you dreaming about her? You didn't even know her."

"I know." Renee sighed. "It was weird. I met her in some open field somewhere. Nothing but tall grass for miles. We talked about you for a while."

"What d'ya say?" Michelle's eyes widened as she leaned forward.

"Just the same stuff you told me. How you knew her." Renee thought back, recalling the rest of the dream. "Then reality slipped in and I remembered she'd killed herself and I reached out to her. I told her she was a beautiful and intelligent young black woman and there was a place for her in this world. I told her to get help for her depression; to seek guidance before it was too late."

"What did she say?" Michelle's mouth was wide open.

"Well, she started to fade and she was staring at me. Her eyes looked so confused. Then, before she completely disappeared, she told me she felt fine."

"You lying?"

"No. That's how it happened. It was eerie, and I just want to forget it."

"You know what it means?"

"I couldn't tell you." Renee took a sip of juice.

"No," Michelle said. "I'm not asking you. I'm telling you."

"You're a dream interpreter now?" Renee laughed.

"No." She leaned back, picking up today's issue of the *Sun Times* from the floor. She handed it to Renee. "But I can read. Turn to page fifteen."

The article was again reported by Chris Jackson. Kimberly was to be buried today in her home town of Philadelphia. The university's memorial would take place on campus this afternoon. Chris went on to explain that he was in possession of certain information that suggested Kimberly hadn't killed herself and further police investigation was necessary. He couldn't print the information because he didn't have strong confirmation and didn't want to risk a lawsuit. He urged anyone who knew anything more to call him or the police. The article ended with a comment that made Renee wonder.

It is suggested by some that Kimberly was severely depressed, which her family denied to me over the phone again today. The memorial on campus is being held as a result of almost seventy-five students and faculty appealing to the university because they were unable to travel to Philadelphia. Seventy-five. All of them claiming to be friends of Kimberly Janis. Would a woman be able to gather so many acquaintances after being here only six months if she was severely depressed and unbalanced?

"That's a good point," Renee said with a nod.

"About her not being so depressed?" Michelle asked.

"I have my doubts." Renee shook her head. "I don't know why. I just do. Tell me more about her, Michelle."

"I don't know much." Michelle shrugged, returning her attention to her food. "We just talked about stuff. Nothing too personal."

"She didn't have any enemies? Any crazy ex-boy-friends?" Renee thought almost every woman had a crazy ex-boyfriend in her past. For her, Alex came as close to that as anyone.

"I do remember . . ." Michelle paused, biting her lower lip. "She had an ex from Philly who was kind of bugging her still, but that was all she said. She didn't say how or anything. She also had kind of a problem with Alan's ex. Apparently Alan wasn't exactly free when he hooked up with Kimmy. Her name was Tamia something or other. Just the usual scorned woman stuff. Prank phone calls, you know. She didn't like to talk to people about her personal problems. I think she wanted people to think everything was cool. She seemed to be reluctant to tell me what she had.''

"Maybe that's the information Chris Jackson has that he can't print.'' Renee looked on the inside cover of the front page and found the paper's number. "I'm gonna call and see if I can get it out of him.''

"You're really tripping over this, aren't you?'' Michelle asked. "I mean, you didn't even know her except a couple of e-mails.''

"I know.'' Renee couldn't explain her growing interest to herself let alone to anyone else, but she couldn't ignore it either. "I know.''

"Hello, Mr. Jackson,'' Renee said as he finally picked up the line, introducing himself right off. "My name is Renee Shepherd and I'm calling about your article in this morning's paper.''

"Yeah,'' Chris responded unemotionally. "You have something I can use?''

"I'm curious as to why you believe Kimberly's death wasn't a suicide.''

"Are you a friend of Kimberly's?''

"I never really knew her,'' Renee answered, "but I have some questions, too.''

"Based on what, if you don't mind my asking?''

Renee told him about the messages that went between Kimberly and herself only hours before her death. She also repeated Michelle and Nick's opinions of Kimberly's behavior from dinner earlier that week.

"I'm interested,'' Chris said. "What made her come to you?''

"I'm an author. I've written a few books on nutrition

and health and I've covered the topic BFK sponsors. She works with my sister at Augusta. I guess she felt I would know people who could find out the truth about these things or had experience in these areas. I know it doesn't make a lot of sense, but I think she was desperate and grasping at straws when she contacted me."

"You said your sister works at Augusta?"

"Yeah." Renee listened as a long silence followed.

"I need to see those papers she sent you." Chris sounded as if he'd suddenly made an important decision. "They might have something to do with her murder."

"Who do you think could've murdered her?" Renee asked, not wanting to believe the accusation, although she knew she suspected the same. "She'd only been here six months."

"I have some ideas," he said suspiciously, "but I don't want to tell you over the phone. Can you meet me outside Loyola Union? It's where the memorial service is being held."

"I . . . I suppose." An inner voice told her she was getting more involved than she should.

"Great. I'll see you out front at noon. We'll talk then." He paused loudly. "And, Renee?"

"Yes?"

"Six months is plenty of time to make an enemy if someone's waiting to be one."

Chris hung up before Renee could say goodbye. She hung up much slower, contemplating what she should do. Part of her wanted to believe it was suicide, not wanting to accept that anyone would hurt this young girl. Only, if it wasn't true and someone had murdered her, he or she were out there with no penalty, and justice needed to be served. No matter how little a hand she could give, Kimberly deserved it.

Renee took another sniff of this morning's azaleas from

Evan, a smile conquering her face and spreading throughout her insides. It was ironic that two situations, Evan and Kimberly, remained in the forefront of her mind at the same time. They both evoked strong feelings and thoughts, only from completely opposite ends of her emotional spectrum. They both made her wonder what she was getting herself into.

Renee arrived at Loyola at eleven forty-five, but Chris Jackson was already there. She spotted him immediately. He looked like a reporter to Renee, or at least her idea of one. Of normal height, Chris had a medium brown complexion. He looked like a student himself, a serious expression fighting his devil-may-care eyes. He was disheveled, looking uncomfortable in a jacket and tie. When she reached him, he was deep in concentration, looking straight ahead at nothing in particular, but as soon as Renee positioned herself in his tunnel of vision, he quickly adjusted with a wide smile. He was pleased.

"You must be Chris Jackson." Renee held out her hand.

"Wow," was all Chris said, continuing to stare while shaking her hand.

"I'm Renee Shepherd." She was amused by his approval, although she wasn't looking exactly her best in the black pants suit she'd borrowed from Michelle's closet. It was a little loose with the legs a bit short, but it being the middle of June, she hadn't packed anything in black that was appropriate for the occasion.

"You're not what I imagined." Chris straightened up, clearing his throat.

"And exactly what was that?" She followed Chris as he led her into the building, rumbling with students and faculty.

"I don't know." He messed with his tie, making it look

worse than before he'd touched it. "I suppose I expected more . . . and less . . . I don't know."

"An older, boring intellectual type?" Renee asked.

"Well, sort of." Chris smiled in embarrassment.

"It's funny," Renee said. "When you're an intelligent and successful woman, some people still assume you're either old or unattractive."

"Please forgive me," Chris begged. "I'm a brother of the nineties, really. I myself am looking for a sister who makes a whole bunch of dough, because I don't figure I ever will."

Sensing a compliment was somewhere in that comment, Renee continued along the corridor until they stopped outside a door marked CONFERENCE ROOM D.

"This is the room," he said. "Do you have those papers Kimberly e-mailed you?"

Renee reached into her purse and handed over the folded sheets. She stepped aside as arriving people entered the room. She watched Chris as he studied each sheet carefully.

"Can I trust your confidence, Ms. Shepherd?" Chris's eyes were glued to the papers as he spoke.

"It's Renee," she corrected. "And yes, you can."

"Kimberly Janis called me the day before her death." He eyed Renee with a secretive squint. "She left a message for me, telling me she'd appreciated the investigative skills I showed in a recent article on racial discrimination at a big Chicago law firm. She asked if I'd investigate BFK. She didn't know what was going on, but she knew something was wrong."

"Did she say who?" Renee whispered even though no one was around them at the moment. She thought of Nick. She hated herself for doing so, but couldn't help it.

"No. It was a long enough message as it was." Chris bit

his lower lip in frustration, then said, "You know Evan Brooks?"

"Yeah," Renee responded. "He's executive director of Augusta."

"But do you know him?"

Renee wondered what Chris was alluding to. "Not intimately, but I've spent some time in his presence. What does he have to do with this?"

"Have you noticed any weird behavior on his part in regards to Kimberly?"

"What are you getting at, Chris?" She didn't want to hear this.

"My first thought is this Nick Hamilton is managing the funds. That's too simple. If Nick was stealing, then Kimberly could've gone to Evan. Evan is above everyone. But she didn't." He rubbed his chin. "Why not? Maybe she wasn't sure she could trust him. Maybe he's the one."

"Evan would never . . ." Renee stopped in the middle of her sentence as the events from earlier that week suddenly jogged her memory.

"What?" Chris asked.

"He seemed extremely curious about her a few days ago." She wasn't sure exactly what she was trying to say with her words. They were only coming out as she thought them. "When I told him about the messages, he was interested to say the least."

"And?" Chris asked, ready to soak in her every word.

"It makes sense," Renee explained, not relishing Chris's apparent delight at her news. "Evan is a caring person, and he was just concerned. As the director, I'm sure he wants to report the truth to the public and he has to listen to every side before he can do that."

"Then why did he refuse every one of my phone calls? I asked for only five minutes of his time, and he flatly refused every time."

"If he believes she killed herself, then what would he say?" Renee sensed herself feeling it necessary to go on the defensive, but wasn't sure why. "He issued a statement with condolences, right?"

"Yeah." Chris shrugged, then sarcastically said, "In form letter style. Very caring. It brought me to tears."

"What have you got against Evan Brooks?" She was beginning to sense something personal at play.

"In my personal opinion," Chris said, placing a polite hand flat to his chest, "he's just another rich guy who can write off his lifestyle as charity when tax season comes around."

"That's ridiculous, Chris." Renee shook her head. "Evan has done a lot for the community. He took that job at Augusta because he wants to give back. He appreciates his fortune and wants to share it."

"You sound as if he's certainly shared something with you." Chris leaned back, giving Renee a judgmental once-over.

"That's out of line." Renee's tone matched her stern impression, but inside she was uncertain. She didn't know Evan well enough to defend him so strongly. So what made her want to?

"I'm sorry," Chris apologized. "You just seemed so defensive on his behalf, for someone who just spent a little time around him."

Renee didn't respond. He was right. She'd done more than speak with him briefly, but not enough to defend his character so strongly. It was only an urge to . . . she was speaking of the man she hoped he was.

"So. What else did you notice?" Chris asked.

"Nothing." Renee remembered seeing Evan at Kimberly's desk and the interlude with the young woman outside Augusta yesterday, but wasn't ready to speak up. It was all

Chris needed to fuel his obvious contempt. He wasn't open to being objective in Evan's case.

"You don't mind if I hold onto these?" Chris held up the papers she'd given him. "I'm going to have to study them more to see if they hold any information. I might give them to the cops if it'll get them to reopen the case."

"Fine." Renee headed for the memorial room, knowing Chris was directly behind her.

The fake wood walls were palely decorated with an assortment of chairs and tables lining the room. It was full of people, mostly students in blue jeans, reminding her of Chris's earlier question in the paper. Would a girl with so many friends commit suicide? Renee looked around. She knew sometimes people with hundreds of friends and family to lean on chose to take their own lives anyway, because their despair had gone beyond any hope, making them feel alone among a sea of loved ones.

"Speak of the devil," Chris said, looking toward the far right corner of the room.

Renee followed his glance. She felt her heart jump at the sight of Evan Brooks. He was so attractive, standing above everyone, smiling with a powerful magnetism, conversing with a crowd circled around him. Renee saw how his appeal reached everyone. Those around him, students and adults alike, couldn't take their eyes off him, hanging on to every word he said. He enjoyed it, too. Evan would never be accused of being shy.

She couldn't take her eyes off him either. Dressed in a pair of black slacks and a plain dark blue button-down, he still looked better than any suit in the room. Not that there were many. Who could notice if there were, Renee thought. As soon as her eyes reached him, all she could see was Evan.

When he suddenly lifted his eyes from those in the circle around him, they went absolutely nowhere but to her, directly catching hers and holding them. To Renee it was as if not only did he know she was here, but he knew exactly where she'd been even before he saw her. She felt the flirtatious smile return to her face, but not as it had before. It was more knowing now, less uncertain. He returned her smile with a gentle one of his own, but not with just his mouth. He smiled with his eyes as well, and Renee felt herself take a deep breath as a feeling of warmth spread over her. Could one smile have such an effect? His could. His did.

"He seems to be taken by you," Chris said, placing a hand casually on Renee's shoulder.

As Evan saw the touch, Renee noticed his smile fade before he returned to being center stage among his admirers. Renee felt her heart drop at the misunderstanding, and she wanted to be angry with Chris, even though he wasn't to blame.

"Not that he's any different from every other guy in this room," Chris continued. "Do you think you can get me an interview?"

"So you can grill him?" Renee asked with a smart smack of her lips. "I don't think so."

"Hey," Chris said, grabbing a young Japanese girl's arm as she walked by.

The girl was at first struck with startled anger, but within a second of looking at Chris, she calmed a little, looking nothing more than annoyed. "What's up?"

"You get my message?" Chris asked in a whisper, pulling her to him.

"Yeah, I got it." The young woman, all of five feet tall with a boyish short haircut that flattered her large eyes, spoke impatiently.

"Well?" Chris asked, then seemed to notice that both women were staring blankly at each other. "Oh, yeah.

Renee, this is Jenny Sukata, a classmate of Kimberly Janis. Jenny, this is Renee Shepherd. She's visiting Chicago."

"You knew Kimmy?" Jenny asked.

"Not exactly." Renee didn't want to explain the e-mail situation again. "We were distant acquaintances."

"So?" Chris asked Jenny, finally letting go of her arm as she pulled away.

"He said he'll see what he can do." Jenny looked around. "You're asking a lot. He's barely past being a rookie."

"He's done it before," Chris said.

"Should I step away?" Renee asked, feeling like a third wheel.

"I'm sorry." Chris smiled. "Jenny's man is a cop. I'm trying to get him to get me Kimberly's file cause it's coming out of his precinct."

"That's legal?"

"No," Jenny said emphatically.

"He's cool," Chris said. "He's a brother. He's helped me out before. Jenny, you got to talk to him."

"I have, Chris." She placed both hands on her petite hips. "I'm not doing any more."

"What about Detective Griggs?" Chris asked.

Jenny pointed a finger at him. "He's not going to tell on another cop."

"But this guy is a racist."

"He's a cop," Jenny said. "Cops are cops. What can I tell you. Besides, you can read about Griggs in the paper."

"Just ask him again." Chris pressed his hands together at his chest in prayer.

"How did you meet her?" Renee asked after Jenny turned and walked away.

"Poking around some of Kimberly's friends a couple of days ago." His frown showed his disappointment. "When I found out she knew my police source, I couldn't believe my luck. Or so I thought. She's starting to flake out on me now."

"What's this about a racist detective?" she asked, finding the situation much more complex than she'd imagined. "What would he have to do with this?"

"Detective Robert Griggs." Chris's face held all the disgust one could. "He's had racial complaints against him for years. Most recently a lawsuit by the family of a young black boy who he beat the living tar out of. Said the kid was resisting arrest. He was twelve. A good slap would've calmed him down. The kid was still in the hospital four months later. He caught him stealing a cupcake."

"Why is this guy not suspended?" Renee was horrified.

"He was. Without pay for two months." Chris shoved his hands into his pockets with force. "You know what expensive lawyers can do for you. They had to take him back, but put him on university police support, which is supposed to be a huge demotion among the blue."

"What are you hoping to get from him?"

Chris let out a laugh with sarcasm edging every bit of it. "He's not gonna give me anything. He blames the press for his predicament now. I'm just real curious why Kimberly's case was shot down so soon, and he's the senior detective on the scene."

"Any luck with Kimberly's other friends?" Renee asked, accepting a cup of punch offered her by a passing gentleman in a white jacket.

"Nothing really. The same stuff, but nothing concrete. Nothing to lead me to a murderer."

"She had an ex," Renee said, remembering her earlier conversation with Michelle. "She had an ex-boyfriend from Philadelphia who Michelle remembered her mentioning was bugging her."

"Who?" Chris's eyes lit up. "What's his name? Tell me exactly what she said."

"Slow down," Renee said, taking a sip of punch. "Michelle never got a name. I told you over the phone they were casual. It's just what I told you."

"Some of these kids must be friends of Kimberly's." Chris looked over Renee's shoulders with jumpy excitement in his eyes. "I'm gonna ask them if they know anything about an ex."

"Chris." Renee grabbed a hold of his arm. "This is a memorial."

"I'll be tasteful." He winked. "Stick around. We'll talk later."

Renee gave him one last glare before he set off. She remembered the memorial for her parents as if it were yesterday. Unrealized grief could come to a fore at any moment. She hoped Chris wouldn't push them right now.

Renee turned her attention to Evan, hoping Chris's exit would help him understand they weren't there together. At least not in the way Evan's expression seemed to imply. Evan wouldn't look at her, focusing on those surrounding him. Renee's frustration tempted her to go right up to him, but she didn't want to turn the attention of the circle to herself. She actually found it interesting to just watch him, his commanding air of self-confidence was attractive and inspiring. His stance was intelligent and spirited, his eyes holding a compassionate wisdom. Yes, she enjoyed watching him, but also wanted some of his attention for herself.

"Ms. Shepherd?"

Alan Smith stood next to her, a Styrofoam cup of punch in his hand. She thought he looked well, considering. He was wearing a black suit, with the tie loosened and one side of the shirt hanging halfway out of his pants. His eyes were tired and weary, and Renee felt a deep compassion for him.

"Hi, Alan." She placed her hand on his shoulder. "Call me Renee. We're the same age."

"I'm sorry." He forced a smile. "I guess, you're kind of famous and successful. I thought . . . well, most famous and successful people are kind of silly like that, you know."

"Not me." She wanted to say something to make him feel better, but she knew words weren't what he needed now. When someone you care for passes away, a grieving person needs an ear to listen more than words of reassurance.

"I saw you come in with Chris Jackson." Alan nodded his head in the direction Chris had gone. "You friends with him?"

"Not really." Renee wondered if Alan had been reading the papers or was purposefully avoiding them. "Actually, I just met him today."

Alan shook his head. "These reporters. They think everything is more than it is. All they care about is a story. Poor Kimberly."

"Aren't you even a little curious?" Renee asked. "Chris strongly believes . . ."

"I hate to be rude," Alan said, interrupting her, "but I really don't need to hear this. It's hard enough dealing with her death, but to have someone try to use this to advance his media career."

"Is that why you think he's doing this?" Renee noticed Alan's tone taking a harsher turn.

"I dated Kimberly for four months." Alan's eyes lowered to the ground. "It took less than a second to fall in love with her. A lemons into lemonade kind of girl. Understood my thing, you know. It's just sometimes she let the drama in her life get to her, and she got a little depressed. Why is that so hard to understand? I'm not saying she was a manic depressive needing medication, but she got down a little more than the usual person, you know? The more this issue is harped on, the more those who knew her have to keep telling everyone how she was. None of us wants to do that. She's dead. Do you have any idea what it feels like to have to tell everyone she had problems now? That's not how I want her to be remembered.''

"I'm sorry, Alan.'' Renee felt a little guilty she'd continued the conversation. "I won't mention it again.''

"Thanks.'' He smiled. "I'd just like to remember her the way I knew her. Not always like that, but energetic and optimistic. She wasn't mentally ill or anything like that.''

"I'm sorry you couldn't get to Philadelphia for the funeral,'' Renee said.

"Too many obligations on such short notice.'' Alan shrugged. "I don't know her family very well either, and they seemed kind of upset that I got her stuff from work. I guess they felt that was their right.''

"Alan.'' Renee felt for him. He had a right to be there now. "I'd love to visit BFK headquarters sometime. Just to look around. I wrote a book that included some of the issues surrounding children's nutrition and I'm still very interested in the topic.''

"Anytime.'' Alan reached into his back pocket and pulled out his wallet. He handed her his card. "Come soon. I pretty much live there, so I'm sure I'll be there whenever you decide to stop by.''

He thanked her for coming before making his way to a crowd of friends and comforters. As Renee watched him accept their condolences, she felt the irony of love. There was so much about it that was good, better and more valuable than anything in the world. Only the price you paid, the risk you took was greater than anything in the world.

"Hello, Renee.''

She immediately recognized Evan's voice as she swung

around to face him. He was standing only a couple of feet from her.

"Hello, Evan." His name slipped so comfortably from her lips, as if she'd said it one hundred times before. Those electric eyes pierced into her. "How are you?"

"All right." He smiled in a way of saying he was pleased at the least. "I read your books."

"Which one?" she asked. The rest of the room was disappearing again.

"All three."

"Since when?" Renee was amazed with each of her books running over three hundred pages.

"Since Monday. After we met at Augusta. I ran to the bookstore." Evan stepped closer, his eyes never leaving hers. "I'm sorry I never read them before. They're very good. You're very talented."

"The real talents are my sources and my editor. I couldn't have done it without them." Renee could smell his cologne as he stepped closer. She liked its scent, masculine without being overwhelming. It was his nearness that made her senses go wild. She felt the constant urge to smile, but this man was no joke.

"I'm looking forward to your next one."

Renee was doing all she could to hear his words. Her mind was going blank as she stared at him. She was deathly afraid of making a fool of herself. "It will be out pretty soon."

He positioned himself to stand where he was for a while, placing his dark hands firmly on his strong hips. "Good for you. What's this one about?"

"Taking a lot of the fat and sodium out of old-fashioned soul food recipes." She liked his attentiveness. It wasn't a cover. He was genuinely interested and she appreciated the respect. "You know the traditional fried catfish, fried chicken, sweet potato pie, buttery pound cake."

"Keeping the taste, though." He waved a playfully warning finger.

"Of course." Renee laughed. "It isn't soul food without the flava."

"I'd love to get my copies signed."

"I have a book signing next Wednesday," she said. "Show up at Black America Booksellers at two and you'll get your wish."

Evan nodded. His eyes wandered over her again as if savoring the moment, before recharging the conversation. "I see you're friends with Chris Jackson."

"Not really." Renee was flattered by his attempt to hide his jealousy, but wasn't into playing games. "I don't want you to misinterpret anything. I just met Chris this morning."

"That's good to know."

There was that honesty again, Renee thought. His words, his expression showed he was very relieved. He didn't think to hide it to keep the upper hand. Didn't need the upper hand. She was immensely intrigued by that. She liked it almost as much as she liked him being close.

"That leads me to my next question." Evan lifted his finger as a reminder. "First I have to apologize for not sticking around yesterday."

"I understand," she said, although she really didn't. She wished she could be honest with him. "She was a friend?"

Evan blinked, his smile fading. "No. But back to the point, we were talking about you giving me a call. I won't push for an update, but if you're looking to offer, I'm looking to hear it."

"I was going to call you." Renee blinked. She wanted to ignore that his prompt no answer about the woman from yesterday nagged at her. "The flowers again this morning were beautiful."

"Not too much three days in a row?" he asked with caution.

"Not at all," she answered, shaking her head.

"Will you have dinner with me tonight?"

Renee tried her best to hide her delight, but was sure some of it showed. "I thought that move was supposed to be mine."

"It was." His brows formed a regretful frown. "You just said you were going to call. I'm saving you the time. Besides, I'm not into chancing it."

"You don't believe much in mystery do you?"

"Not true. There's a whole bunch of stuff you don't know about me, Renee." He gently touched her shoulder, his eyes trailing her neck, returning to her face. "But when I see something I want, I go after it. What I want now is to have dinner with you."

He was intimidating, but Renee figured Evan's candidness deserved as much in return. Besides, if she'd had the slightest doubt before, his touch on her shoulder immediately erased it. "I'll have dinner with you."

"I can pick you up at seven if that's all right?"

"Yes, but you need my address."

"I have it. Your sister gave it to me Tuesday when she gave me your phone number."

"She's thorough if anything." Renee had never thought she'd appreciate Michelle's attempts at matchmaking. "She told me about your conversation."

"She was very helpful."

"She's expecting a raise from all this," Renee said. "That's her objective."

"We'll have to see." Evan glanced at his watch and grimaced. "I have an appointment in twenty minutes and I have to get going. This seems to happen every time with us."

"You work on Saturdays, too?" Renee sensed her great

reluctance to see him leave. She so selfishly enjoyed his attention.

"A good man's work is never done." He winked with a laugh. "Likewise for the rest of us. I have a contributor who asked to meet with me. Big-time money. I'm not at liberty to confine him to nine to five."

"As well you shouldn't."

"Can I give you a ride anywhere?"

"I promised Chris I'd wait for him." Renee said regretfully. "I'll see you at seven."

"Seven it is."

His eyes seemed to flash at her, sending a warm sensation flowing through her long body. They said their goodbyes. Renee watched him leave, still feeling the heat from his touch on her shoulder. How could it be, she wondered? How could someone have such an effect on her from a brief, seemingly insignificant touch?

Her euphoria was interrupted as, just before reaching the door, Evan stopped and turned to his left. Renee followed his gaze to the corner of the room.

It was her again. The young woman from outside the building yesterday was looking just as disturbed today as she eyed Evan. She blinked nervously then turned away, her figure getting lost in a crowd of people. Renee watched as Evan continued to look in the girl's direction for a few seconds before turning and heading out of the room.

Renee had to know who this girl was. What was her connection to Evan? What was his hold on her, disturbing her so. She knew it was none of her business, but she didn't care.

Doing his best to contain a smile at an unjoyous occasion, Chris returned to Renee's side only moments after leaving.

"I've got some news about Kimberly." He leaned in close for the whisper. "I just talked to five of her friends. A couple of them gave me the same thing, saying she'd been acting a little unusual the last month or so of her life, but none of them felt she was depressed enough to kill herself."

"What do they mean by unusual?" Renee asked. "Did you get any concrete definitions?"

"They said she seemed edgy and very preoccupied." Chris popped a breath mint in his mouth, returning the packet to his back pocket.

"That sounds more like what Michelle said. She said Kimberly seemed paranoid."

"So it makes more sense that her behavior was sparked by fear than depression." Chris tapped his forehead with his finger. "She knew someone at Augusta was on to her."

"Or she was being harassed by her ex," Renee added. "Her death doesn't necessarily have to do with Augusta, even though she was concerned about it at the time. She had other problems more pressing to her safety."

"I've got to find out more about that guy."

"There's another possibility," Renee said as she remembered. "Alan Smith, Kimberly's boyfriend, has an ex who wasn't too happy to be the ex."

"Name?" Chris pulled out his pad.

Renee shrugged. "Can't help you there. All I know is what Michelle told me."

"More questions to ask her friends. I wonder why no one mentioned the spurned ex before."

"She probably hasn't told them. Michelle got the distinct impression she didn't want to talk about it."

"I'd like to talk to your sister if that's all right with you?"

"It has to be all right with her." Renee said. "She's not too comfortable with the girl being someone she knew and her own age at that."

"I have to get back to the paper, but can I come over tonight? Maybe if you're there, she'll talk to me." He paused, clearing his throat. "Then, if you're not too busy, maybe we can grab a bite to eat somewhere."

"I'm sorry, Chris," Renee said respectfully. "I have plans tonight."

He quickly wiped the disappointment from his face as it appeared only for a quick second. "Evan Brooks?"

"Evan has asked me to dinner and I accepted." Renee saw the cautious look on Chris's face and she met it head on. "I'm not really interested in hearing your opinion of Evan Brooks."

"Fine." Chris paused, his eyes filling with light again. "What about tomorrow night?"

"Chris," Renee said, respecting his young persistence. "Aren't you a student?"

"Grad," he said defensively. "I'm twenty-three years old if that's what you're wondering. You can't be much older. At least you don't look it."

"Thanks for the compliment, but I'll have to decline." She tossed her cup in a nearby trash can.

"Friends then?" He held out his hand in a peacemaking effort.

"Friends." She smiled as they shook in agreement. Renee looked around the room for the mystery girl, but couldn't find her. She would find a tactful way to ask Evan about her tonight. She'd have to.

"Today went well. I gotta say. Still, the more I get, the more I need to find out."

"You believe in objectivity right?" Renee asked. "Telling both sides."

"Of course I do. I'm a journalist." He opened the conference room door, letting Renee exit before him.

"Then you should also know that Alan Smith told me personally that he's seen her get depressed more often than normal."

"I'm not saying she didn't get depressed. I'm only saying she didn't kill herself."

"Did you get any more on the ex from Philly?"

"His name was Ben Monty." Chris pulled the pad from his back pocket and looked over the first sheet. "A couple of them said he works at a radio station in Philly. He hit her once or twice. She got a restraining order against him, but he'd test it every day."

"Like if the order said not to come within fifty feet of her," Renee said, "he'd stay fifty-one feet from her apartment. That kind of thing." She was grateful Alex, her ex, wasn't that bad even though he had been reluctant to let her go.

"Exactly. She and her parents agreed it would be best if she left Philly."

Renee felt her anger rising. "He's the crazy one, and she's got to leave her home town. Sounds fair."

"Ironic as hell." He flipped the pad and returned it to his pocket. "They thought they were making it safer for her."

"Did the police check out this ex?" Renee couldn't stand to think of what the parents were going through. She hated living so far from Michelle. Hated it.

"Probably not." Chris stepped aside for passersby. "I know this Detective Griggs is dirty. He has a hand in this. I'm checking it out. I'm gonna find out more about this Alan Smith her friends and you are talking about."

"You don't know who he is?"

"Just like you, I know he's Kimberly's last boyfriend, but I didn't get . . ."

"He's the director of BFK." Renee was surprised Chris hadn't figured that out yet. Chris's expression was almost dumbfounded.

"That's very interesting" was all he said.

"You aren't drawing another conclusion are you?" Renee asked.

"No." Chris smiled at Renee's intuitiveness. "This just adds another angle."

"Well, if he's her boyfriend, he should know about her behavior." Renee knew she was contradicting herself, but she was still hoping it wasn't murder. "He'd even know more than her friends."

"She's only been here six months," Chris said with a look of skepticism on his face. "I can see close friends, but lovers? How close could they've been? They probably just saw each other now and then. What I wonder is why she didn't tell him about her suspicions?"

"Maybe she did," Renee said. "Maybe he just didn't believe her. He's never mentioned it, but he's never been asked. He seems to have been honest with me so far."

"Maybe I'll ask." Chris rubbed his chin as his eyes squinted.

"Listen," Renee said. "Alan seems truly saddened by Kimberly's death. You should leave him alone today. At least today."

"Maybe he's faking it for the attention. Some people are like that. I'll have to look into it, objectivity being my middle name. I'll see you later."

"Bye, Chris."

Renee watched Chris down the hallway. She felt she should've been relieved his attention was off of Evan, but it seemed similarly ridiculous to suspect Alan. Why would Kimberly have still been dating Alan at the time if she suspected him or was afraid of him? She remembered Michelle saying Alan had picked up Kimberly's things from the office, making it seem as if they still had a relationship until the end. Anything was possible, Renee understood, but it wasn't likely.

Caught up in her thoughts, Renee didn't notice Nick

walking toward her and was startled when he called her name.

"Hello, Nick," she said. He looked all business in a blue suit and with a briefcase in hand. She was getting used to the eternal look of impatience on his face.

"What are you doing here?" he asked.

"I came for Kimberly's memorial." Renee couldn't help but let his words rub her the wrong way. It wasn't so much the words as the way he said them. His tone.

"You don't even know her. Why do you care so much?"

Renee glanced at her watch. She didn't have to answer that. Be cool, she told herself. Michelle loves him.

"I've got to go. I have an appointment."

"So do I." He straightened his tie. "I'm in and out of here faster than lightning."

Without a goodbye, he brushed past Renee and headed for the conference room.

"How caring," she whispered before turning and heading outside.

As she stepped out a side door of the building, Renee expected some fresh air as she inhaled deeply, only it wasn't as fresh as she expected. She exhaled quickly with a quiet cough when she tasted the cigarette smoke. Looking to her left, she saw the odor was coming from Alan Smith. He was standing in the corner, unaware of her presence, coolly smoking a cigarette. It wasn't that in itself that Renee noticed, but the look on his face. He seemed calm and almost at peace, appearing extremely relaxed. There was no telling the cause, Renee thought. Maybe he felt closure after attending the memorial. Maybe smoking was his own release. Maybe Chris was right and Alan was in this for the attention. Renee knew it wasn't the worst thing anyone had done, but then cleared the thought from her mind. She'd seen Alan up close and believed his grief to be real. She was just letting Chris's doubts cloud her judgment.

She decided not to bother Alan and instead went in search of a taxicab. She didn't want to think of poor Kimberly Janis or the circumstances surrounding her death right now. It was too upsetting. Instead, she focused on tonight. She was more than simply excited about it and wanted to knock Evan off his feet with a stunning outfit. She had some shopping to do. So, back to the Magnificent Mile. Something red was in order.

It worked.

SIX

When Evan saw Renee in the fitted, ruby-red satin Donna Karan dress that stopped only inches above her knees, anyone within a mile could see he was floored. At first sight, he photographed her with his eyes, resulting in a charged smile that sent her pulses racing. She didn't try to hide her pleasure at his approval. The satisfaction was sweeter than she'd imagined.

Renee hadn't done so much primping since the party last New Year's Eve in New York, but even then there wasn't too much to do. Her natural features, trim figure, and long legs were automatic. She'd set her hair several hours before and it spiraled softly around her feminine, oval face, which was done up with modest earth tones accentuating her seductive eyes and full lips. Nothing heavy in the hot summer. The dress didn't hug her curves tightly, but slid around them caressingly. Never one to bring too much attention to herself, never needing to, Renee knew she'd get some stares tonight, but the only stare she was concerned about was from the handsome man who sat across from her at One-Sixty Blue, considered the higher class of basketball star Michael Jordan's two Chicago restaurants.

Renee didn't win that looks contest hands down. She made sure to compliment Evan as he'd been so kind to do to her a few times already. His casual evening V-neck shirt laid on him, hinting at the lean but muscular definition underneath. The designer glasses were gone, allowing Renee to see the softness and appeal of those light eyes that mesmerized her. She found herself drawn to their compelling gaze enough to make Evan a little nervous, which Renee found refreshing considering she didn't think he was capable of being so.

"It's nice, you know." He blinked, smiled, showing his perfect teeth. "Not to be the only one staring for a change."

"I'm sorry." Renee felt a blush sweep over her. "I was being rude."

He frowned. "You'd be rude to stop. I know I can't stop staring at you."

"Fine, then." She flipped him a coy, confident smile. "I won't."

"I wonder," he uttered. "When will the real Renee Shepherd come out?"

"What do you mean? You think I'm putting up a facade?"

"No. That's not what I meant. What I know of you is perfection." Evan leaned forward, his face only a foot from her own. "You're beautiful, sexy, intelligent, and independent. You're also a little shy. I know you've had some unfortunate things happen to you in the past, but from the outside, it seems you haven't got a problem in the world now."

"You'd prefer me to?" Renee felt a shiver down her spine as his hand gently covered hers atop the table.

"I'd prefer to know the real you," he whispered as he

stared intently into her eyes. "I want to know your doubts, frustrations, and fears. What's important to Renee? What does she live with she'd rather not? What can't she live without?"

"That's pretty personal." She found his touch dangerous to her libido and slowly withdrew her hand. He was so close. She needed to slow down.

"I know," he said. "I'd tell you if you wanted to know."

"You barely know me." Renee believed him. Didn't doubt him for a second. Her head was starting to spin.

"You show more than you think." Evan leaned back as the waiter placed their food on the table.

"How do I do that?" How self-assured he seemed in his judgment of her piqued her curiosity.

"Take Monday night for instance," Evan postured. "It was more than obvious that you don't care for Nick Hamilton, although you tried very hard to hide it."

Renee cleared her throat, her eyes blinking nervously. "I'll admit, we haven't gotten off to a good start, but I'm trying for Michelle's sake."

"If it helps to know, we were all surprised to hear the news. We knew they'd been dating, but they aren't an obvious match up."

"Tell me about surprise." Renee sighed. "I mean, three months isn't nearly enough time."

"I'm gonna have to disagree with you there," Evan said. "I've known people who knew they were meant for each other after three minutes and were right."

Renee blushed as his silent gaze seemed to last forever. Was he telling her something, or simply flirting, which seemed to be a part-time job for him? Either way, she felt like she could stay in this moment all night long.

"I'm just surprised it was Nick," he added after an extended silence.

"Why so?"

"I don't know Nick very well." Evan shrugged. "No one really does. It just seemed to all of us that he'd go for some high-powered executive type. Someone as bloodthirsty to climb the corporate ladder as he is. Who else could relate to him?"

"It's my opinion that Nick wants to be the only one with ambition in his marriage." Renee rolled her eyes. "An accessory. Now, he does want someone with education for presentation purposes, but I think he really wants a trophy wife whose only desire is to make him look good to the corporate honchos."

"I can't imagine Michelle settling in the role of an arm piece," Evan said. "At least not from what I've seen of her. She seems ambitious and expressive. She has a little of your independence."

"She's young and in love." Renee batted her lashes to mock infatuation. "She probably believes she'll change him. I know she's smarter than that, but I'm sure even Albert Einstein missed a step or two when he was in love."

"Is that it?" Evan seemed surprised.

"Isn't that enough?" Renee asked.

"Yeah, but I don't believe that's all there is to it."

"Enlighten me." She leaned back in her chair, crossing her arms against her chest.

"I think you want to hold on to Michelle." Evan smiled with confidence as if welcoming the invitation. "It's understandable. She's the only family you have left and the thought of her having her own family, one she would have to make her priority, is very upsetting to you."

"Are you suggesting," Renee said, feeling her temper slowly rise, "that I don't want her to marry Nick for selfish reasons of my own? Just so I can have my sister all to myself?"

"Maybe not consciously, but . . ."

"For your information, Evan Brooks, I have spent the

last eight years wanting only the best for Michelle because she's been cheated, and . . ."

"So have you," Evan interjected.

Renee sat silent, only able to stare at Evan, who stared right back. Out of the blue, she had an urge to cry. Bawl her eyes out. She refused to give in. Evan had struck a hidden chord with her and it disturbed her. He was too perceptive for her liking. She was sure he was wrong. There was no way she was jealous of Nick. Maybe, Renee agreed to herself, there were some unresolved feelings about Michelle going off to live her own life, no longer depending on her big sister, but there was certainly no desire to keep her sister from doing that. From being happy.

"I would like to change the subject." Renee tore her eyes from his, tossing her hair in a defiant gesture. She wasn't about to let him know his words had affected her so deeply. Besides, it was time for him to be probed a little bit. "I have a question for you."

"Fire away."

"Friday, when you came to my car outside . . ." she began.

"I remember." He dug his fork into his food. "By the way, you're a pretty good singer."

She fought the smile, but it was stronger than her will. "Continuing, you left me to go talk to someone. A young woman."

Evan's smile faded. Stone serious. "Yes."

"I saw her again at the memorial today." Renee knew she'd struck gold. His expressions were priceless. She wondered if she'd get an answer. "I was just curious. A friend of yours?"

"No." His eyes went to his plate as he wiped his mouth. "She's just someone I know. Why?"

"It's probably none of my business," Renee added, beginning to feel bad for bringing the subject up. Why should she? It was an honest question. "I was just curious if she was a friend, but you just said she wasn't, so . . ."

"Her name is Tamia Griffin. She's just an acquaintance I needed some work-related information from. I don't know much more than that." He tried to force a smile, but his eyes showed the truth. He didn't want to talk about this.

"I've gotten too personal," she conceded, assuming she'd gotten as much as she was going to. "After I just told you you were getting too personal."

"It's okay. I understand why you'd be protective of your relationship with your sister."

Evan returned to his food. "I only asked because I get the impression that you haven't indulged yourself in a long time, and you deserve it. Michelle wasn't the only one who missed out because of what happened eight years ago. I'm thinking, because you were twenty, you thought your childhood years, the ones when you need your parents the most, were over. So it was Michelle that was cheated the most. Only, you never stop needing your parents. I'm thirty-five, and sometimes I'd give anything to be able to call my dad up and ask for some advice. You were cheated, too, Renee."

"I've made a success of my life," she said, his words were begging the tears to come. "I'm happy with what I've accomplished."

"You should be. Not many people have three successful books before the age of thirty. Now, what about the other things in life? Like . . ."

"Don't say, what about a man." Renee held up a hand to stop him. "I don't need a man in my life to be happy."

"I know that." Evan laughed. "I'm not trying to get slapped. I wasn't going to say that."

"Maybe I do focus on Michelle too much," Renee said, "but she's just a kid and . . ."

"She's an adult," Evan corrected her kindly.

"A very young adult," she corrected back, becoming frustrated by his challenges. "I'm prepared to let her go when the time comes that she can take care of herself."

"What will you do then?" Evan asked as his eyes assessed her.

"You tell me." She grinned, not willing to give him the pleasure of knowing he was getting to her. "You seem to know so much tonight."

Evan laughed. "I think you're going to become like those parents who send their last kid off to college. They don't know what to do with themselves. They were just parents, and had stopped being individuals a long time ago. They try to do things like get a pet to fill the void, but it doesn't work."

"I'll have plenty to do with myself, so don't worry about me." She grinned to hide her discomfort. "Let's change the subject again, please."

"So it must be fun being a famous author." Evan took a mouthful of scampi chicken. He laughed at her off-guard stare. "Well, you asked to change the subject, didn't you?"

"I suppose I'm surprised," she said. "You're so persistent. I didn't expect you to give up so easily."

"You'll tell me what you want to when you're ready." Evan shrugged with confidence. "There's no need to push."

Renee wasn't so sure she liked the confidence with which he made that statement, but she was more disturbed by the fact that she didn't doubt him.

There was a short, tension-filled silence as they both dug into their meals, exchanging occasional glances and flirting smiles. Feeling recovered from the personal tone of the previous discussion, Renee started a new conversation, making sure to stick to safer topics like her career and the famous people Evan met while working with D.C. and

Chicago area politicians. Returning to what urged her to write her first book unintentionally brought the conversation to Kimberly Janis.

Renee noticed again that the mere mention of Kimberly's name brought an unusual reaction from Evan. She hated the thought, but Chris's comments forced themselves back to her memory. She contemplated keeping her mouth shut, but wanted to hear Evan erase the doubts, if only by expressing some doubts of his own.

"Do you really believe Kimberly killed herself?" Renee asked, despite the voice inside telling her not to go there. Not tonight. "Some people are suggesting it wasn't suicide."

"I wouldn't worry about them." Evan's expression became stone serious again. "People try to make events seem more important than they are so they can preoccupy themselves. Real life is like television to them."

"Chris Jackson," Renee said, taking a moment to add a nervous, disbelieving laugh. "Chris seems to think someone at Augusta had something to do with it."

Evan's mouth tightened, his eyes widening. Renee sat silent as she watched him internally contemplate the news. Each second without a response made her more nervous. She was almost ready to beg him to say something, anything, when he finally chose to.

"Did he give you any names?" Evan's voice was calm and controlled, his gaze steady.

"He thought it could possibly be a superior." Renee chided her yellow streak, unable to mention Evan's name directly. His reaction to her words confused her. She couldn't tell if he was intrigued or upset. It seemed like both to her.

"Chris Jackson has no clue." Evan shook his head with an annoyed frown. "I think he's looking to make himself famous. He didn't even know Kimberly."

"She contacted him once." Renee lowered her head to the table, playing with her food.

"When?"

"The day before her death." Renee kept her eyes on her plate. "She didn't tell him much except that she suspected something was going on. Maybe someone was taking money from the donation pool? What Chris found interesting was that when he spoke to some of the people who saw her regularly, they all said Kimberly wasn't one to get depressed enough to kill herself."

"Maybe she was good at hiding it." Evan leaned back in his chair, seeming suddenly without an appetite as he frowned at his food.

"Maybe." Renee's heart told her to end the conversation now, but her mind urged her to go on. "A few of them noticed she seemed preoccupied and paranoid. You know, the way people are when they suspect something is going on or they suspect someone suspects something is going on."

"Can you do me a favor Renee?" Evan asked after eyeing her seriously for a moment.

"Yes," she responded without hesitation.

"Leave this issue alone." His brows lowered as he leaned across the table. "If there's more to it, it could get dangerous for you."

"Dangerous how?" Was this advice, a warning, a threat? Renee couldn't ignore the sudden chill that crept inside of her.

"If you're right, and the wrong people find out what you suspect . . ." Evan shook his head with indecision. "Well, I don't know. Just leave it alone."

"But . . . but if she . . . was murdered." Renee couldn't believe she was feeling fear, but she was. "Someone should . . ."

"There are people who do that for a living," he interjected. "Not you or I. I'm sure Chris will tell the cops anything he has."

"Not if he thinks they're in on it?"

Evan smiled. "Nothing like a good conspiracy story. Look Renee, Chris is grabbing at straws. Don't let him drag you along with him. It'll be a waste of your vacation."

"I suppose," she said, even though she didn't agree at all.

Evan looked down at his watch. "I hate to be rude, but I have to make a follow-up call to a donor. I'll be right back."

She nodded and with a smooth, quick move he got up and walked away from the table. Renee swallowed hard to hold down the shiver of fear she felt. She clung to the earnest look in his eyes, wanting desperately to believe he knew even less than she did. She wanted desperately to believe his only intent was concern. She was grateful for those few minutes apart, giving her time to pull herself together, time to tell herself she was being silly.

Dinner was quiet and courteous for the rest of the evening. They engaged in more small talk. Evan's charm took control and, within minutes, Renee's concern was replaced with attraction, interest, and excitement. She enjoyed talking with him. He was so candid with his emotions, which she found rare. He didn't seem hung up with excessive pride or pretensions, but was open and not afraid to show some vulnerability. His behavior, in turn, encouraged Renee do be the same, being more open than she usually would be and enjoying every minute of it.

As the restaurant wasn't far from Michelle's apartment and the night temperature in the warm and breezy low seventies, Evan had parked his Mercedes convertible and he and Renee walked to the restaurant. Walking back, the change of scenery created new topics for conversation that allowed Kimberly Janis to leave Renee's thoughts.

"Are your books in there?" Evan asked while they walked along the side streets of Chicago. He was pointing to a small corner bookstore.

"I don't think so," Renee answered, taking a good look at the shop. "It's a real small store. My books do best in the big chains and Afrocentric book stores."

"That makes sense."

"Chicago is a fantastic book market," Renee said, feeling safe about a familiar topic. "A big percentage of my sales are from this area."

"Which would be more of an incentive for you to move here." Evan nodded decisively.

"Is that so?" Renee smiled, thinking now maybe this topic wasn't as safe as she once thought.

"Let's face it, Renee." Evan's eyes kept straight ahead. "Chicago is the best city in the United States. It has the best stores, the best sports, tons of culture and now we learn it ranks very high on the list of book buying. That alludes to intelligence."

"Now Chicago has the smartest people?" she asked, unable to contain her laugh.

"It's a fact that we've raised the most Nobel prize winners in our many neighborhoods." Evan seemed to be fighting hard to contain his laughter. "We have some of the best universities in the world. Northwestern, University of Chicago, University of Illinois, De Paul. Loyola ranks up there, too. Which brings me to another incentive."

"Let me guess," Renee interrupted. "Michelle."

"Family is everything," he said loudly with a finger raised in the night air. "With Michelle getting married, you'll be lucky to see her whenever, but your chances are better if you're in the same city."

"Thanks for the broadcast." Renee's tone was sassy.

"Just trying to help you out." Evan finally laughed after having kept it in the entire time.

His laugh was strong and deep and Renee found it sincere and appealing. She wasn't sure when, but sometime in the midst of all the laughing and walking, Evan Brooks had taken her hand in his. She hadn't resisted because she didn't want to. She felt a warm sensation at his touch and a seductive comfort at his closeness. She allowed his gentle grip to continue all the way to Michelle's apartment door.

"I suppose this is good night." Evan's face held a softness as he looked into Renee's eyes.

"Yes it is." She felt silly as the shyness from him standing so close again returned to her. She wasn't sure she wanted the night to end, but knew it had to.

"I'm not a desperate man, Renee. I assure you." His tone was confident and tender. "At the risk of sounding so, I'd love to ask you out again."

"You don't sound desperate." She reassured him with her eyes. "I would love to see you again."

"You'll consider my well-made points on the benefits of living in Chicago?" He smiled, erasing some of the tension in his brows. He was obviously more at ease than he'd been a second ago.

"Of course." Renee laughed softly. "I was seriously considering Chicago already, but any incentives you can bring to my attention are appreciated."

"In that case . . ." Evan stepped even closer and whispered, "Here's one more."

With a quick and smooth hand, he took hold of Renee's soft cheek. His fingers slid down the strands of her hair as he drew her face to his. A dizzying current raced through her and Renee felt her heart leap, knowing what was coming. She closed her eyes and felt his lips melt into hers. A volcanic flame swept through her body and fireworks exploded. She was lost in the smoldering, steamy embrace and the touch of his lips ignited wild sensations through her entire body, making her limbs quiver.

His lips teased and tantalized, savoring every second. Renee tasted back, drinking in the passion. Then suddenly, the kiss deepened and Renee felt herself moan at the desire circling in the pit of her stomach. It urged her to pull her body closer and lift her arms to his trim waist. She loved his masculine smell and the gentle urgency with which he held her face. His lips were soft but demanding, and she met their request with her own. As they melted into one, her chest heaved and she knew he could feel her arousal. The heat she was feeling couldn't be confined to her. Wanting, wanting, wanting . . . it was all raised a level as she heard Evan moan and felt his tongue touch her lips. Renee knew this was all going too fast for her, and she had to do something before she began to love it too much. She used the last bit of reserve she had left to push away.

"Was I too fresh?" Evan's voice broke, his breathing heavy as he lowered his hands to his sides. "I'm sorry. I just meant to give you a good night kiss."

"I'm not angry." Renee was having her own loss of breath.

"I just couldn't . . ." Evan sighed heavily.

"Please, Evan." She placed her hand on his chest, but quickly removed it because the feel of his muscles under her skin sent a shock through, threatening to rekindle her desire. "I understand. It's a hot summer night and we've both had a few glasses of wine."

Evan's eyes shifted nervously around the hallway. It was well lit, silent except for a stereo blasting something in the distance. "I guess I should get going."

"I had a great time, Evan." Renee was just now feeling her heart beat return to normal as he stepped away. Did it have to end? Yes, she knew it did.

"I'll call you tomorrow," Evan said. Seeming to catch himself, he smiled. "If that's okay."

"You can call me tomorrow if you'd like." So he noticed he was a little presumptuous. He was also a little flustered. Renee was flattered to know the kiss had a similar effect on him as it had on her.

"Good night." He gave her one last approving glance as he waited for her response.

"Good night." She left him standing there as she opened the door and entered the apartment.

Renee placed a shaky hand to her chest as she leaned against the door in the dark. She'd never been kissed like that before. She'd expected to kiss him; had wanted to since the moment he'd come to pick her up for the evening. She hadn't spent time imagining it, but knew if she had, she could've never imagined it being that great. It was brief, seemingly innocent, but the speed with which it took her body over with desire was almost frightening.

Even though it was only ten thirty on a Saturday night, Renee wasn't sure what Michelle's plans were, so she made a point to be quiet as she tiptoed to her bags, grabbing her night clothes and making her way to the bathroom. Changing, brushing her teeth, and washing her face, she couldn't get rid of the smile of satisfaction she had. She felt like laughing for no reason other than she could. She felt silly, giddy, and somehow along with that, sexy. Very sexy, even though she didn't look so in her yellow cotton pajama jumper, which she covered with an even less sexy tattered blue bathrobe.

As she tiptoed toward the sofa, a soft glitter caught the edges of her right eye. Turning to see what it was, she saw a small, gold trimmed, cream-colored envelope that looked like it had been slid underneath the front door.

It was from Evan, Renee knew it as she hopped to retrieve it. He must have slipped it there after she'd gone to the bathroom! Flowers, letters. The romanticism made her heart flutter. She saw her name typewritten on the front.

"Maybe he put the letter together before the date," she told herself, noticing the typing.

Renee's smile quickly faded as she realized the typed letter was not at all romantic.

STAY OUT OF KIMBERLY JANIS'S DEATH OR IT COULD GET DANGEROUS FOR YOU.

Renee read the message again, not believing its intent. She shook her head in shock, unable to speak a word. She was being threatened now!

"Michelle! Michelle!" Renee ran screaming to her sister's room, and just as she went for the door, it flew open. Michelle stood in the doorway, half asleep, her red satin nightgown flowing to her feet.

"What is it?" she asked in a groggy, tired voice. Her eyes blinked repeatedly. "It better be a fire."

"Look at this!" She grabbed Michelle's hand and slapped the letter in it. "This was slipped under the door tonight."

Michelle took a while to comprehend the letter, but the moment she could, her dark eyes lit up.

"Nick!" She turned, calling behind her. "Wake up!"

Renee decided to ignore the fact that Nick was spending the night. She didn't like it, but she knew Michelle made her own decisions.

"What?" Nick's voice was more annoyed than concerned when he appeared in the bedroom doorway in nothing but a pair of black boxer shorts.

"Renee got a threatening note." Michelle handed him the letter. "It was slipped under the door tonight."

"Have you two been inside all evening?" Renee asked. "Did you see anything?"

"We rented a movie." Michelle spoke slowly as she tried to remember. "Then we ordered pizza and that came at eight or so. I got the pizza. There wasn't anything there then."

"We watched the movie until about nine thirty, then turned in." Nick returned the letter to Renee. "It must've happened after that. We would've heard the swishing sound of paper that thin on the hardwood floor from the sofa with it being so close to the door."

"And I checked the locks before we headed for bed." Michelle frowned as she looked at her watch. "That was only an hour ago. There wasn't anything then."

"Has anyone been threatening you?" Nick asked. "Have you been getting phone calls?"

"Not until now," Renee answered.

Then suddenly, Renee remembered Evan's words over dinner. He'd said them almost exactly the way they were written on the note. *It could get dangerous for you.* But the kiss.

"What is it?" Nick asked. "What's that look for?"

"It's nothing." Renee was now more depressed than scared. "Only earlier this evening Evan had told me it could be dangerous if I continued to ask so many questions about Kimberly."

"You think Evan could have something to do with this?" Michelle asked.

"Of course not," Renee snapped back. "I don't think he was even aware I was asking around about this, which I'm not really. Besides, he was with me tonight."

"That doesn't mean he didn't have anything to do with it," Nick said, rubbing his tired eyes. "A smart person would pay some kid a buck to do it. That way anyone entering the building would let him in without any questions and Evan couldn't be traced if the kid got caught."

"Did he get in the building?" Michelle asked.

"He walked me to the door." Renee found Nick's explanation far fetched.

"So at least we know he didn't do it himself." Michelle put her hand on Renee's shoulder.

"How do you figure that?" Nick asked.

"She was here the whole time," Michelle explained. "She kissed him and he walked away. You kissed him right?"

"I didn't." Renee felt her stomach turn.

"You didn't kiss him?" Michelle pouted. "The roses alone deserved a kiss."

"I mean I didn't see him walk away." Renee sighed, her head lowering. "He was outside the door when I came in. He hadn't left yet."

"Oh." Michelle bit her lower lip, but apparently wasn't giving in yet. "But you were right at the door weren't you? You would've heard . . ."

"I was in the bathroom," Renee said.

"He could've done it then." Nick shrugged. "I mean, who knows. Maybe so, maybe not."

"Do you have any other reasons to suspect him?" Michelle asked.

"It's nothing really." Renee let Nick's point sink in and didn't like the fact that he was starting to make some sense. "That reporter, Chris Jackson, thinks he has something to do with Kimberly's death. Only, Chris has something against successful men, men like Evan. He's jealous of him and wants him to be guilty, so I'm not placing too much faith in his suspicions."

"When did he tell you this?" Nick asked. "How do you know Chris?"

"I met him this morning. He was interested in seeing the e-mails and the e-mail attachments on BFK Kimberly sent me. The brochures and the financial statements."

Nick hit the wall. "You didn't say anything about financial statements last time. Damn that Kimberly. She can't go sending BFK information to anyone. That's confidential. Now you're giving it away. If it gets out to the public, people will think I let it out."

"Oh, that's nice." Michelle slugged Nick in the chest. "Curse a dead girl."

"I don't think it was that important," Renee said, although this wasn't the point.

"Oh." Nick seemed a bit relieved. "We just don't want our competitors getting info . . ."

"Competitors?" Michelle asked. "You're nonprofit, jerk. You think so corporate."

"Anyway," Renee stressed, realizing they were getting off the subject. "Chris and I met for Kimberly's memorial at the school."

"So someone in that room might have murdered Kimberly," Nick said.

"You said you didn't believe she was murdered," Michelle said. "You said she was depressed."

"One doesn't cancel out the other." Nick crossed his arms. "I might be changing my mind now."

"If she was murdered," Michelle said, "wouldn't that make you a prime suspect? You worked with her."

Nick rolled his eyes. "That doesn't mean anything. Besides, I had an alibi. I was in a cab coming home from the airport. I called you from the cell phone, remember?"

Michelle shrugged. "Oh, yeah. Whatever."

"Why do you think the murderer was in that room?" Renee asked. Evan was in that room.

"How else would whoever sent this note know you were interested in Kimberly's death? You haven't told anyone. All everyone knows is that Chris Jackson is investigating and you were seen with him. Maybe he got a letter, too."

"Oh, yeah! That reminds me." Michelle brushed past

her sister and headed for the kitchen as both Renee and Nick followed.

"Here." She handed Renee a message pulled off the refrigerator. "Chris called after you left. He left this message for you on the machine."

Renee read the message urging her to call him no matter what time she got in. She contemplated not calling him, not interested in hearing more doubts about Evan planted in her mind.

"Nick." Michelle turned to her fiance who was standing in the doorway to the kitchen. "Check all the locks and windows again. Just in case."

"Okay." He started to go, but quickly turned around to face Renee. "What are you going to do about the letter?"

"I guess I'll go to the police in the morning." Renee wasn't sure what to do. It was still hitting her that someone had threatened her. She refused to believe it was Evan.

"They won't do anything." Nick waved a dismissing hand in the air. "Bunch of losers. They won't do anything unless you get a direct threat to your safety. That letter could be a viewed as a warning from an anonymous friend concerned about you. Either way . . ."

"Nick's right, Renee," Michelle nodded. "I know this girl who was sent threatening letters by her boyfriend, but because he wrote the words just so, they couldn't classify them as threats and didn't do anything until he broke into her apartment and tore apart her stuff. Maybe this isn't even like that. Maybe Evan left it because he's concerned and just didn't want you to know."

"I don't think Evan had anything to do with it either way." Renee fought the doubts welling up inside of her. "I'm almost certain whoever did send this put it in the doorway between the time you two went to bed and I got here. And they weren't sending it out of concern. Besides, why would Evan want to hurt Kimberly?"

"Kimberly and Evan didn't like each other," Nick said.

"What do you mean?" Renee felt the anxiety and frustration adding to her fear and confusion.

"I didn't notice that." Michelle turned to Nick with a confused expression.

"I worked with her, so I noticed stuff other people didn't." Nick shook his head. "It was nothing, really. Only she used to say he was a jerk. I think he made a pass at her or something and started blowing her off after she turned him down."

"That's sexual harassment," Michelle yelled out.

"That's debatable," Nick said with a cold tone of voice. "He could've just asked her out like I did with you. That's not harassment. After a while, there seemed to be a lot of tension in the air when they were both in the same room. Especially so the last couple of weeks. Nothing to kill someone over. Kimberly still might have killed herself. Maybe Evan left the note because he doesn't want you snooping around and finding out why she hated him. He wants to look good to you."

Renee thought she was going to be sick. This was too much. Could it be that all of her opinions about Evan were wrong? Could it be that the man that she couldn't get off her mind was a sexist jerk? Could it be that the man she thought was so refreshingly honest was hiding something as awful as murder? Could any of these suggestions by Chris or Nick be true about Evan? She didn't want to believe this, but couldn't really ignore them any longer. Not now that she'd been threatened herself.

"Why don't you both go back to bed?" Renee plopped down on a kitchen chair. "If I do anything, it won't be tonight."

"You're not gonna get any sleep." Michelle headed for the refrigerator. "Not out on that sofa bed all by yourself. I'll sleep with you."

"Michelle," Nick whined childishly.

"Very mature, Nick." Michelle grabbed a bowl of cherries from the refrigerator. "This is a great time to be selfish. Just go to bed."

After a stunned stare, Nick quickly retreated.

"Check the locks," Michelle yelled after him.

"Thanks, hon." Renee winked at her sister, proud to see her stand up to Nick and give him an order for once. Maybe she would be all right.

"You gonna call Chris?" Michelle headed for the living room with a bowl of cherries in her hand.

"I suppose."

Renee took a deep breath, hoping Chris wouldn't give her another piece of bad news about Evan. She wasn't sure she could take more. Within a span of four hours, she'd gone from elation to passion to now fear and mistrust. All of those emotions related to one man, who was becoming more important to Renee than she'd expected him to. She had already decided not to tell Chris about the note. At least not tonight. She needed time to think of what she was going to do about it.

"Hello?"

"Chris? Hi, it's Renee Shepherd. You left me a message telling to call no matter what time it was."

"Renee. Oh, yeah."

"Is it too late to talk?"

"No." There was a short pause. "I found something out."

Renee heard a faint whimper as she spoke. "Did you find a clue in the papers Kimberly sent me?"

"There's something there. I'm looking into it, but I haven't found it yet."

"Then, what?" Renee knew she was being short, but couldn't help it. Her stomach was turning and her patience thinning. Manners weren't the most important thing to her right now.

"You remember Jenny Sukata from the memorial?" Chris asked, seemingly unaware of the sharpness in her tone.

"Yeah," Renee said. "If I remember right, she was pretty annoyed with you for trying to get her to ask her boyfriend to squeal on another cop."

"Whatever the case then, she came through for me. Her boyfriend's name is David Fox. Fox talked to Detective Hartman, the junior detective to arrive first on the scene with Detective Griggs. They're partners, but Hartman hates Griggs, so it wasn't too hard for Fox to get him to spill his guts to another cop. Hartman told Fox that Kimberly was almost a whole fifteen feet from the building when she finally reached the ground. That means, unless she can fly, she was pushed or thrown off that ledge."

"Wouldn't this have been in the police report?" Renee knew she was going to be sick now.

"That's the thing," Chris said. "Hartman told Fox that Grigg's filled out the report right in front of him and put her at around eight feet, which is no big deal when someone jumps. When Hartman spoke up about it, Griggs told him to leave it alone if he didn't want any trouble of his own. Griggs is the senior officer of the two and you know how cops are about silence. Griggs gives the orders and Hartman followed."

Leave it alone was another phrase Renee remembered Evan using earlier that evening.

"This has to be reported, Chris."

"We can't. That information was off the record. If I violate that code, I'll never get another cop to say a word to me ever again, and that could be the least of my problems. That's not all."

"More?" Why not, Renee thought.

"I found out that Alan Smith's ex made it pretty clear to her own pals that she wasn't happy about being dumped for Kimberly. They were reluctant to tell me earlier because they didn't want me to suspect her. I talked to your sister tonight and she piqued my curiosity. If Tamia is as angry a sister as I think she is, we may have another motive on our hands."

"Who?" Renee heard the name and it immediately rung a bell. Was this the mystery woman Evan told her about earlier?

"Alan's ex is Tamia Griffin. Why? You know her?"

"She was at the memorial today." Renee's words were barely audible. She left out that she'd first seen Tamia outside Augusta with Evan.

"That's interesting. I didn't see her."

"Why are you telling me all this?" Renee asked.

"I've only told you because I'm dying to tell someone and I feel like I can trust you. Don't ask me why, but you seem honest and I think you're interested in the truth."

"Is that why you wanted me to know?" she asked. "To confide in someone?"

"I wanted you to know so you'd be careful. You had dinner with Brooks tonight. I know we got other leads, but I want you to keep a look out for that guy. If I'm right and Griggs purposefully lied on the report, it must have been a bribe that convinced him to do so. A lot of money would have to cross hands for a man already attracting heat to put himself at more risk. In Chicago, police bribes cost serious dough because of the competition. Evan Brooks is the only potential suspect with the kind of money and connections that could change a police report."

"Thanks Chris." Renee's gratitude was lost in her sorrow.

After hanging up, she stayed in the kitchen for a while, needing to be alone. Michelle was right. She wasn't going to get any sleep tonight. Gone were the pleasant memories of her dinner with Evan. Gone was the enticing passion from the brief kiss she'd hoped would linger into her slumber. They were replaced with doubt, confusion, and fear. It all made her realize how far ahead of herself she'd gotten. She'd let the attraction, the romanticism get to her. She'd let the lazy smiles, piercing eyes, flowers, and candlelit dinner table tell her she knew who this man was. But there was a lot she didn't know about Evan. Maybe a lot she'd rather not know.

What she did know was that Kimberly Janis had definitely been murdered. Renee no longer doubted that after the letter she received and Chris's news about the police report. She knew she had a choice. She could do as the letter said and stay out of it and try to enjoy her vacation. She could return to New York none the wiser to the truth, letting Chris follow through and do what he could. Only Renee knew she wouldn't do either of those. She pictured a frightened Kimberly trying to uncover the truth, believing there was nowhere she could turn. No one she could trust.

Kimberly Janis had turned to her for help, and Renee was going to do what she could. Right now she knew that she and Chris were possibly the only people who could get to the truth and find justice for her family and for BFK if it was true someone was cheating the organization. Renee only hoped the truth didn't lead to Evan Brooks like Chris was determined to see it do. Until she knew for sure, she felt it was best to keep her distance from Evan no matter how hard that would be. She almost regretted the dinner with him now, because she knew the pleasant memories and teasing contemplations of the future would make it all the harder to stay away from him.

SEVEN

It was ten in the morning when Renee finally woke up with red puffy eyes. She was happy to have at least gotten a few hours of sleep. She awoke with immediate remembrance of the previous day's events. The tragedy of it all was that a young woman had been murdered. The heartbreak was that the man Renee was developing strong feelings for could be behind that murder. The uncertainty was her own safety as Renee contemplated the letter she had received along with Evan's words from the previous night.

She felt a little selfish, victimizing herself in this. Although the letter had been threatening, Kimberly was the real victim here. Renee remembered herself at the age of twenty-one. As she started accepting the loss of her parents the year before, she remembered feeling a hint of excitement for her own future. Life as an adult was just beginning. Kimberly had been robbed of that future.

Still, Renee knew she couldn't ignore the fact that

despite her new feelings of fear where Evan Brooks was concerned, she was extremely attracted to him. It was more than a physical attraction, which worried Renee the most. A physical attraction could be forgotten with time and distance. She was concerned about the emotional attraction that had been awakened after last night. He seemed to see her from the inside out, to know her feelings as much or more than she knew them herself. He seemed genuine and real, not full of pretenses or wearing a facade. She'd been so excited about exploring further what had started last evening, but now her excitement had dimmed. Dimmed, but was nowhere near gone.

She would have to try and keep away from him. It would be hard, she knew. It would be a battle between her better judgment and her newfound impulsive emotions, but she had faith in herself and her ability to resist.

That ability was tested sooner than Renee expected as she answered the phone on her way to the shower. It was Evan on the other end and the mere sound of his voice made her alert and responsive.

"Did you get a good night's sleep?" His voice sounded cheerful and friendly.

"Evan?" Renee said the name even though she knew it was him. She was stalling, trying to muster the courage to do what she had to do.

"Yes, it's me." He sounded amused by that. "I was just talking to a friend of mine. Her name is Sandy Pete. She's a physician's assistant at Cook County Hospital. I was just telling her about you and she said your name was just added to the guest list of a dinner she's attending Friday night. Are you planning to go?"

"Uh . . . yes. My agent booked it for me." Renee was at a loss for words. She was torn. Both glad and frightened to hear the sound of his voice at the same time.

"Are you all right, Renee?" Evan asked. "Did I wake you?"

"No." What could she say? *I'm sorry, I think you're a murderer. Can I call you back when I know for sure?* If her suspicions weren't true, she could ruin any chance she had with him. He would think she was crazy.

"Well," Evan said after a brief silence. "I was wondering . . . I mean I was going to the dinner, too. Augusta has donated to some of the charities and hospitals the organization sponsors and . . ."

"I'm sorry, Evan," Renee interrupted, sensing an invitation coming on. She had to refuse now, because if he actually asked her along, she wasn't so sure she could do it then. "I really have to get going. I have a lot to do today."

There was a short pause. Renee knew it only lasted seconds, but it seemed like hours to her. In the short time she knew him, she'd begun to care about Evan Brooks, and despite her doubts about him she didn't like hurting his feelings.

"I understand." His tone contradicted his words. "I'll call you later. Possibly this afternoon or tonight."

"Why don't you let me call you." Renee knew she was doing a one-eighty on her words from last night, but so much had happened since they'd said good night. "I know I told you you could call, but I wasn't thinking. I'm going to be very busy today."

"Sure." The underlying tenor of his voice showed his hesitation. "Goodbye, Renee."

"Goodbye."

She hung up the phone with her heart in her throat. She could tell he was hurt and that was her last intention, but there were some important questions that needed to be answered. She could have come right out and asked him herself, but she was too chicken. What if he did have something to do with it? He surely wouldn't admit to it over the phone. Even if by some miracle of miracles he did confess all, she wasn't so sure she wanted to hear it. Would she be in still more danger?

Renee groaned out loud as she stood in the hallway. The man she'd been with last night was no killer! He was funny, warm, and honest to the core. She knew those beliefs were backed up by her heart and emotions, but she also knew that wasn't enough. She may have felt like she'd known Evan Brooks for a long time after last night, but the truth was that she didn't. She would have to know more to prove to her doubtful mind what her heart begged her to believe. She hoped Chris had been serious about following up on Ben Monty from Philly and Tamia Griffin. She needed some proof to thwart off her doubts and she needed it now.

"Would you get into this?" Michelle nudged her sister with an elbow as she whispered in her ear.

Renee returned from daydreaming about Evan, back to reality. Reality was the DuSable Museum, one of the most famous African-American museums in the country. She'd been excited to see the Henry Ossawa Tanner paintings and photographs exhibit when Michelle told her it would be there during the second week of her visit. Tanner was one of Renee's favorite African-American artists—one of the few things she and Michelle agreed on.

The only problem was that Renee wasn't at all concerned with art right now. Evan was the only thing on her mind. She'd felt awful the day before when he'd called and she'd turned him away. She kept hearing the rejected sound of his voice. She was certain he wasn't used to being rejected. She'd been so affected by his tone, more than she realized at first. Her feelings for Evan were stronger than usual and had come faster than usual. She'd known he was going to be trouble from the first moment she met him. Only she'd thought it was going to be a good kind of trouble.

She decided to go to the police with the threat she'd received later that afternoon. She figured she should at least get the word out. Like Nick and Michelle told her, she was told nothing much could be done except for her to file a formal report and the police would keep a record of any more letters or phone calls as she updated them. They'd asked her the general questions, including why she was interested in Kimberly's death and what she had to substantiate that interest. Unfortunately for Chris, Renee placed the blame on him. Reluctantly, she added his suspicions of Evan but included Ben Monty and Tamia Griffin, adding the last two with emphasis. She didn't even think of telling them about Chris's suspicions of Detective Griggs, knowing that, as a journalist protecting his source, Chris would never back her up.

She left the station feeling less accomplished than before and spent the rest of the afternoon and that evening reliving all of her encounters with Evan, hoping to find some conclusion about who he was from them. The first time outside the elevator, that same night at DiVincis, the impromptu lunch at Pomodoros, in Kimberly's office afterward, outside Augusta last Friday with Tamia, the memorial and the dinner that night. Going over each encounter, she had to admit some suspicion was valid.

Noticing her depression, Michelle forced her to get out Monday and visit the museum. Renee had hoped the outing would take her mind off Evan, but nothing seemed to be working.

"I'm sorry," Renee said as they stepped along with the small crowd of people. "My mind is wandering."

"This stuff is so cool." Michelle's eyes lit up at the sight of art. "Henry crossed over all of the color barriers just by doing what he wanted to do. That's not always easy now. I can't imagine what it was like in the 1800s. It's inspiring. I've been thinking about painting, you know.''

"I thought it was sculpture," Renee said. In the last year, Michelle had changed her mind regularly when it came to her future aspirations. Dancing, teaching, sculpture, acting, graphic design.

"It's too confining." Michelle shook her head, squinting her eyes and nose. "Takes too long. Paint is never ending, and with a splash and splatter you have it. What you feel is out there."

"What about acting?" Renee was trying her best to keep from thinking about Evan. She was always interested in Michelle's career goals, just happy she was beginning to develop some. For the longest time any career-related questions had been met with a long-winded sighing *I don't know.*

"I thought you said acting was frivolous." Michelle placed a hand on her hip and threw her a sardonic stare.

"Correction," Renee said offhandedly. "I said acting without ambition was frivolous. Not in general. It's a hard way to make a living. You have to have a goal, direction, connections. You have to be very good and very lucky to get noticed. Otherwise you're going to college to be a waitress."

"You don't think I could do it?" Michelle stood still, allowing the crowd to pass them by.

"Michelle." Renee spoke with impatience. "I didn't mean that and you know it."

"I think you did." Michelle shook her head with a defeated frown.

"Don't put words in my mouth." Renee knew her tone was harsh, but her temper was short these days. "I never once said you couldn't do anything. I've always encouraged you to do what you wanted, knowing you'd be great at it.

I wouldn't have brought the topic up if I didn't think you were capable."

"I guess I should feel so blessed." Michelle rolled her eyes.

"Okay, Michelle." Renee threw up her hands and sighed. "You want to fight, lets go ahead and fight. You're obviously not happy unless you're fighting with me about anything and everything."

"How would you feel if you went out of your way to do something nice for someone and they were this unappreciative?" Michelle looked around the museum. "For example, take them to a nice exhibit to have them completely ignore it and you."

Renee retorted in anger. "I suppose it's the same as you'd feel when you try and help someone realize their dreams and try to support them in their transition from child to adult and they take every moment to slap you in the face with defiance and comparisons."

Renee regretted her words as soon as she said them, knowing they'd been straight out of frustration with no tact or concern for Michelle's feelings. She realized she'd made a big mistake as Michelle, who had stood open-mouthed for a moment, turned and ran out of the building.

Renee ran after her and found her sitting on a concrete bench, looking down at her hands. Michelle didn't acknowledge her older sister as she sat down next to her. Renee stayed silent for a moment, wanting to gather her thoughts and her temper before she spoke again. When would she find the right words?

"Michelle." She placed her hand on her sister's thigh. "I'm sorry. That didn't come out the way I intended."

"How did you intend it exactly?" When Michelle looked up, her large eyes were filling with tears.

"I'm frustrated, honey." Renee shook her head and

sighed. "I don't know how I intended it. It's just that a lot has happened to me since I've been here, good and bad. I guess I'm frustrated with some decisions you've made and I'm certainly disappointed in your opinion of my feelings about you."

"Why do I always have to be so grateful?" Michelle asked, her young eyes pained with confusion. "I feel like I'm supposed to get on my hands and knees and thank you every day for what everyone else gets so easily."

"You don't, Michelle. You have every right to the chance you're getting." Renee was reluctant to speak, unsure of the right words. "Don't take this the wrong way, but everyone doesn't get this chance so easily, even though they should. You are lucky, but I don't want you to bow to me in any way. I just want you to appreciate the fact that a college education is special."

"I know that," Michelle said with a nod. "I didn't mean it like that."

"I didn't think you did." Renee ran her long hand down the back of her sister's head, letting her long, thick hair run through her fingers. Their mother always ran her fingers through their hair to calm them, soothe them. It was so comforting as she talked to them about everything, but nothing. "Forgive me. I didn't mean to ignore what you've done for me today and I'm sorry for my withdrawal. I have a lot on my mind, but I appreciate your planning this for us. I appreciate your remembering one of my favorite artists."

"I'm sorry, too." Michelle wiped her eyes as a faint smile appeared. "I know you probably should be left alone right now to think out what you want to do about this situation with Evan."

"Maybe I should." Renee felt the emotion swelling up inside of her, upset with herself for her inability to communicate effectively. This was better than she could remember ever doing, but she knew that simple *I'm sorries,* although necessary, weren't the only answers to their problems.

"I guess we should go." Michelle stood up. "I have to meet Nick for dinner anyway. You guys never got together, you know."

"I'm sorry," Renee said. "We'll do it soon." Her brief interactions with Nick, as he was at the apartment regularly, had improved, but she couldn't say her opinion of him had changed. "Why don't you go on, honey. I'll take a cab home. I want to walk around."

"It'll start getting dark in a little while, Renee." Michelle looked around uncomfortably. "I don't know."

"I'll be all right," Renee smiled as she waved Michelle away. "I know PK's best by heart, remember?"

Renee was referring to a move Patricia Kelly, now Robeson, had taught the two of them during their self-defense class together years ago. It was her most recommended and Michelle's favorite way of getting out of an assailant's grip. They'd nicknamed it PK's best.

"Oh, yeah." Michelle laughed. "PK's best will do ya. Get home soon, so you won't have to use it."

Michelle stood there for a while with an uncertain smile before they said their goodbyes. As Renee watched her walk away, she felt the hurt caused by their strained relationship. It was getting so that every other discussion they had ended with an argument. These temporary bandages weren't going to work forever. She had to do something.

Relationships were confusing, and Renee was even more confused about the one, or the possibility of the one, she had with Evan. She'd hoped she could get him off her mind, staying away from him, but it wasn't working and now it was invading her time with Michelle, making her testy and short tempered. Since yesterday morning time had been at a standstill. It seemed like weeks since she'd spoken to him on the phone.

She had to do something about Evan and she needed to do it now. There wasn't time to wait for Chris to follow his leads and get back to her. Besides, his view was too tainted as far as Evan was concerned. Renee realized she was on her own, so she'd ignore her feelings in search of the truth. When she found that truth, she'd seek justice for Kimberly Janis, a chance at love for herself, and a chance to reach Michelle once and for all.

"Where do I start?" she asked herself.

Her only connection to Kimberly was as good a place as any. She didn't have the papers anymore, having given them to Chris on Saturday. What she did have was BFK and an open invitation from its director. Renee decided to start her own investigation first thing in the morning.

Alan Smith's expression was pleasant surprise when Renee appeared in his humble office doorway at BFK's headquarters on Erie Street.

Renee greeted him with the friendliest smile she had. "You busy?"

"Not right now." The young man, dressed in khakis and a white T-shirt, stood up from his chair. "Nice of you to come by."

"I was in the neighborhood." She entered and sat across from Alan as he motioned her to do. His space was much like the entire BFK office, makeshift. The boxes, bland furniture, and mostly bare walls made it look like any day now, they'd be moving into their real offices. "I thought I'd stop by real quick to learn a little more about BFK."

"I'm glad you did." Alan cleared his throat as he leaned back in his chair. "BFK is my baby. I can answer any questions you have."

Renee liked his friendly tone, making her feel comfortable. "Why don't you tell me what you think of the organization?"

"I'm crazy about the program." Alan leaned forward, entwining his fingers with each other. "We started a couple of years ago with an idea and a lot of eager volunteers. A lot of our children weren't getting the proper nutrition necessary for their mental and physical growth. It would be nice if heart and determination were enough, but we all know they're not. Nutrition affects mental growth. We had the heart, but needed organization and money, so we called on Augusta for funding and administration and formed a union. Now we're able to distribute a little over one hundred thousand dollars worth of healthy food to Chicago area families each year."

"That's fantastic after only two years." Renee was inspired and encouraged. She wished more people were as committed to helping others. "You must be proud to be a part of something so beneficial."

"I've sacrificed the last two years of my life to make BFK a success. I've already been approached by community leaders in Los Angeles, New York, and Detroit interested in starting the program in those cities. No other organization under Augusta has gone national."

"That's good to hear," Renee said, respecting his allegiance and pride in his accomplishment. She knew she was about to tread on dangerous waters, but thought best to enter on a high note. She took a quick swallow and asked, "What about Kimberly?"

"What do you mean?" A hint of caution hit his face.

"How did she get involved with BFK?" Renee didn't want to rush, but she was determined to find out the truth. Besides, Alan looked in better spirits than he had at any time she'd seen him.

"Through Augusta." A somber expression formed on

his face. "She wasn't a volunteer or anything. She . . . we met at a finance meeting with all the other groups."

"Her only involvement was through financing?" So, it was clear that the fraud involved money.

"Occasionally at that." He shrugged. "She didn't have more to do with BFK than any of the other programs. At least I don't think. I didn't have much to do with the money once it got here. Just the administration, management."

"I know you don't want to believe Kimberly was murdered," Renee said, "but would she have any reason to believe there was something suspicious going on with the financing?"

"I don't see where it would come from," he said. "Nick is obsessed with perfection with the numbers. He'll tell you everything if you ask. You have to ask, but he'll tell you. If he's good at anything, it's keeping track."

"What about something that could happen before Nick got his hands on the money?"

"Where is this coming from?" Alan asked. "What aren't you telling me? Someone been stealing from us?"

"It's nothing really," Renee said, shaking her head. "Kimberly may have . . ."

"Does this have something to do with Evan Brooks?"

Evan's name wasn't the one Renee wanted to hear. Any more mention of him in connection with Kimberly wasn't good. "Did Kimberly tell you about any confrontations she had with Evan?"

"She never told me anything specific. His name came up occasionally. He's the big guy, so, of course, it would now and then. I mean really, a lot of BFK donors write their checks out directly to him even though he says he tells them not to. Kimberly never liked to talk about Evan. I think there was some bad blood between them."

"How do you mean?" Renee persisted, although she didn't like the direction her search was taking her.

"She didn't like him." Alan shrugged. "BFK, Augusta, and things related were sort of an off-limit topic for us. This is my career, not a part-time job like it was for her. We just didn't want it to come between us."

"I understand." Renee was clearer now as to why Kimberly might not have told Alan what she suspected. "What about those last two weeks? Did she break the rules and say anything out of the ordinary about Evan or BFK?"

"Nothing about BFK," Alan said. He paused, like he was thinking about something. "The last time I talked to her was early in the afternoon the day she . . . you know. All I remember is that she didn't want to do anything. She was in one of her moods."

"Her depressions?"

"Some of that." Alan's tone saddened. "Depressed, angry. Mad at me, her job, her friends. She couldn't give any reason. She never did, she was just not in the mood to go out or even talk on the phone."

"I understand," Renee said, although she was even more confused than before.

It was possible that she was murdered and was in one of her states at the same time. One did not necessarily have to negate the other, but Renee wasn't satisfied with that conclusion.

"What about Tamia Griffin?" Renee noticed the lift of his brow as she said a familiar name. "You aware she was harassing Kimberly?"

Alan let out a disbelieving sigh. "That's ridiculous. Tammy is not the kind to . . ."

"Kimberly probably didn't tell you because she didn't want to look like the whining girlfriend, but she told some other people."

"Tammy just called me today." Alan shook his head. "She had only nice things to say about Kimberly. She was at the memorial."

"I saw her," Renee said. "I'm not suggesting she's a murderer. I really have no reason to . . ."

"How do you know Tammy was harassing Kimberly?" Alan asked, apparently not yet ready to accept this conclusion.

"Kimberly told my sister Michelle." Renee felt like an ogre bearing so much bad news to this already grieving man. "They worked together. Chris Jackson also got the news from some other kids Kimberly knows. I mean knew."

"Are you really following his lead?" Alan's grin was out of pity. "I mean, Chris Jackson will print anything to get people to read his column."

"I don't know about that." Renee hadn't done any research on Chris, but had gone with her own intuition, which told her he was all right.

"He may be in left field," Alan said. "He's been there before."

"Even about Detective Griggs?" There was another hit.

Renee could see she was full of surprises for Alan. She sat and watched his face as, for a moment, he had nothing to say.

"So you've heard of him," she said.

"Who hasn't?" he answered, leaning even farther toward her. "What I'm surprised at is, how you know about him?"

"Chris Jackson."

He laughed. "Figures. Look, Renee, I know all about Griggs's rep. I've come across him several times in my community work. I do some counseling for boys at the YMCA and the James Jordan Boys & Girls Club. Kids in the hood see everything, and they tell me. I know very well what he's about. Even more than Chris. I've already spoken with him and his partner about Kimberly."

"What did they ask?" Renee sensed his hesitation. "If you don't mind. I'm curious. Not word for word."

"You're a persistent one." He smiled, crossing his arms over his chest. "It lasted all of fifteen minutes. The day after her death, they came by BFK. Griggs asked me where I was. I said home, which was true. I was surfing the net. The time is logged by the service. I went to the billing section and printed the record out for them. His partner, Hartfield, Hartman, or something like that asked if I'd spoken with her. I told them about calling her earlier to see if she wanted to do something. They asked if I knew anyone who would want to hurt Kimberly. I said no. Griggs thanked me and left. Haven't heard from them since. If they thought it was a murder they would've gone into it a little more in depth, don't you think?"

Renee agreed, but didn't believe the reason was the same. She thought it was more likely the detectives didn't want to make this a murder investigation. "Was that all?"

"I called a couple of days ago to follow up." He looked away, pausing, reflecting "You know, just in case. What's the report? It was case still closed. All the same. I'm not calling again."

"What about Ben Monty, her ex?" Renee asked, speaking cautiously, knowing she was already getting too personal. "You said the cops asked you if you knew anyone who might want to hurt her. You said no."

"You mean that sorry brother from Philly?" Alan smirked, rotating a pen from hand to hand. "He's a punk. A coward."

"He was stalking her."

"First of all, he's in Philly. Second, from what Kimberly told me, he's all bark and no bite."

Renee shook her head in disagreement. "He had enough bite to make her leave Philly and come all the way to Chicago." Renee was looking for any clue to lead away from Evan. Maybe she was pushing too far.

"I don't know." Alan sighed. "Maybe there was more

to it than Kimberly told me. This stuff about Tammy, Ben. She wasn't telling me everything. I don't know why. I still don't think anyone killed her."

"What about the possibility, Alan?" Renee couldn't understand his resistance. "You cared for her didn't you?"

"It's because I cared for her that I can't believe it." He lowered his head with a pause only for a moment. "I'm her boyfriend. I feel guilty. I . . ."

"You weren't there to save her," Renee said, sensing his emotions. "It's not your fault. You can't feel guilty about something you couldn't have prevented or foreseen. You obviously didn't know all of what was going on with Tamia, Ben Monty, or Augusta that concerned Kimberly."

"I was her boyfriend. I should have . . . done something."

"I understand, Alan," Renee felt awful for persisting. She had gotten caught up in the excitement of finding out the truth, each answer leading to another question. Alan was upset. That was obvious. "I'm sorry."

"It's all right." He forced a smile. "Listen, let's just move away from that topic. How about a tour of our offices?"

"If it isn't a bother, yes." Renee stood up, grabbing her black leather purse from the floor.

"We're only a couple of offices." Alan led her down the hallway, pointing here and there. "Most calls for donations are done out of Augusta. We call our more faithful donors from here. I'll usually call them myself. Sometimes Evan even dirties his nails."

"Donations doing well?" Renee asked as they stood in the room where the calling was done. There were flyers and posters for BFK all around. Most with pictures of Alan surrounded by several smiling kids. Some with pictures of Alan alone.

"Going great for the last six months especially," Alan answered, rubbing his hands together. "We hit an all time high three months ago. It's amazing what I've ... we've done."

"Do you get along with Evan?" Renee asked. "I mean businesswise?"

Alan shrugged as he righted a picture on the wall of himself holding an award for something. "Evan's all right, but he likes to take the credit a lot. Doesn't give props where they're due sometimes."

"You're saying he doesn't respect you?"

"It's like this," Alan said. "I'm BFK. Okay? This is my baby. The second I came to him for funding, Evan wants to do this and that."

Renee was surprised as she began to realize, even though Alan was committed to his cause, he wasn't as selfless as she'd first thought. Maybe talking about Kimberly upset him.

Alan continued. "Everything is always Evan Brooks. The heavy hitters always want to talk to Evan. The reporters always want a picture of Evan. It's like it's all him. Like he's doing it alone."

"But he's executive director of Augusta," Renee said. "He's also well known in the city."

"Yeah, because of his daddy." Alan smirked again. "But how am I supposed to establish myself, make a name for myself in the public? I have aspirations, you know? I'm going national. Los Angeles asked if Evan can come out there with me. BFK isn't about Evan."

Renee sensed his frustration building. "Okay, Alan. Don't get so upset. I'm sure everything will work out."

"It better," he said as if reassuring himself more than anything. "Because things have gotten out of hand. I've done too much to make BFK a success."

Anxious to leave, Renee held her hand out to Alan. "I really should get going. Appreciate the time."

"It was my pleasure." A smile reappeared, the smile

in all the brochures and posters, as he shook her hand vigorously. "Please excuse me if I seemed angry. Things have been hard on me recently, and I seem ready to jump off the handle for any reason."

"I understand, Alan. I really do." Renee knew her questions hadn't helped the situation any. "Let BFK be a good distraction for you. You're doing a great job. I'll be adding it to my list of monthly donations."

She followed Alan to the front of the office.

"Don't think I won't follow up," he said. "Maybe you can help me write a book on BFK and my life."

Renee left feeling worse than she had before she came in. Her purpose for pursuing the truth was for the truth itself, but also to clear any doubts she had about Evan. Instead, she had more doubts about Evan than before and was now all over uncomfortable with Alan, whom she'd thought she would like very much.

Who was Evan Brooks after all? She wondered if what she knew was a lie. Had she made up this image of a man she wanted to be with all on her own? Was he the self-confident, caring, and humorous man who seemed so interested in sharing something special with her? Or was he a liar, an unlikeable guy interested in her for one thing. Or worse even, maybe he wasn't even interested in her for that, but only to find out what she knew about his misdeeds?

"Misdeeds?" Renee repeated the word to herself. Stealing, plotting, and cheating were misdeeds. This was cold-blooded murder. She knew from the heaviness of her heart what the truth could be. She was determined to hold on to the possibility of Evan's innocence. She'd been alone for a while now, and she was ready to have someone in her life. With Evan, she saw the possibility of more than companionship and sex. Evan didn't seem like an almost-all-the-way kind of guy, and Renee felt, for the first time, that maybe she wasn't either.

Renee tossed her bags on the sofa and flicked on the window air-conditioning unit. It was turning out to be a hot one today. She thought to take a cool shower. By the time she got out, the air should be flowing.

As she passed the telephone in the entranceway to the hallway, she noticed the answering machine blinking. Three messages. She pushed the button. Michelle had told her she didn't mind, and as much as she didn't want to, Renee knew she was hoping one of the messages was from Evan. Or better yet, she thought, one was from Chris telling her Ben Monty or Tamia Griffin was the murderer and Evan was free and clear. The other was from Michelle saying she'd come to her senses and broke it off with Nick entirely. The third was from Evan, asking her out to dinner.

No such luck.

"Michelle. It's Nick. Stop by Silverston's and pick up my dry cleaning on your way into work. You don't need a ticket. I called and told him you were coming. You'll need thirty bucks."

Renee smacked her lips. "She's a college student, you jerk. She doesn't have thirty dollars. Pick up your own laundry."

Evan's voice was strong, but Renee could sense the uncertainty in his message.

"Renee, this is Evan. I was hoping we could speak today."

Brief, to the point. Nothing emotional in his words or tone, but Renee's reaction was to feel her heart drop into her stomach. His voice held none of the cocky, self-assured tones it had in the past. Tones that, as much as she hated to admit it, she was attracted to.

Deep down inside she could admit she found some pleasure in knowing she mattered enough to him to affect him like this. Only she hated that she was. She could only wonder how much longer she could stay away from him.

"Hey, Renee." Chris Jackson's voice came scratchy over the machine. "Uhm . . . yeah. This message is for Renee Shepherd. This is Chris. I'm on my way to Kimberly Janis's apartment. Her brother is back in town to set things up for the movers. He said he'd give me some time. She's at 1234 Diversey Parkway. Apartment 2-0-0-4. If you're interested."

Renee could almost feel the cool bathwater soothing her, but she knew it wasn't going to be stronger than her desire to learn more about Kimberly. Her life and her death.

She didn't have time to figure out where Diversey was. Grabbing her purse and keys, she darted for the door. She hailed a cab in less than a minute.

Chris met her at the door to apartment 2004 after buzzing her up. Pulling her aside, he whispered his instructions

"I'll ask the questions. He's a little edgy. If you ask, he'll need to qualify. The more work he has to do, the less he'll talk."

"What did you ask me here for?" Renee jerked away from his grip. She wasn't in the best mood and definitely not of the attitude to be grabbed by the arm. "Decoration?"

"You look around. Get an overview of the place while I talk to him." Chris stepped aside so she could enter. "You're my assistant. I'll introduce you."

Renee walked past him toward the young man sitting on the huge wool-covered sofa. He was wrapping plates in newspaper and gently placing them into a box. Renee saw the familiar look in his eyes and she felt the urge to cry. She didn't know his name, but she felt his pain and wanted to hug him.

"I'm Renee Shepherd." She held a hand out to the

dark-skinned man. "I'm so sorry about Kimberly. I've lost loved ones, and I can honestly say I know how you feel."

His face was drained, his eyes limp with grief as he shook her hand. He tried to form a smile, the edges of his full lips attempting a weak curve. "I'm Marshall Janis. Thanks."

Renee saw the look on Chris's face as he sat across from them. She returned it. He couldn't have possibly thought she would lie to this man.

"You work for the paper, too?" Marshall asked, returning to his work.

"No. I'm here out of concern for Kimberly. Maybe Chris told you about the e-mails."

He looked at Chris, no expression, waited, then turned back to her. "Oh, yeah. That's you. The author."

"Yes." He could hardly think, Renee could see. She felt tears welling in her throat. "I guess to confess, I'm very interested in finding out more about her."

"She was . . ." Marshall sighed, looking at a pastel teal plate. As if it held the rest of his sentence, he held it up for Renee to see. "Colorful."

Renee placed her hand on his shoulder. "So many people came to love her in the short time she was here."

"Marshall," Chris interjected. "You were telling me earlier that Kimberly was a little more emotional than most, but not depressed."

"Nothing clinical," he answered after a moment. "I mean, nothing she wouldn't tell us about. Those pills were not hers."

"What pills?" Renee asked.

Chris cleared his throat. "Marshall got a quick glance at the police report. It says Prozac was found next to Kimberly's computer. Two pills."

"Did you follow up on the prescription?" Renee asked.

"There was none," Chris said. "No bottle. Nothing. Just two pills."

"Obviously a plant," Renee said. "Someone planned this."

"I'll get you a copy of the report," Marshall said with a weak voice. "The police are mailing my parents some version or other of it."

"Good luck with that," Chris said, ignoring Renee's glare. "I'm not trying to upset you, Marshall, but I've told you about Detective Griggs. I think he's hiding something."

Renee noticed a poster of the Philadelphia skyline at night on the wall behind her. "Did the report say anything about Ben Monty."

"There's been no sign of him," Marshall said, his somber eyes showing a flicker of anger. "We had to urge the cops to look for him because the cops in Chicago ruled it a suicide. The Philly detectives thought it was too early to say that, too. So they tried Ben's home in Philly, but there's been no answer. They've been trying since the morning they discovered her . . ." He paused, staring at a cup this time. "Her body."

"He could still be here," Renee said, her soul aching to console this man she didn't know. She felt like the most horrid person in the world for feeling some sense of happiness at this latest news. If Ben Monty wasn't at home in Philly, he could be here. The coincidence would be too much. He did it.

Chris stood up and started pacing around the barely decorated studio apartment. He stopped at the desk, running his fingers over the laptop, left open. "Does this have Internet access?"

Marshall shrugged his shoulders. "Yeah," he said. "She loved surfing the net. She couldn't afford her own account, so she logged on to her work address on Augusta's intranet, icon."

A vision of Evan, sitting at Kimberly's computer flashed

in Renee's mind. "I don't think you'll find anything there." She couldn't believe she was saying this. No he was doing something else. Not erasing evidence.

"They didn't mind her doing that?" Chris asked as he walked to the bare mattress that used to be her bed. "At Augusta?"

"Alan told her to." Marshall's look made it clear he didn't want Chris sitting there and Chris promptly jumped up and stepped to the dresser. "He did it from his place all the time. Didn't cost extra or anything."

"What did you think of Alan?" Renee asked.

Marshall turned to her with a half smile. He set the box full of dishes aside. "Alan seemed cool. I only spoke with him once or twice over the phone, but Kimberly was crazy about him. After Ben, I thought she'd be a recluse for a while. Alan prevented that, so he's okay to me." He let out a painful laugh. "All for what, this?"

"What did she think of other people at Augusta?" Chris asked, returning to his initial seat. "Her superiors."

Renee knew what he was getting at and she fought her anger. She wanted to know, too.

"You mean Nick?" Marshall shook his head. "Kimmy thought he was a jerk. He was a snob, she said. He treated her like he'd rather not have her around, but she wasn't bothered. She said she could handle him."

Renee inhaled and mustered the courage to finish what Chris started. "What about Evan Brooks? Augusta's director?"

Marshall paused, seemingly trying to recall. He looked exhausted from grief. "Oh, yeah. The bald guy with the glasses."

"You've met him?" Chris's eyes lit up.

"No. Kimmy described him. She didn't like him. She said he was too aggressive, too pushy. She said he made her uncomfortable."

Renee was glad she was already sitting. She had to continue. "How so?"

"Sexually?" Chris's eyes followed Marshall as he stood up and walked to the balcony door. The balcony.

Renee wanted to strangle Chris for insinuating sex had something to do with it, but she knew it was relevant.

Marshall opened the sliding glass door, but stopped short of stepping outside. "No. I can't remember that. She didn't like him. That's all I know."

Renee had heard enough. She could only think of how aggressive he'd been with her and how, at first, she didn't like it. She'd given in since. Kimberly hadn't. No, she said to herself. There was no reason to believe he'd made sexual advances to her. There were plenty of reasons for two people not to like each other. It didn't have to be sex. "Marshall, do you know a girl named Tamia Griffin?"

Marshall kept his back to both of them, staring out over the balcony. "Chris told me about her. Kimmy said Alan's ex was pissed off with her, called her some names. I hadn't heard anything recently."

"I'm checking up on her," Chris said. "It's weak, but she's suspect number three."

"Ben Monty is number one, right?" Marshall asked. He took one step onto the balcony.

"Yeah." Chris stood up. "With him missing right now, he's got to be. Evan Brooks is my second suspect."

Renee turned away from both men. She wanted to leave. She wanted to go back to New York. She wished she'd never met Evan Brooks. She wished she'd never heard about Kimberly Janis. She wished Marshall Janis wasn't about to bring her to tears.

She stood up from the sofa. She wanted to run, but instead she turned from the door, toward the dresser next to the bed. She saw herself in the mirror. Her eyes were welling up. The first tear fell, splashing onto a picture lying on the dresser. Next to the picture were a pair of dolphin earrings, a Disney watch, and a bus token. Little things.

"Renee?"

She turned around to see both men standing at the balcony window staring at her in bewilderment. The tears were flowing even though she was silent now. She looked at Marshall. "You never get over this loss. You learn to deal with it, live with it. You hold on to the memories, believing you'll see her again. It won't go away. Sometimes it will come back hard and seem like it never tempered. No matter that, you'll be okay. Life goes on."

Chris stood in silence as Renee came face to face with Marshall. Probably thirty or so, he looked like a teenager in an Eagles T-shirt and cut off jean shorts. His tears were streaming, but he was smiling wider than he had before. He held out his hand as Renee handed him the picture from the dresser. The picture of Kimberly and Marshall Janis together. Kimberly had one arm around Marshall and was holding a black and white cat with the other. It rested like a baby in her arms.

"Pepper," Marshall said. "She loved that cat. Acted stupid over it, like it was a human baby. She couldn't bring it here. The landlord said no pets. She was going to look for another place that would take them so she could have Pepper with her."

Renee smiled. "See, I told you. Memories. Now you're smiling."

"We'll find out who did this," Chris said. "We'll stay on top of this and make sure the police listen. We'll get to the truth. No matter what and no matter who."

No matter who. Renee heard those words repeating themselves in her head.

Chris kept his hand on Renee's shoulder as she leaned against the wall outside Kimberly's apartment. She wasn't crying anymore, but needed a second.

"Who was it?" he asked in a whisper. "If I can ask."

"My parents. Eight years ago." Renee felt like a fool, carrying on. She couldn't explain how it just hit sometime. "I'm fine, really. I just lost it for a second. I'm sorry."

Chris laughed. "Don't apologize. I think you helped Marshall feel a lot better. Bummed me out, but I think you helped him."

Renee heard a weak laugh work its way out. "Good and I'm sorry."

"Listen." Chris leaned away. "You can head home if you want to. Marshall said the cops talked with the only neighbor on this floor who was home at the time. She's right down the hallway. I'm gonna go talk to her."

Renee stood up straight. "No, I'm fine, really. I want to be a part of this." She paused taking a strong breath. "No matter who, right?"

"Cool." Chris smiled before turning and heading down the hallway. "I like having a sidekick."

Just as they reached the apartment door, the door swung open. A blond woman, at least six feet tall, stuck her head out. Her hair was in curlers. She was wrapped in a satin bathrobe. She was yelling at the top of her lungs.

"Ward!" She looked at Chris and Renee standing outside her door, staring at her. "You two seen a little boy? Ten years old, red hair, red T-shirt, black shorts?"

Both of them shook their heads.

"Ward! You little . . ." She took a second to compose herself. "He's always walking off like he's some grown up. I'm gonna beat his little tail. Watch."

"Are you Eva Bell?" Chris asked.

She looked him over once before folding her arms across her chest. "Who wants to know?"

He held his hand out to her. "I'm Chris Jackson, a reporter for the *Sun Times.*" He let his hand fall to his sides as he realized she wasn't going to shake it. "I'm writing about the Kimberly Janis case."

She rolled her eyes, turning to Renee. Her brows raised. She wasn't satisfied.

"This is Renee Shepherd," Chris explain. "She's my assistant."

Renee smiled. First sidekick, now assistant again. Chris was enjoying this too much.

"I'm Eva." The woman leaned against the doorway. "What case? I thought it was a suicide."

"Honestly, Ms. Bell . . ." Chris shook his head for obvious dramatic effect. "A lot of people don't think so."

"What did you see or hear that night?" Renee asked.

"That darn boy." Eva looked again down the hallway. "Look. I'll tell you what I told the detective."

"Griggs?" Chris asked. "Detective Griggs?"

"I guess so." she shrugged. "Sounds right. Anyway, I heard someone knocking around ten or so. Real loud. I had my television on, but I could tell it was a woman. I clicked the mute button. Whoever it was called her a bitch, among other things. Most of it was muffled, but I heard that. I wasn't about to open the door, you know. I didn't want to get caught in the crossfire. I peeked through the peephole. She's too far down the hall. I couldn't see anything. The girl living there screamed a few words back. Told her to go away. Next thing, the girl was gone."

"Was that all?" Renee was sure she was talking about Tamia Griffin. If only someone had seen her. She wanted to feel better about this, except she'd witnessed the two unusual interactions between Tamia and Evan.

"You never heard a scream?" Chris asked.

Eva shook her head. "Why would I? She killed herself right? That's what the paper said. No, there was no scream. If someone had pushed her, she would've screamed on her way down. From what I hear, no one heard a scream."

"She could've been unconscious or even dead before she was pushed," Renee said.

"How about anything unusual?" Chris was writing on his pad. "You know, strange . . ."

"There you are you . . . you little bum." Eva's eyes set on the young redhead walking toward the three of them. "Where have you been?"

"Downstairs at Steve's place." He spoke with a lisp as his face held no concern, no fear of punishment.

"Thanks for telling me." Eva's hands went to her hips. "You're not an adult, you know."

"Duh." He rolled his bright blue eyes.

"Get in this apartment!" Eva pointed. "And watch that mouth." She turned to Chris. "Any strange what?"

"Cars maybe." Chris smiled at the young man who wasn't obeying his mother but standing outside the apartment staring the visitors down. "It's a lot to ask, but this is a permit parking area. You might notice an unusual car here and there."

"Nope." She reached for the boy, but he evaded her grip and giggled.

"How about you?" Renee bent over, coming eye to eye with the boy. "Did you see anything, Ward?"

"How do you know my name?" He spat the words out, his eyes excited at being included in the conversation.

"Heard your mother calling you." She looked at Eva. "Do you mind if I ask?"

Eva shrugged. "Answer the woman and get in this apartment. Cars. You notice any new cars out front from that night the woman died?"

His face changed. It wasn't a memory a ten-year-old should have. "Is she still dead?"

Renee felt her heart stop for a moment. She didn't know why this question touched her so deeply. If only . . . "Yes, dear. She's still gone. She won't be coming back here."

He stepped in between them, leaning against his mother. "She was okay. I liked her music. She played it loud. Puff Daddy was a favorite."

"Did you see anything or not?" Eva grabbed his arm, pulling him inside. "Hurry up."

He pulled free of her, throwing her a defiant frown. "Okay. Let me think. Man. Always pullin on me."

Renee could see Chris's patience wearing thin, but he kept his mouth shut. She wondered if Eva had taken the time to sit down and talk to the child about death, loss. She doubted it. Most people didn't know what to say. They didn't understand themselves. They don't know what they believe, so the kids are left wondering, fearing.

"There was a smooth car that ain't been there before." Ward smacked his mother's hand away. "It was red or something like that. You can take the top off, but this one was on. It made a cool sound when it drove off. I saw it."

"How could you see it?" Chris asked.

Renee remembered Evan's car from passing it on the way to dinner. A ruby red Mercedes convertible. A chill went down her spine.

"He hangs out on our balcony all night," Eva said, finally pushing the boy all the way in. "It faces the glorious parking lot. Some view."

"Does he know the make?" Renee asked, knowing she was reaching now. "The name? Mercedes, Nissan, BMW."

Eva looked back. Ward was nowhere to be seen and she didn't appear the least bit interested in seeking him out. "Look, my show is on. I gotta go. I told all that to the cops."

"About the car?" Chris asked.

"No." She was already shutting the door. "Ward was off running somewhere when they were here."

As the door slammed shut, Chris turned to Renee. "So, that might be a clue. We got to find out what Tamia and

Evan drive. Ben's car would probably be a rental. In reality, that car could've been anyone, but if it's . . ."

"Evan drives a red Mercedes convertible." Renee felt no desire to hold on to secrets anymore. Could she really protect Evan from Chris's biased opinions anyway? Did she even want to?

Chris looked Renee sternly in the eyes. "You're giving this up? I've sensed your reluctance to suspect Evan since the beginning. Something must've changed. Was it Marshall?"

"Partly." She nodded and they both turned and headed for the stairs.

"There's more?"

"Yeah," she said. "There's more."

Chris salivated as Renee told him everything she'd been holding back about Evan. She told him about catching him at Kimberly's computer, outside Augusta with Tamia, the dinner warning, the note slipped under the door, the look between him and Tamia at the memorial.

"We have to find out the connection with him and Tamia." Chris's eyes were dancing as they stopped at his car. "That's the key. It's something between them. I think . . ."

"I really can't talk about it anymore." The bright June sun was scorching and Renee had had enough of it for one day. She'd had enough of everything for the day.

"Where d'ya park?"

"I hailed a cab. You want to be the highlight of my day and drop me off at the apartment?"

With a compassionate smile, Chris obliged.

He pulled up to the brown brick apartment building. It was late and the streets were starting to jump. Neither Chris nor Renee spoke during the short drive.

"Look, Renee." Chris turned sideways and placed a hand on Renee's shoulder.

"I'm sorry, Chris." She shook her head, her hands gripping her thighs. "I'm acting completely weird. I can't explain it myself."

"You don't have to." He scooted closer. "How could you imagine, huh? You thought the guy was the answer to your dreams. You had no idea he'd be trouble."

She looked at him and had to laugh at his fake pout. She knew then she'd found a good friend. She accepted his open arms and hugged him tightly. Just as she did, her eyes focused on the red Mercedes convertible double parked across the street.

She was frozen as Evan's eyes, electrified with anger, bore into her. In a second's time, he turned away and sped off.

"What?" Chris asked as she pushed away. "What is it?"

"Evan." She couldn't see the car anymore, but she could still see his eyes. Guilt swept over her. "He was parked across the street."

Chris swung around, looking everywhere.

"He's gone," she said, resting back in her seat. "I guess he was waiting for me. He saw us hugging."

"How close are the two of you?" Chris frowned.

"I can't tell you, honestly," Renee answered, every word the truth. "I think we're a lot closer than I'd care to admit. It's a feeling I've had since I met him. A sense."

"Trouble," Chris said as if reading her mind.

EIGHT

"Make it out to Charleen Bartlett, please."

Renee obliged, giving her best regards, closed the book and slid it back to the older woman. She pasted on a friendly smile for Charleen even though smiles were hard for her now. Despite the warm welcome she was receiving from the men and women arriving for the book signing, Renee's thoughts flipped from Kimberly to Evan and nothing else. She thought of the innocent girl whose life was cut short. She thought of Evan's angry eyes across the street from the apartment. She thought of Kimberly pleading for help, advice, anything. She thought of Evan's lips and the fire she felt when they touched hers. Renee would give anything to be absorbed in books and signatures, but a signing seemed so insignificant when murder and a lost chance at love consumed her mind.

The last thing Renee wanted was to be selfish and complain of a temporarily broken heart when a young woman was dead, two parents without a daughter, Marshall without a sister, and Alan without the woman he had loved. It was only that she had, before these new revelations and still now, felt there was more to her and Evan than a vacation romance. She was certain so much more was about to happen, if it hadn't already.

She wanted desperately to wipe the thoughts from her mind as she signed a book for Antoinette Clark, an aspiring nutritionist at De Paul University, but she knew that would be impossible as soon as she met the next person in line.

"Hello, Renee."

Evan Brooks's smile gave no indication that he was as familiar with her as he was. It gave no indication that he had seen her hugging Chris Jackson. It was unassuming and kind, as if he was doing his best not to intimidate her, upset her.

His name slipped softly from her lips. "Evan, what are you doing here?"

"I told you I'd come." A frown appeared briefly as he slid his copy of her book across the table. "Remember the memorial?"

Renee tore her eyes from his and opened the book. She'd forgotten her invitation to him, which seemed like months ago. "How would you like me to phrase it?"

Evan only stood there, a puzzled look on his face.

"Renee," he asked. "What's going on? Why are you avoiding me? What's between you and Chris Jackson?"

"Evan." She spoke in a whisper, her tone turning harsh as she eyed him. "I'm working here. Now is there any particular way you would like this signed?"

"Yes. Sign it to the man I kissed last Saturday night." Evan's words were quietly spoken as he bent over the table, his eyes holding a determination that let her know he wasn't the type of man to be brushed away so easily.

As her temperature rose, Renee tried to hide the effect his intimate comments had on her. Without a response, she opened the book and signed only her name, then slid it back to him.

"I want to speak with you when you're finished." Evan's tone was unwavering. He meant what he'd just said.

"It'll be awhile." Renee only glanced at him for a moment. *If he wasn't so gorgeous.* If his eyes weren't so piercing.

"I'll wait," was his only response as he retrieved the book and stepped aside.

Renee felt a tug at her heart as she saw him walk away from the table. She didn't think she was capable of feeling such a way for someone who could be a killer. It wasn't possible, was it? She knew she was having a hard enough time trying to stay away from him, but his appearance only heightened the already strong attraction.

So, she thought, he said he would wait. Renee knew she had to come up with something. Evan wasn't a man to accept empty explanations. Did she have the courage to tell him her suspicions? She knew she didn't, couldn't.

There were more people than Renee had expected and even though she was pleased, she was also exhausted after signing the last book. Her mouth hurt from smiling non-stop. She hadn't forgotten about Evan, not for a second. His was the first face she looked for as she stood up from the table the book store owner had set up for her. When she saw him sitting on a nearby love seat, a feeling of joy came over her. That was the last emotion she'd expected to feel, but it was undeniable. He had waited. In more than a small way, that meant something to her.

It wasn't that she wanted to speak with him. She actually dreaded it, not knowing what she would say. Rather, it was that he'd done what he said he would. She could trust him at his word. He was patient. That was what she needed if there was to be any chance for them.

She almost didn't want to disturb him, watching him

from a distance. As he stared out the large window watching the passersby on Michigan Avenue, Renee took in his profile. There was strength in every inch of his face. Clean-cut and well dressed. She found it more than difficult to keep her blood pressure down as the sternness of his jaw contradicted the tired look in his eyes in such a sexy way. He looked like a man who could do something he shouldn't if he had to, but not murder. It could never reach that point, could it?

"All finished, Ms. Shepherd?"

Stacy Ford, the owner of the bookstore, clasped her hands together in an excited manner. She was a middle-aged woman with raisin brown skin and dark brown eyes. Her thickly braided chocolate brown hair had a striking streak of white, which matched the flashy blue pantsuit she wore with sequins pasted here and there. She'd been overjoyed to meet Renee, always happy to do signings because of their effect on a store's sales.

"Yes, I suppose." Renee turned from Stacy to Evan who had heard her name being called and swiftly started toward her.

"You're probably starved," Stacy said. "I have some snacks for you in the back room. Come on."

Renee followed, knowing Evan was right behind her. Stacy led them toward the back room, cluttered with boxes and stacks of books. There was an old sofa in the middle of the room and next to it, an end table with coffee, finger sandwiches, and cookies.

"It isn't much, but . . ." Stacy stopped in the middle of her sentence as she saw Evan standing in the doorway.

"Stacy." Renee stepped aside as Evan approached. "This is Evan Brooks, a friend of mine."

"It's very nice to meet you, Stacy." Evan was his usual charming self. "This is your store?"

"Yes." Stacy's words came out in a breath as she pulled

her head all the way back to look at Evan face to face. "Stacy . . . Ford."

"I've been looking around. It's very impressive." Evan attempted to remove his hand from her strong grip after their shake, but she clasped both her hands around his.

"Me, too," Stacy responded, her mouth as wide as a saucer as she delightedly looked him up and down. She had no idea her words made no sense.

Renee found the scene amusing. She took a seat on the sofa, satisfied to see that Evan had that effect on someone besides herself.

"I'll be sure to shop here from now on," Evan said, finally able to get his hand back. He turned to the sofa and sat beside Renee.

Renee was more than aware of his closeness. His gentle but masculine smell was now familiar and she fought the urge to scoot closer to him. She tried hard to concentrate on Stacy who was still in a trance over Evan. Anything to keep from looking at him and those mesmerizing eyes.

"If you come," Stacy said with a little more composure, "I'll give you half off. Promise."

"You got a deal." Evan was so used to attention from women he showed no signs of embarrassment.

"I'll let you two alone for a while." Stacy winked as she backed out of the room until she fell into a stack of books that went sliding all over the floor.

"No, let me. Let me. You sit." Stacy waved to Evan who began to stand up with the intention of helping her. As he sat back down, she started piling the books on top of each other. Despite her efforts, each book seemed to want to stay on the floor because one slid back down as soon as another was added. This went on for a several seconds, until Stacy cursed under her breath, pushed the remaining standing books to the ground and stormed off.

Renee wasn't sure if it was the scene before her or something more, but a sudden burst of laughter erupted from within her, and Evan joined right in. It wasn't just the humor of the moment, it was a gamut of emotions expressing themselves through her laughter. The last two weeks had been pressing on her for many reasons and she needed to let some of it go. The stress, concern, and worry was building up and occupying her every waking moment. So she laughed. She laughed and felt herself calm down for the first time in a while.

Then suddenly, Evan's laughter stopped and Renee turned to face him. His stone serious face and smoldering eyes quieted her. She could only stare into them as he reached a hand out to her arm and commandingly pulled her toward him.

Renee heard a voice in the back of her head telling her to resist, but it was too dim. It had been drowned out by the voice of desire and passion that yelled at her to get closer, to kiss him and touch him. She wanted him with no requirements and had never felt that before. The danger of it all excited her beyond words.

His lips claimed hers in a hungry, possessive way, unlike the tenderness of the last kiss. They demanded, and much like their owner, weren't going to take no for an answer. Renee felt the pit of her stomach swirl and every bone in her body fell limp as his touch sent a fire raging within her. She didn't hesitate to wrap her arms around his neck and pull herself even closer. As his lips devoured hers, Renee let out a moan. She was losing her mind, she knew it. She wanted to. She felt his hands grab her waist, squeezing her. She wanted him to squeeze even harder. She pressed her lips to his, opening his mouth. Her tongue entered and connected with his, forcing a tortured groan from deep within him. Its urgency only served to ignite Renee's passions, making her feel powerful.

She ran her hands down his back, feeling the muscles

beneath his thin summer shirt. She only wanted more with every touch she got. His fervent hands all over her said the same. Could she ever get as close as she wanted to? It didn't seem so, as she felt him pull her tighter. More.

"Renee." The word came under a husky deep breath as Evan separated his mouth from hers. His lips trailed her neck and shoulder with a greed like he knew what he touched belonged to him. Renee was reeling from the constant shock waves flowing through her body. Nonstop.

She gave in to the pressure of his weight and fell backward on the sofa. He moved his body to lie atop hers, supporting himself with his elbows at the edges of the sofa.

"Evan," she moaned, the desire threatening to take her over. "Evan."

His lips returned to hers, his tongue penetrating, searching and wanting. His hands found a crevice between their chests and cupped her breasts. He gently caressed them, erotically stimulating, promising. She felt the heat through her blouse, her bra, all the way to her soft flesh. Through to her. Her head was spinning, his caresses making her wild.

She could feel through her dress and his pants that he was aroused. The realization threatened to render her completely mindless. As his legs rubbed against her thighs, Renee knew they were heading for a direction they couldn't go. They were in a book store back room. The reminder was barely there. She screamed inside for her wits to return to her and quickly tore her lips from his. As she turned her head to the side, Evan's lips returned to her neck, making it all the more difficult for her to resist. But she was determined.

"Evan, no." Renee pushed him away, hard this time, trying to lift his body from hers. "Stacy could come back."

She looked into his eyes as they opened again. He was so deep in desire, it seemed difficult for him to comprehend her words. She could tell from the cloud his eyes seemed to hold, he was confused as he lifted himself from her. His eyes never left hers.

"Renee, I . . ." His voice was deep through strong, sharp breaths.

"I can't believe this." Renee quickly pushed herself up from the sofa, only to have to sit again as the blood rushed to her head and her knees buckled.

There was a moment of silence as both of them took a second to regain their composure. As reality hit her, Renee was astonished at how quickly, without hesitation of any kind, she'd come to him. She was embarrassed and angry, knowing everything was much worse now.

"I'm not sure what just happened," she said, sliding down the sofa as far from Evan as possible. "But it might be best if you leave."

"I'm sorry, Renee." Evan shook his head, seemingly angry with himself. "I'm not sure what happened either, but I think we should talk about it."

"I have nothing to say." Renee finally found the strength to stand, even though her knees were still a little weak. She turned with her back to Evan, not trusting herself to follow through if she looked at him again. She wished she could stop wanting him, if only for a second!

"I don't believe that." Evan stood, taking a step toward her. "I don't know what's going on, but I'm getting mixed signals. Hot, then cold. I want an explanation."

"I don't owe you anything." Renee hid her embarrassment behind anger. The truth was, she had no explanation. Her body did the exact opposite of what her mind told her to. It was involuntary, without reason.

"I know you don't, but we need to have some communication. We seemed to click last Wednesday when we had lunch. Then, Saturday was fantastic. Afterward, you said it was all right to call you. Then I call and you give me the cold shoulder to say the least. Then I see you hugging that reporter whom you told me you barely knew. You do the cold shoulder act again today, even though you invited me to come here. Just a second ago you were a more than willing partner when I kissed you."

She turned to give him an intimidating scowl, but the man that she knew wouldn't back down and he didn't.

"You were willing," he repeated earnestly. "And nothing you can say will make me believe otherwise. It was something special and we both felt it. Now, you're looking at me like I'm a leper."

"I don't know who you are," Renee said. "If I've been sending mixed signals, it's only because you're pushing me."

"If that's what it is, I can lay off." Evan ran a frustrated hand over his bald head. "I just thought. No, I know there's something special between us and I didn't want you to go back to New York without having the chance to show you that. I may have pushed. If so, I apologize."

"You just need to lay off." Renee folded her arms across her chest, not knowing what else to do with them. She wanted desperately to tell him everything she knew, but she couldn't.

"I will if that's it." Evan stepped closer, raising a keen eyebrow. "Is that really all there is to it? I get the feeling there's something more."

"No." She turned again, her back to him. She felt her emotions stirring at his closeness again. What was this hold he had on her?

Evan didn't respond for a while, making Renee all the more nervous. Could he tell she suspected him of murder?

"Evan." She turned to face him, mustering the strength to look him in the eye. "I'm sorry, but I need time."

"I'm a man, Renee," he said with a gentle but defiant

tone. "I don't like to be dragged around. I have pride, just like any other man."

"I know you do and I'd never attempt to harm that pride." She sighed, deeply affected by the hurt look on his face. It had to be Ben Monty from Philly. It had to.

"I hope you'll call me before you leave." He headed for the door, turning one last time to face her before exiting. "I'm not sure what you think of me, but I can care for you Renee. I want to care for you. I already do. I wouldn't smother you or try to possess you. I'd accept your independence. I know I'm the right man for you. That is, only if you're ready."

Renee refused to cry even though she wanted to. She wasn't even sure why that was. She was only sure that things were more complicated now than ever.

She believed Evan cared for her and wasn't interested in her for only one thing or for what she knew about Kimberly. She believed it because she saw it in his eyes and felt it in his touch. She didn't want to believe he could have anything to do with Kimberly's murder and there were no facts indicating that he had. Everything she knew was circumstantial. Circumstantial, but enough for her to be cautious.

To be near him was risking too much. From their electrically charged encounters, she knew this was more than a crush or vacation romance. As Evan had said, this was something special. Could it be love? The thought frightened Renee to death. She'd been so careful to guard her heart, only allowing a select few a place in it. They were only those she couldn't help but love. But to love meant to risk losing, and she'd lost enough to last a lifetime with the death of her parents. She wasn't sure she was strong enough to love more people.

But what if Evan had something to do with Kimberly's death? If she allowed him a place in her heart and that turned out to be true, Renee wasn't sure she could bear it. She wasn't ready. Not right now.

If she was wrong and Evan had nothing to do with Kimberly's death, would she be ready? She was almost certain she would be, but would he still be waiting? That wasn't certain. He'd told her he had pride, not that she didn't know that. She knew he wouldn't wait around forever whether she decided to stay in Chicago or not.

Her mind was going crazy with hope and fear. Her heart was fluttering with questions and needs she'd never asked or felt before. Renee understood her feelings for Evan were special. She understood that Kimberly was murdered by either Ben Monty or Tamia Griffin. These understandings didn't clear up a thing, only bringing more questions she was far from answering.

Renee's grumbling stomach forced her to reach for a sandwich.

Thursday didn't start off as Renee had hoped. She wanted to wake up in her bed in New York, the past two weeks a dream from which she could remember the good and forget the bad, but it didn't happen. Instead, she awoke to the sound of garbage trucks in the alley and the couple upstairs arguing about the telephone bill. Michelle was still marrying a jerk, Kimberly was still dead, and she was still falling for Evan.

For distraction, she spent the morning visiting some acquaintances she'd made in the area through book interviews and association meetings. It was nice to see people she hadn't talked to in a while, but no matter what, Evan stayed first and foremost on her mind. Even the news that a former dietician who was a self-proclaimed man hater when Renee had met her two years ago was now a happily married, stay-at-home wife and pregnant with twins wasn't enough to push Evan into the back of her mind.

She hoped to clear her mind of its cluttered thoughts with a jog along the lakefront, only Evan was imprinted in her head. Nothing was getting rid of him. The scenes of couples in love as they walked and rollerbladed hand in hand along the concrete path beside her didn't help. It only made her miss him. She finally gave up and returned to the apartment.

She knew Michelle would be home soon, speaking the praises of St. Nick Hamilton who had canceled lunch with Renee for the second time. Tales of how much Michelle loved him were the last thing she wanted to hear.

What she did want was to take a long, hot peach-scented bubble bath and fall into a bed. Not a sofa bed, but a real soft, plush bed with down pillows all around her. She wanted to forget about everything and everyone for at least today. But as she stepped onto the second floor, Renee knew that hope would be delayed a little longer.

Standing in the doorway to the apartment was Tamia Griffin. She looked as apprehensive now as she had the last two times Renee had seen her. This was not a woman at peace.

"Can I help you?" Renee hesitated as she searched her purse for her keys. Should she be scared? She wasn't.

"The door downstairs wasn't locked," she said. "You should know."

"Thanks for the information," Renee responded, not yet standing at her door. She took another step. "You're Tamia Griffin?"

"How did you know?" She scratched her tawny-shaded cheek with a long red fingernail.

"People talk," Renee said, staring the girl down. She wanted to see something, anything to make her believe this girl wasn't a killer. She didn't look the part. "I know you were Alan Smith's girlfriend before Kimberly. I know you were harassing her."

"That's what I came to see you about." Her stance straightened as her tone harshened. "You and Chris Jackson been asking around about me like I killed Kimberly."

"Did you?" Renee asked, trying to brace for an answer she didn't expect to get.

Tamia's mouth dropped, then closed again. "Would I be here talking to you if I did?"

"How did you know where I live?" Renee placed both hands on her hips. Did Evan give her this address?

"Chris Jackson. He called me, asking all kinds of questions. He said if I had anything to add I should call him. I got his machine. I'm not leaving a message about murder on an answering machine." She exaggerated the last two words. "I know you were at the memorial with him and he mentioned you when I called. Michelle's address is in the student directory."

There was an awkward moment of silence as the women eyed each other. Renee knew then that Tamia wasn't a murderer. Chris didn't think so either. He would've never given her access to Renee if he thought she was.

"What do you have to add?" she asked, feeling hopeful for a second. She had to be cautious. Every question she got answered only raised more questions about Evan.

"Okay. To back it up, Kimberly and I used to be friends." Tamia flipped her braids with her right hand. "When she first got here. We used to talk and stuff. Then, she stole my boyfriend."

"I understand that." Renee felt sorry for her, but this wasn't the issue. So, Kimberly wasn't perfect. No one is.

"I had words with her." Tamia's eyes shifted. "You know. I feel bad now cause she's dead, but I was pissed. I was at her apartment the night she died. Alan was almost mine again and she snatched him back."

Renee's eyes widened, standing at attention. "What do you mean almost yours again?"

"He called me. I mean, I called him. He was starting to understand that Kimberly wasn't for him." She smiled as if she held a secret too juicy to tell. "You see, Alan loves attention. He likes to be the great guy. He needs to be reminded how down he is. Regularly. He's gonna run for public office one day. Wants to be a black Kennedy."

Renee was reminded of her visit to BFK. That description sounded about right. "What made you think you would get him back?"

"I could feel it." She shoved her hands into the pockets of her khaki shorts. "He told me there was no future for Kimberly and him. He told me he hadn't appreciated my support."

"What changed?" Renee wondered why, with all this news, Alan seemed so hurt by Kimberly's death. He was planning to break up with her. She thought Chris must've been right when he said Alan was only out for attention.

Tamia lowered her head and spoke somberly. "Then I saw him the next day with Kimberly on campus. He was holding her hand. I saw him kiss her. She did something. The next day, I went to her apartment to confront her. She never even let me in. I left. That was it. I swear."

"I believe you," Renee urged after a moment's hesitation. "Tell me how you know Evan Brooks."

"How do you know . . ." She held a confused frown for only a moment, then let it go as if nothing surprised her anymore. "I don't know him. I didn't at least. He called me the day after Kimberly died. He asked me to come to Augusta. Said he needed to talk to me. Needed to. I think he connected my name to her because we used to be friends. He probably thought we still were. I set him straight on that. He was asking me questions I would have no idea how to answer."

"What kind of questions?" Renee couldn't imagine what Evan was doing? Didn't sound like a murderer's behavior to her. Asking around, introducing himself to Kimberly's friends. Asking about her death.

"What I know about her depression. Who were her friends. Who were her enemies. When I set him straight on my relationship with Kimberly, he just looked at me weird and that was it. Like he didn't want nothing to do with me anymore."

"You told Chris this?" Renee was certain Chris was elated to hear about more suspicious behavior on Evan's behalf, even though this was more confusing than suspicious.

Tamia nodded.

"So what was it you had to add?" Renee realized the look she'd seen on Tamia's face at the memorial was fear. Evan's initial encounter with her confused her, and she didn't know what he was after. Renee was all too aware of how intimidating he could be.

"I forgot one of the weird questions Evan asked," Tamia said. "Chris wanted to know if I remembered."

"What was it?

"He asked me if I knew Kimberly's e-mail password." She shrugged her shoulders. "Like I would know."

The image of Evan at Kimberly's computer flashed in Renee's mind. With every answer, another question.

Tamia headed down the hall. "Look, I gotta go. I just wanted to add that. I wanted to help. I hated Kimberly for stealing Alan from me, but I didn't want her dead. I felt guilty thinking she'd killed herself 'cause I was messing with her. I didn't even know she was a depressive, or whatever you call it."

"She wasn't," Renee said. "She didn't kill herself. She was murdered."

"Not by me. I was at home. I live less than five blocks from her. My roommate was there when I got back way before Chris said she was supposed to have been pushed over."

"Why were you at her memorial?" Renee's question had nothing to do with anything. She just wanted to know.

Tamia's eyes softened, showing her youth, uncertainty. "I guess . . . I wanted to . . . I was sorry she was dead, you know. I went for Alan. I wanted him to know I was there for him. I know it seems cold, but I was hoping to score some brownie points."

"Is there anything else?" Renee wanted to chide her, but couldn't. These small sins seemed so insignificant compared to the big one on her mind coming closer every second.

"Chris Jackson seemed to think Evan might have killed her? What do you think? I mean, what I heard of him is he's a big philanthropist. A good person. Alan never liked him, but most people did."

"Chris doesn't have any proof that Evan did anything," Renee said. "So there isn't any need to go saying anything about this to anyone, all right?"

"Whatever."

Renee watched as the young girl disappeared down the staircase. She'd defended Evan again despite her own misgivings, in order to protect his name. With each piece of information she got about Kimberly and the mysterious circumstances surrounding her death, the more Renee felt the answer lay with Evan, whether or not it was he who killed her.

She felt so torn inside as she entered the quiet, peaceful apartment. She honestly believed she was falling in love, real love, for the first time in a way that could be stronger than her fear of loss, the hold her grief had on her. Why did it have to be with Evan Brooks? Why did it have to be with a man who could be a murderer or at least have something to do with the murder of a beautiful, intelligent, and young black woman?

The irony wasn't lost on Renee as her mouth formed an inch's worth of a smile. She'd protected the deep chasm of her heart from men her whole adult life. Sometimes it was harder than others, but always manageable. The one time she opened up and started to wonder, dream, and contemplate, she was thrown this curve, this unbelievable situation.

She thought back to when she met Evan, wondering what she could have done to avoid this, but it was useless. From the beginning, her heart and body had a mind of their own. There was nothing she could've done, and all she could do now was hold on to the little bit of hope she refused to give up. Simply refused.

After setting her things on a nearby chair, Renee reluctantly picked up the phone and dialed Chris's phone number. She planned to leave out her momentary lapse of self-control in the back room of the bookstore the other day, calling with hope that Chris had made progress on Ben Monty, but she knew her chances were dimming. She knew the answer to Kimberly's death was right here in Chicago, not Philadelphia.

"Hello?" Chris answered the phone sounding out of breath.

"Chris? This is Renee. Are you all right?"

"A little out of breath." He paused for a moment. "Just got in. Hate to miss any phone call. You never know. Could be the story that puts me over the top."

"I can call later. After you're situated."

"No," he protested. "What is it?"

"Tamia just left here. She had more info."

"Lay it on me, sister."

His seventies reference passed over Renee's consciousness as her mood left no room for a sense of humor. She told him everything she and Tamia discussed.

"This doesn't look good for the privileged one," Chris said.

"I don't want to believe it." Renee knew she sounded defeated. "It looks like you may be right. What about Ben Monty? Have you found anything on him?"

"Had a buddy check it out. I'm telling you, Detective Griggs didn't do *any* follow up. What little time the cops spent looking for Monty was a waste. They had him all the time. Efficiency huh? I started feeling lucky when my guy told me Monty was arrested three times for stalking ex-girlfriends. Only, it turns out, on the night of the murder, he was on lockdown for that third arrest. He'd violated the restraining order on the latest love of his life. He's still there, can't afford bail."

Renee saw her last feather of hope fly out the window. "Do you think he could've paid someone to do it?"

"He got fired from his job three months ago. He was getting evicted. He doesn't even have enough money to be broke. Besides, these types of psychos that stalk women don't pay someone to do their dirty work. They do it themselves. That's the whole point. That's how they get off."

"I know, you're right." Renee sighed. "So he's out as a suspect?

"Out," he repeated. "But I have some other leads I'm working on. Still, Brooks looks to be my number one guy."

"What other leads are you talking about?" Renee felt a glimmer of hope return. She would hold on to anything that could point the finger away from Evan. Substantiated or not.

"I can't tell you yet," he protested.

"Chris!" Her tone of voice gave away her frustration.

"I've told you everything I know. What happened to all that stuff about trusting me?"

"Listen, Renee." Chris tone was serious. "I can tell from the sound of your voice you're more involved in this than you're letting on. Even more than you've confessed to me. Now, do you want to repeat that part about your telling me everything? Have you really?"

Renee's first intent was to deny his insinuations, but she thought about it for a second and gave up. There was no use in hiding it. "You really have that reporter's keen eye, don't you?"

"You've got to be careful," Chris said. "At least for now."

"I know and I am being careful. It's just ... It's just hard."

"Can I do something to take your mind off all of this? Maybe a dinner between friends."

"Between friends?" Renee asked.

"If that's all you want."

"Friends sounds good." Renee needed a friend right now. At least.

"So, it's dinner then?"

"Not tonight. I promised Michelle dinner tonight. I came to Chicago to visit her and we've barely spent more than a couple of hours together."

"Some other night, then?" Chris asked.

"I have an association dinner tomorrow night at the Palmer House Hilton downtown. I could use a friend."

"What time?"

"Starts at seven and it's formal," Renee said. "I know you young guys can be a little reluctant to dress up."

"I'll rent a tux and pick you up at six thirty."

"Why don't we meet at seven?" A pickup sounded too much like a date for Renee, and she was never at a dinner before it started. She wasn't ever anywhere before it started. "How about outside, in front of the hotel?"

"See you at seven tomorrow."

"Chris?" Renee asked.

"Yeah?"

"Maybe you'll share some of your new leads with me then?" She was as polite as she could be without letting him know how desperately she needed to hear there was someone besides Evan on his mind.

"I'll think about it."

Renee's smile was much bigger this time as she replaced the receiver. What little she knew of Chris, she liked. He made her feel comfortable. The complete opposite of Evan, who made her senses go wild, her body react in involuntary ways, and her temperature hit the ceiling.

Knowing only a warm, long bath would make her feel comfortable right now, Renee headed for her carry-on bag placed behind the sofa. She remembered bringing her bath crystals and placing them there. Making her own personal spa. That would be the perfect touch. Maybe she couldn't get Evan off her mind anytime soon, but her body would feel great in an hour.

Renee searched her bag, a little confused at its disarray. She'd carefully placed the items in small plastic containers, sealable bags, or folded them to keep everything neat, but they hadn't stayed that way. Folded items were unfolded, sealed items were unsealed or halfway sealed, and some of the containers were open. Renee thought it only reflected her state of mind. The past two weeks had been hectic and keeping her bag tidy was the last thing on her mind.

She finally found her crystals and grabbed them. Michelle wouldn't be home for a couple of hours, giving Renee enough time to rest and enjoy. She checked the locks before escaping to the bathroom. She locked the bathroom door, too. She hadn't forgotten the threat placed at her doorstep, although she was glad she hadn't gotten anymore. When she finally slid her aching, bare body into the hot, bubbling water, she felt another day of unease begin to release and wash away. Soon, she was ready for a nap.

As she snuggled under the sheets on Michelle's bed, the only thing she couldn't get off her mind was the kiss she'd shared with Evan at the book store the other day. She could swear she still felt the imprint of his pleasingly rough lips against hers. She couldn't remember feeling such passion. Even though she hadn't been with a lot of men, Renee knew what she'd felt while in his embrace was special. Never had she experienced such abandonment of restraint, such a willingness to give, to take, and to share.

Would she ever forget his touch? Would she have to? She knew it would take much more than a bubble bath to wash her feelings for Evan Brooks away. She knew no amount of crystals would soothe her like his arms would. She needed to know the truth and would have to face that truth when it came, no matter what it told her.

Renee stared into the crowded parking lot as she sat in Michelle's car outside Augusta's building. Michelle had canceled last night's dinner due to Nick's request for his fiancée to join him for a business dinner at a country club in suburban Glencoe. Renee had been in fact relieved at not going out, but upset at a foiled attempt to spend more time with her sister. Instead, she spent the night alone in the apartment watching television and doing everything she could to keep from thinking about Evan. Nothing worked.

After arriving home that night, Michelle promised to make it up to her.

"I don't have any classes tomorrow," she said. "We can go to dinner."

"I have the association dinner tomorrow night." Renee lay on the bed as Michelle dressed in her pajamas.

"Oh, yeah." Michelle sighed with a flighty sigh as she strung her hair into a ponytail. "Then let's just hang out. We'll shop for a dress, unless you have one already."

"No, I don't." Renee sat up. She was never averse to the idea of shopping. "Good idea. When?"

"Gotta work. I'll take the bus to work. Pick me up at Augusta around one."

Renee obliged, not wanting to let Michelle in on her apprehension over a possible encounter with Evan Brooks. Besides, coming up with an idea, Renee was anxious to get to Kimberly's computer. She believed she knew the Internet password Evan had been asking about. She'd do her best to avoid Evan and cross her fingers for luck. She had to put finding the truth above her own fears and, more importantly, her own desires.

She checked her watch as she reached the third floor. Michelle was expecting her around one and it was twelve thirty. She peeked around the corner before entering the finance department. As she'd guessed, most everyone was at lunch. The only people there were a few students who weren't likely to question her if she acted like she knew what she was doing.

Remembering the last time she approached Kimberly's office and found Evan at her computer, Renee decided to peek before entering. It was empty inside, but before she could enter, she was met with a surprise from around the corner.

"Renee! What are you doing here?"

"Alan." Renee tried to conceal her surprise with a pleasant smile. "What are you doing here?" She hadn't meant to return the question, but was caught off guard, feeling pressured to say something immediately.

"I was discussing BFK going national with Evan." His eyes moved from Renee's face to her hand, still on the door knob. "I thought I'd stop by and see if there was anything of Kimberly's left that I needed to get."

"Didn't you do that already?" Renee asked.

"Yes, but . . ." Alan sighed. "It was upsetting and I had to leave. I thought maybe her family would leave something if they knew it wasn't hers. You know, any memories."

Renee placed her hand on his arm, not sure what to feel. She wanted to believe him. Felt something was there. Tamia had seen him and Kimberly kissing the day before her death. Maybe they had decided to try again. She wasn't sure. Alan was playing the part well. As if one would think he wanted to hold on to any memento from his lost love. As if on cue, his expression changed from emotional to inquisitive.

"What are *you* doing here?"

"A curious glance, I suppose," Renee lied. She was sure grieving a lost loved one looked good on a public figure's resume. "I'm picking up Michelle, my sister."

"I've met her," he said with a familiar nod. "She's engaged to Kimberly's boss. Nice kid."

"You know Nick well?"

"We've talked a few times about the programs. I'm one of the smaller organizations, so he doesn't waste too much time with me, but he's proud of what I've done with BFK financially."

"Michelle isn't off until one, so I thought I'd give myself a tour of the offices."

Alan took a step away from her, his eyes still watching her hand. "Well, there's really no need to go in there. As a matter of fact, there's no need for me to go in there. It would only bring up memories best left alone."

Renee agreed with him before turning to leave as they said their goodbyes. She waited around the next corner until he was out of sight and returned to the office, shutting the door behind her. She searched for a lock, but there wasn't one. If Alan returned, she'd simply have to tell him the truth. After all, if he really did care for Kimberly, which Renee was starting to doubt, he should want to know the truth, no matter how painful it would be. Renee sure knew she did.

The office was completely empty except for a file holder, a phone, and a computer on the desk. Not even a stapler or roll of scotch tape in sight. Renee propped herself in the chair and turned on the computer. It was an older version than her own, but she quickly adapted and found the online program. She knew most people used a password uniquely familiar to them. At home, Renee's password was E-A-T-R-I-G-H-T. When Kimberly's computer asked for the password, she typed in P-E-P-P-E-R. She crossed her fingers and closed her eyes as she pressed the ENTER button, knowing if she was wrong there were no alternatives and her risk would be for nothing.

She was counting on her earlier conversation with Marshall and his reaction to the picture she'd handed him. It was all she had.

She opened her eyes. A wide, accomplished smile lit her face as the online program began to form icons and the hard drive made the familiar boot-up noise. She was in. She went directly to the mail box to check for outgoing mail.

Nothing. It was empty.

Mail sent.

Nothing.

Incoming Mail.

Nothing.

She went to the File Manager and clicked on the download menu, which would contain a copy of any mail with attachments like the first letter Kimberly sent her in New York.

Nothing. Completely empty. As if it never existed.

Renee knew most mailboxes kept letters for at least two weeks, usually longer. The few correspondences between Kimberly and herself should still be available for retrieval. Someone had deliberately erased every piece of mail Kimberly Janis had sent or received in all of that time. Maybe Evan was successful in finding out Kimberly's password from one of her friends. Everything was gone.

Could Evan have forced Kimberly to tell him before he threw her off her balcony?

Renee inhaled, surprised at herself for asking that question even hypothetically. He wouldn't have asked Tamia for the password if he knew. The scene two weeks ago of Evan searching files at this same computer brought the question on. She decided to check her regular word processing files for anything. Anything to show this computer had even been used.

Nothing.

Someone had deleted everything! Renee gritted her teeth at the empty screen. She was certain there had been files here when she saw Evan in the same seat she was in now. Now they were gone. There weren't enough coincidences in the world, she thought. Renee felt her stomach turn queasy and her breathing pick up pace. She was angry for herself and for Kimberly Janis.

"What are you doing in here?"

Renee swung around in the chair. She caught her breath, stunned to see Evan Brooks standing in the office doorway. She had been so caught up in her search for files, she hadn't heard the door open.

"I . . . uh . . . I." She quickly switched the POWER button on the computer off and stood up, facing Evan. She wondered how she could explain herself out of this situation. She wondered how, despite everything she now knew, part of her was still happy to see him.

"Why are you looking at Kimberly's computer?" His voice was strained, his eyes wide.

"I was . . ." Renee was well aware of the fear that swept through her as he stepped closer. "I was looking."

"What were you looking for?" Evan stepped farther into the room attempting to close the door behind him.

The move frightened Renee. Instinctively, she yelled, "No!"

"What's wrong with you?" Evan asked, looking very perplexed.

"Don't you dare close that door," she ordered, feeling her whole body shake.

"What?" Evan swung the door open again. "Are you afraid of being alone with me?"

"Should I be?" Renee forced the most obstinate stare she could form as she kept her distance.

"What does that mean?" There were hints of anger and annoyance trailing his voice now. "What have I ever done to make you afraid of me?"

"You tell me, Evan." Renee grabbed her purse from the desk and pressed it to her chest. "What happened to Kimberly's files? What happened to her e-mail?"

"How would I know?" Evan went to flip the computer on. "Why are you looking for them?"

"You were here," she said, her voice a little weak and uneven. Was she really saying this? "I saw you at this computer last week going through her files. Now they're gone."

He paused a moment, as if contemplating whether or not to ask how she'd seen him, but decided it wasn't important. "Yeah, I was at her computer last week. I needed to figure out what was Augusta-related, what wasn't. I was cleaning up her computer, getting rid of her personal files for her replacement."

"Kimberly Janis was murdered." Renee felt a little more confident as she stepped around him, moving closer to the doorway. "She didn't commit suicide."

"You've already expressed your views on that issue to me." He turned from the blank computer screen to Renee. "I told you to stay out of it."

"Or it could be dangerous for me was the way you described it, if I remember right."

"Yes, and after that letter you received, I would think you'd listen."

"How did you know about the letter?" Renee asked, knowing she hadn't told him. "You *did* send that letter."

"No!" Evan shook his head in disbelief. "How could you think I would threaten you?"

"How else would you know about it?"

"Your sister just told me less than a half hour ago. I was concerned about how you've been acting lately and she told me what happened."

"I asked you to slow down." Renee didn't believe he'd bother to lie, knowing she could turn around and ask Michelle. "Don't you listen?"

"I wasn't going to bother you," he explained. "I was just concerned. Now I'm even more concerned. What happens between the two of us I said would be up to you and I meant that. I'm talking about your safety now. I want you to stay away from this."

"Or what, Evan?" Renee's words were laced with suspicion.

He took a second, but quickly realized what she was insinuating. His facial expression changed from confusion to hurt. Renee felt her heart fall. There was no turning back. Despite the proof, despite her fear, she cared for him and felt horrible as he looked at her just now.

"You think I had something to do with Kimberly's murder?" His voice almost cracked as he appeared amazed by his own words.

"I don't know who did it," she answered sharply, "but I know someone did."

"Renee." Evan reached for her only to stop as she quickly backed away.

"I have to go, Evan." Renee turned and sped out of the office. Her heart was beating faster than ever.

Heading for Michelle's desk, she refused to look back, although she knew Evan was standing outside the office watching her walk away. The tense moment still with her, Renee jumped and screamed as Nick Hamilton busted through the door she was headed for.

"Renee." Nick forced a tense smile. They didn't seem to come easy for him. "What are you doing here? Don't tell me Michelle made another lunch date."

"No. I'm picking her up," she answered nervously, wondering if Evan was close behind. "How are you, Nick?"

"I'm fine." He looked around the department. "The front entrance to Augusta leads to Michelle's department going the other way. Why did you come through here?"

"I thought I would stop by to see you." She was going to continue with her lie, but didn't see the need as Nick wasn't interested in what she had to say any longer.

"What's he doing over there?" Nick was preoccupied with Evan, who started walking toward them.

"He was in Kimberly's office." Looking back, Renee noticed Evan's eyes weren't on her. He was looking directly at Nick and with the angriest look she'd ever seen him have.

"What for?" Nick was suddenly nervous, blinking rapidly. "He never cared about her."

"He's been asking Kimberly's friends about her," Renee said, confused by Nick's response. "He was asking some questions about her. Mainly what her Internet password is.''

"It's her stupid cat," Nick said. "Everyone knows that. She talked about it all the time like it was her stinking kid."

"He says he just wanted to clear things up for Kimberly's replacement.'' Turning her back to him, Renee could hear Evan's steps.

"Do you remember that day you came for lunch and I was in a meeting in his office?'' Nick never looked at Renee, his eyes staying on Evan. "Evan said we weren't going to fill that position anytime soon, so no one needed to bother with the office. So, he was lying if he told you that.''

"Nick?'' Renee felt fear creep over her. He was getting closer.

"Get out of here,'' Nick answered. "Michelle is waiting for you.''

Renee wasn't sure if he was back to his cold, dismissing self or was purposefully trying to get rid of her for her own sake. Either way, she jetted out of the room, not looking back at either man again. Heading for Michelle's desk, she knew she wouldn't be able to get Nick's look off her mind. He'd been afraid of Evan Brooks. She wondered why. Did he know what she knew? Did he know more? He knew enough to be afraid, and so did she. It amazed her that, despite what she knew so far, she didn't believe Evan would hurt her. It seemed irrational to believe this, but she did. The fear that had almost paralyzed her earlier and stayed with her now was of the truth, not of Evan.

"Renee! Renee!''

Renee was broken from her trance by a sharp fist in the shoulder. She returned to the middle of the evening gown department of Nordstroms at the Old Orchard Shopping

Center in Skokie. Michelle was holding up her fifth recommendation for the evening, a sequined cherry-red party dress.

"Pay attention, ditsy. What about this one?" Michelle held it against her body and swung her hips from left to right, making the dress sway.

"Too red." Renee shook her head.

"Red is sexy," Michelle said with an exaggerated pout. "Red is seductive."

"I'm attending an association dinner with a friend." Renee grabbed the dress and returned it to the rack. "Sexy and seductive isn't the combination I'm going for."

"What are you going for?" There was a note of impatience in Michelle's voice.

"Something formal," Renee answered, ignoring her sister's rolling eyes. "More demure and not so short. For Pete's sake. I'll get picked up by the cops in that dress."

"It has to match the green shoes, too," Michelle added with a sweet smile. After not getting a response from Renee, she frowned and asked, "Do you want to do this or not? What's wrong with you?"

"Nothing," Renee lied, not wanting Michelle to get involved in the mess her life had suddenly become. "I want to do this, but I told you I was tired."

"Tired from what?" Michelle placed a hand on her hip. "Hanging out doing nothing? You're on vacation. Your life is a vacation."

"Michelle." This was Renee's turn to show impatience. "Let's move on."

"It's about Kimberly Janis, isn't it?" Michelle followed her sister to the next rack of dresses.

Just hearing the name that had changed her life made Renee sigh. "Why do you ask?"

"Why are you so curious about this?" she asked. "Don't you think it's dangerous? I mean, if it's true."

"It *is* true, Michelle." Renee glanced around, noticing no one was within ear shot. "Kimberly Janis was murdered. I can't tell you everything I know, but Chris Jackson has some pretty good evidence and so do I."

"Like what?" Michelle was whispering as she moved in closer. Her eyes widened in intrigue.

"I really don't want you to know. It's for your own safety."

Michelle pouted. "Renee, you treat me like a child."

"All I'll tell you is that it may go as far across as the police department and as high as . . ." Renee hesitated.

"As high as?" Michelle's anxiety showed. "As high as what, who, where?"

"That's all Michelle." Renee returned her attention to the dresses, frustrated and confused by the fact that she was simply unable to point the finger at Evan to someone else even though she could do everything but accuse him to his face.

"You still think Evan Brooks is behind this?"

"I don't know." Unwanted emotions returned to her. Michelle's persistence was all she needed now.

"Nick does." She paused for a moment. "He thought it was suicide at first, but you've rubbed off on him. You know, Evan came to my cubicle today."

"I'm aware of that." She gave Michelle a stern look. "You told him about the threatening letter. I wish you hadn't."

"He just seemed so concerned." Michelle gestured with her hand to her heart. "He was adorable. He's usually Mr. Confident, Cool, Collected. This time he was actually shy and it was so cute. He was worried, too. He wanted to know if you still liked him. He seems to think you've been playing him."

"Michelle, you were there when we discussed him possibly having a hand in sending that letter." Renee was sure

Evan hadn't used Michelle's terminology exactly, but it was a sharp stab to her heart to hear that it was obvious to others she wasn't being fair with him. He'd reminded her of his pride, and she was treading on dangerous waters.

"If I remember correctly," Michelle said, "you were the only one who thought he couldn't have sent it. Even if I thought that then, it all disappeared when I saw him today. You should have seen the look on his face when I told him you were going to the dinner tonight with Chris."

"You told him that?"

"He asked." Michelle mocked a pained expression. "He was crushed. This is very romantic."

"Don't talk to him about me anymore." Renee's tone was sharp, as intended. "This is a serious issue, Michelle. Not some love story to take lightly, like you tend to."

"Oh, here we go again." Michelle's voice rose slightly. "Like I tend to?"

"I didn't mean anything by that," Renee said, regretting her words. "I'm sorry."

"So now I don't live in reality?" Michelle asked with sarcasm, shaking her head. "You really think you're so much more together than I am."

"Let's not get into that discussion." Renee wasn't sure exactly what she'd meant. "I don't think I'm more anything than you. It only seems like you tend to see every encounter between an unattached man and a woman as a budding romance in the making."

"Your attitude isn't about me, Renee," Michelle responded with a harsher tone than usual. "This is about Nick."

"I don't want to argue with you about Nick." Renee caught herself before her voice went too high. "Not now."

"You're jealous." Michelle gave a victorious smile as she folded her arms across her chest.

Renee didn't respond, only giving her sister a cold glare, then returning her attention to the dresses.

"You don't intimidate me with those looks of yours," Michelle said. "You're copying Mom. It used to work, but I'm not a kid anymore."

"Then don't act like one." Despite her anger, Renee was touched at Michelle's mention of their mother. It didn't happen often.

"I'm moving on in a way you haven't been able to." Michelle's tone was accomplished. "And you're jealous."

"Say that again?" Renee almost laughed at the words, but didn't. Something inside told her not to. It would only make things worse.

"It's kind of ironic." Michelle shook her head. "I mean, I've spent eight years being jealous of you because you had seven more years with Mom and Dad than me."

"Oh, Michelle." Renee reached out for her sister, but Michelle backed away.

"Then I was jealous," she continued, "because you were so smart and successful while I couldn't even graduate from college on time."

"I can't tell you enough times," Renee said, "comparisons are ridiculous and insignificant. We are two different women, eight years apart. We'll always be at different stages in our lives."

Michelle took a second, seeming to contemplate Renee's words, then continued by saying, "Then there were the little things that burned me. Those things I guess all sisters stay at odds with."

"Always have and always will." Renee was glad Michelle could see that now. "We're women. We seek definition and substance in all of our relationships. That's always going to cause challenges, create gaps to fill."

Renee felt her own words were for herself as much as Michelle.

"Maybe so, but now the tables are turned." Michelle walked around the rack slowly.

Renee waited until two chatting women passed by. "We back on the jealousy thing?"

"We've both had boyfriends," Michelle said. "We've both had lovers. But now, I have a fiancé. I'm getting married. It's different."

"I'm not jealous that you're getting married, Michelle. I have my misgivings about the timing and maybe your choice, but I'm happy for you."

"I've always wondered why you never talk about the guys you date." Michelle continued as if she hadn't heard Renee's response. "You dated that one guy for two years and I had to practically beg every time to get you to talk about him for more than five minutes."

"What is this leading to?" Renee was becoming more uncomfortable as the conversation progressed. How did her love life become the issue?

"Somehow, it relates to Mom and Dad" Michelle went on. "I don't know how. I'm not a psychiatrist, but you haven't been able to open your heart up to a man in that ultimate way. I have, and I don't think you're happy about that."

Renee wanted to tell Michelle how silly she was. She wanted to dismiss this entire conversation, but she couldn't. Her words struck a chord with her and Renee couldn't ignore that. She wasn't sure it was all true, because she could never be jealous of the person she loved the most in this world. On the other hand, Renee wasn't sure it was all untrue. These past couple of weeks, her feelings for Evan had made her face realities and emotions she hadn't experienced before. Had she been unable to or unwilling?

"I haven't been ready," Renee responded after a while. Her tone was calm and controlled. "You can believe whatever you want, but people are ready for a marrying kind of love at different times in their lives. Some people, with parents dead or alive, aren't able to open their hearts until they're a lot older than you, older than me. It could be now, ten years from now or more. Each person has his or her own time.''

"Sounds lonely," was Michelle's response "Sounds pretty lonely.''

Renee had no retort as she flipped through the dresses. She was torn between anger and sadness. She thought of her parents, Michelle, and Patricia far away in Japan. An image of Evan Brooks flashed before her, brushing her heart. She was sure, after learning to deal with the grief of her loss eight years ago, that her life had been fulfilling and satisfying to this point. Now, all of the sudden, things were changing. The future didn't seem to hold the same as the past. Renee realized it sounded pretty lonely to her, too.

NINE

"I may be a lowly, vastly underpaid reporter during the day," Chris said with a proud smile, "but with you on my arm, looking this good, I'm definitely *the man* tonight."

"I'll take that as a compliment," Renee responded, standing beside him in the entrance way to the Palmer House Hilton's main ballroom. She'd showed up late. It was seven fifteen when she arrived, and Chris was waiting for her.

She and Michelle were able to stop arguing for five minutes and found the time to actually do what they'd intended—find a dress to match the green suede shoes. After trying on several, they agreed on a sleek, sharp black velvet spaghetti-strapped piece with a green sash swirling from the top of her left waist to hug her right hip. The dress was fitted and flowed down to her feet, flaring just above her shoes with a flirtatious slit up the left side.

Her makeup was sophisticated and soft and her hair was tightly slicked back, a look that always brought the feminine features of her face to the forefront. Chris was more than impressed.

"I know we agreed to just be friends." Chris pushed Renee's chair in for her and quickly took his own beside her at their table. "But after the way you look tonight, I'd like to reevaluate the situation."

"An agreement is an agreement," Renee warned. "But I appreciate the compliment. I've had a pretty bad week and I needed a little dress up to feel better."

"I'm still mulling over what you've told me." His brows tensed. "I wonder what was on those files that had to be deleted."

"Names, letters, places." Renee shook her head and shrugged her shoulders. "Numbers. Who knows?"

"I know what would help," Chris said. "How you could help."

"I'll do anything," Renee said, leaning in closer to him. "I want the truth."

"I know he brushed you off the last time, but try and ask Nick what he knows again." Chris was whispering now that others had joined them at the table. "He worked with Kimberly. He has to know more."

"I'll ask again," Renee said. "He drops by every now and then and he used to act like he didn't care, but after what happened at Augusta this afternoon, I'm sure he's changing his mind. I think he's thinking about it more; where things could connect. He's out with Michelle tonight. Maybe I'll catch him when he brings her home."

She noticed an unusual look on Chris's face. "Wait a second," she said. "You don't suspect Nick, do you?"

"I just want to know what he knows." Chris frowned in response to the disagreeing expression on Renee's face. "I know he's your sister's fiancé and everything. He worked with her every day. He probably never gave a damn what she did, but if he thought hard enough, who knows. As

far as being a suspect, I can't rule him out. Ben Monty
and Tamia Griffin are out. Augusta is all we have left. You
should be happy. That's what you wanted. To hear about
someone other than Evan.''

She nodded. ''Yeah, but not Nick. I couldn't even imagine. I don't want to.'' With that, she threw it from her
mind.

They greeted the couple joining them at the table, a
pediatrician and her husband. The husband had read two
of Renee's books and, much to the doctor's dismay, wanted
nothing but to talk to Renee about herself.

Despite the dazzle and glamour the evening promised,
she couldn't forget her baby sister's words earlier that day.
Forcing herself to address them, Renee hadn't remembered being so perceptive at the age of twenty-one. She
could only remember grieving for her parents, worrying
about Michelle, and trying to finish school. Doing everything she could to keep from falling apart. She had
returned to life, one day at a time. Her first order had
been to make sure Michelle was recovering. Then came
finishing her education. There were so many things to deal
with, including the death of their grandmother only a
couple of years later.

So much love lost. Years and experiences stolen. Renee
had focused all her energy on being both parents for
Michelle, and maybe she'd ignored herself like Evan had
said. She wasn't sure. She only knew that she felt a sudden
emptiness inside that was even stronger than the lack of
fulfillment she'd felt in New York just before coming here.
Part of it had to do with her parents, part with Michelle.
Then there was a part, a very big part that was about . . .

''Evan Brooks.''

Chris's words jolted Renee back to the present. Could
he tell what she was thinking? Was she that obvious?

''Turn around.'' Chris's head motioned forward.

Renee took a deep breath and turned around. It took only a moment to spot him. Despite the fact that every man in the room wore a tuxedo, Evan Brooks made the outfit seem different. His broad shoulders, muscled chest, and tight waist made it hang in a way that no other man's body could. At least not to Renee's eyes. He took her breath away, the mere sight of him. She immediately felt her heart rate speed up and her body temperature rise.

Only he wasn't alone. Renee's heart stung and her eyes narrowed as *she* came into view. This was no sister-in-law. She was almost as tall as Evan, at least six feet, with legs that went on for miles. She had very short chestnut brown hair, cut less than an inch from her head and waving toward the back. Her raisin-brown-colored figure was covered in an African-style dress that stopped just above her knees. She was thin, very thin, and beautiful, very beautiful.

Renee hated that jealousy had shown itself in her heart so quickly. She'd been jealous before. Jealous of people who talked about their parents, of women who wore size-five shoes. Only she'd never been jealous of a woman over a man, and she didn't like the feeling. It made her feel weak.

Who was she to feel this way anyway? Renee asked herself, as she watched the woman allow Evan to guide her into the ballroom. Evan wasn't hers. She'd rejected him and pushed him away. She'd done everything but outright accuse him of murder to his face. He had every right and reason to see other women. Renee only wished they weren't so beautiful.

Maybe she was a cousin or a business acquaintance. Yes, a business acquaintance. She felt a little better now. Only a little.

"Careful," Chris said. "You're starting to turn the same color as your shoes."

"Am I that obvious?" Renee tore her eyes from the

couple and reached for a glass of water. What she really wanted was a gigantic slice of chocolate cake with an extra large scoop of vanilla ice cream on top.

"To those who know." Chris leaned in again to whisper. "You did blow him off, remember?"

"I wouldn't phrase it that way," Renee retorted defensively. "I just have a lot of questions."

"Number one being, why did you murder Kimberly Janis?"

"We don't know he did it." Renee had to catch herself as the other couple at the table turned to her. "He may have something to do with it, but actually killing? Besides, what little we do have is circumstantial. You know who we need to find out more about?"

"Who?"

"That Detective Griggs who reported the wrong place of impact for Kimberly's body to the ground and warned his partner to leave it alone. That same detective who asked the weakest questions to the fewest people before declaring this a suicide, closed case."

"No, no, no." Chris shook his head and spoke with conviction. "This is Chicago, babe. You don't mess with a cop, even a dirty one, unless you got some serious, in-your-hand, preferably on videotape proof. Even then, you're taking a chance. You could be walking down the street, minding your own business. Next thing you know, some cops throw you down 'cause you look like a perp. They pick you up and oops! There's an ounce or two of cocaine in your pocket. How did that get there?"

"All right." Renee placed her glass down. In seconds, she turned away again. She couldn't help it. Her eyes begged to see Evan.

She felt like her breath had been cut off when she spotted him. Not because she saw him again, but because this time, he was staring directly at her. There was no mistaking it. His eyes were centered on her, holding hers still. Renee could feel the purpose in his look. What purpose, she only wished she knew. All she did know was his gaze, his determined stare, frightened and excited her at the same time. There was an incredible magnetism between the two of them. It seemed to consume the room, turning everything a hue of rose. Renee had felt it the moment she met him and it had only grown stronger with each encounter.

His companion was none the wiser as she conversed with others at their table which was twenty or so feet from Renee's. No one else seemed to notice their eyes tunneled to each other. To Renee, no one else was even in the room.

"Earth to Renee."

She tore her eyes from Evan's after what seemed like years. Blinking rapidly, she turned to Chris. His expression held an enviable disgust.

"What is it with guys like that?" Chris sent Evan a searing glance. "Is it the money, the flash?"

"Evan doesn't flaunt his money," Renee said. "He isn't flashy either. What is it with guys like you?"

"Like me?" he asked with naive surprise.

"You assume because a guy has money . . ."

"That he got from his daddy," Chris interjected.

"He's done pretty well on his own," Renee answered back. "Either way, he has money. That all of the sudden makes him a bad guy? Even before this evidence, you had already indicted and judged Evan guilty in Chris's court of public opinion."

With a smirk, Chris turned his attention to the place setting in front of him. It was clear he had no response and Renee decided not to push anymore. It was his grudge and he was entitled to it. Everyone was entitled to one.

The evening went on excruciatingly slowly for Renee. She tried to enjoy the meal and the entertainment as well as the company. It was useless, as her mind and heart were only on Evan. She tried to fight it, but her eyes were drawn to him several times throughout the evening. Each time he was waiting, staring right back. Occasionally, he'd look away to respond to a question, take a sip of wine or a bite to eat, but his eyes always returned to her.

His look seared through to her bones. Renee could feel his eyes touching her entire body. She couldn't fight the intrigue and arousal she felt from this erotic attention and was unsure how to handle the emotions it stirred within her. It became uncomfortable enough for her that as the meal and speeches ended and people began to mingle again, she excused herself from the table. Chris was concerned, but allowed her to go after she promised him she'd return in ten minutes.

Finding a quiet spot down the hall and around the corner from the ballroom, Renee sat down on a rose-colored leather bench and stared into space. It was away from the noisy crowd and bright lights. Away from Evan. She still felt him. She felt his eyes on her, telling her she was his. Her body had never denied that, and now her heart wouldn't.

She was in love. It hit her like a brick. She could try and search for other explanations, but there wasn't any use. There was no denying it. She was in love with Evan Brooks. She had come close to love before, maybe even twice. Neither time had it come close to what she felt now.

Renee wasn't at all prepared for this revelation. It didn't make sense. She'd been in Chicago a little over two weeks and all she could think of was Evan. He'd been on her mind morning, noon, and night, but she never imagined it would develop into this. Love? The attraction was there from the beginning and had grown stronger since, but what amazed Renee the most was that this love had developed despite all the revelations about Kimberly Janis and her death.

"What do I do now?" she whispered. She had no clue.

Whatever her feelings for Evan, she still wasn't sure he had nothing to do with Kimberly's death. She could only wish. Renee felt her heart cringe at the thought of loving a murderer and it nearly tore in two at the thought of being wrong, with no forgiveness from Evan.

"Hello, Renee."

She jumped from her seat as the still dark figure began to move from around the corner and into the dim light. Evan stopped only a foot away from her.

Renee wanted to back away, but couldn't. In an instant, her body wanted to be close to him, to smell him and touch him, but she fought it and stood still. "Evan . . . what are you . . ."

"I had to talk to you." His eyes pleaded with her. "I can't stand the way things are between us."

"Won't your date be missing you?" She tried to hide her insecurities under a ruse of contempt.

"She isn't concerned with me," Evan said with annoyance. "She's an old friend who happened to be in town. She didn't have anything to do, so she came along. I had to come. I needed to see you. Especially now that I know . . ."

"I don't want to hear this." Renee turned her head to the side, staring at the rose-colored walls. Everything was rose. "I don't need to hear this."

"This is not about us." Evan's voice was overwhelmed with concern, his face racked with worry. "It's about your safety. I warned you."

"Another threat?" Renee gasped, taking a step back.

"Renee!" Evan took a moment, seeming to try and calm himself before continuing. "How could you think that? I could never hurt you. I could never hurt anyone!"

"You don't know how much I know." Renee sent him a defiant stare, trying to ignore the place in her heart that told her to believe his every word and fall into his arms.

"I think I have an idea," Evan said. "Why don't you tell me."

"Evan." Renee turned herself away from him. "Please, just go away."

"If you won't tell me what you know," he said, ignoring her plea, "then I'll tell you what I know. I know Kimberly was murdered. I can't say that I ever thought otherwise, but I had nothing to base it on. I know the person or people who did this are aware of you and what you're trying to find out. I know you're in danger. How imminent, I'm not sure, but you are."

"From whom?" Renee asked, her back still to him.

"I can't say yet." Evan's tone was distressed. "I have someone in mind, but I can't say."

"You have no idea, do you?" Renee tried to hold back her tears. "Evan, please go away. I'm too confused right now. I can't discuss this."

"Renee, please." He stepped toward her, his tone a plea for compassion.

"I don't know what to think." Renee felt her knees go weak as she could feel his warm breath on her neck, smell his seductive scent. Even now, she could only want him.

Her chest heaved as his strong hands grasped her bare arms and swung her around. She had a second to look into his deep eyes before they closed and he lowered his face to hers.

Renee felt the life within her explode at the touch of his lips on hers. His kiss was full of hunger with a strong hint of anger and she added confusion and need with her own searching lips. Intense with desire, she heard him moan as she brought her hands to his face. She gripped his head and tried to pull it closer, although they could be no closer. She wanted to be one with him and a mere kiss wasn't enough.

Their lips ravaged each other, each matching the other's

desire, then elevating the passion to a new level. Her stomach swirling with desire, Renee knew she could stay forever in his arms with his mouth on hers. The passion she felt now would never cease. When his lips connected with hers, all doubts faded and only ecstasy ruled.

Renee was unwillingly returned to brutal reality when Evan tore his lips from hers and pushed himself away.

"Evan." She whispered his name as her hands reached to retrieve him and return him to her.

"No, Renee." Evan was out of breath as he grabbed her hands and gently brought them down and away from him.

Renee stood dazed, taking a moment to return from the fantasy and comprehend his sudden rejection.

"It's not that I don't want you," Evan continued. "I want you too much. I think I love you, Renee."

This was too much for her. His words, the kiss. Feeling her knees go weak, she sat down on the bench, still looking up at the man she loved. Her heart sang out that she loved him back, but no words came.

"I want you to think about that," he said, looking down at her with tried affection. "Think about those words and that kiss and you'll know whether or not I had anything to do with Kimberly's death. You'll know who I am. Take your time. I'll wait for us to be together. It's not as if my heart is giving me a choice. Think about it, and please, Renee, be careful."

As she watched him turn and walk away, Renee felt attacked with exhaustion. In the past two weeks she had expended enough emotion for a lifetime. Enough for a year in the past ten minutes alone.

Chris Jackson came rushing around the corner. "Are you okay?" He sat next to her. "What did he do to you?"

"No." If you only knew, Renee thought as she was finally able to utter her first word. *He told me he loved me.*

"I was looking for you and I saw him coming around

the corner.'' Chris looked back for a moment as if he thought Evan was still around. "He looked upset. You look worse."

"I feel worse." Renee leaned back against the wall, her regular heartbeat starting to return to her. She pressed the tips of her fingers to her mouth, the feeling of his lips still so fresh to her. She loved the touch and the taste of him. Everything.

"What happened?" Chris asked impatiently.

"I barely know myself," Renee answered, telling the truth. She remembered the kiss and those words. *I think I love you, Renee.*

"Oh, my God!" Chris let out a gasp as he grabbed Renee's arms by the wrists and held them up.

Before Renee could ask what his sudden surprise was for, she noticed it herself. Her arms. Where Evan had held her and pulled her to him, her skin was beginning to bruise. Renee hadn't even felt any pain, only consumed with the knowledge that she would soon taste his sweet lips.

"Chris!" Before she had a chance to tell him it looked much worse than it appeared, Chris was up and running around the corner.

Renee quickly stood up. She had to pause a moment, her head swirling before going after him. She screamed his name once more before he disappeared into the crowd. She went after him, but her dress, her heels prevented her from keeping pace and she quickly lost him.

As if she needed more worries. Renee frantically searched the ballroom for both men. Chris, under the impression that Evan had been abusive with her, was going to confront him and seeing Evan's current mood, Renee imagined his response. He towered over Chris. It was going to get ugly unless she reached them in time, but where were they?

Several minutes later, she found Chris leaning against

the wall outside the front entrance to the hotel. Evan was nowhere around.

"Chris!" Renee ran to him, checking to make sure he wasn't hurt. He seemed okay. "Are you all right? Where's Evan?"

"I'm fine." Chris stood up straight. "Evan just left with his date."

"I hope you didn't do anything stupid. Those were just hand prints from holding me." She lifted her arm for him to see. "I bruise easily."

"He corrected me on that." Chris let out a quick laugh. "He was nice enough to explain the situation without knocking it into me. I confronted him, all right. My chivalry got the best of me. I was halfway through my threats before I realized how much bigger than me he was."

"I was going to remind you of that." Renee let out a laugh of her own. She hadn't laughed in a while and it felt good.

"He set me straight, although he had a look in his eyes like he wanted to beat me down. I think that had more to do with me showing up here with you than anything I said."

"Chris, I don't know who killed Kimberly Janis," Renee said, "but I'm certain Evan didn't. And I'm one hundred percent sure he'd never hurt me."

"We talked about Kimberly." Chris seemed more frustrated than Renee. "I'm starting to have doubts of my own."

Renee's eyes came alive. "What did the two of you talk about?"

"Not much. He said he could help me. I'm gonna meet him tomorrow morning."

"Let me come!"

"No way." Chris spoke adamantly as he shook his head. "He said he'd give me some important information on one condition. That I keep you out of this."

"I'm not a child," Renee said. "I can watch out for myself."

"I'm not going to fight with you, too. Between the two of you, I'm going with Evan. You could both probably take me, but I think he'd do more damage." Chris held his hand up to stop her. "I promised him I'd get you home safe tonight and that would be it. So, let's go."

"Fine." Renee approached the sidewalk as Chris hailed a cab. This wasn't over, but she'd play it light right now. "I'm done for the night anyway."

As she hastily slipped under the covers that evening, Renee felt exhausted, but not tired. Her heart, her pulse, and her mind were all running at top speed. She heard Michelle and Nick return home from their date. Instead of staying as usual, Nick left shortly after arriving. Renee thought to ask him again about Kimberly, but she knew he suspected Evan and she wouldn't hear any more of that. She'd call him at Augusta and ask him on Monday. She wondered if any more questions were even necessary.

Evan was innocent. Her heart had won over. Renee was only going to think positive from now on, she vowed to herself. She would help where she could, but Evan and Chris would find Kimberly's murderer and he would be put behind bars. Then she could be with Evan. All of the doubts erased, questions answered, and confusion cleared up.

There would be a lot of apologizing on her part, but she was prepared for that. Everything needed to be out in the open and she'd give her heart to him loud enough for anyone within ten miles to hear. He deserved that at least. He would forgive her, she was sure. She'd seen the compassion for her confusion in his eyes tonight. He loved her and had told her so at a time when he knew he was most vulnerable to rejection. That took strength and courage, and Renee couldn't wait to return the reply in a deserved way.

She knew once she uttered the words there would be

no turning back, but she wasn't afraid. No, that was a lie. She was scared to death of baring her soul and placing all her cards on the table, but she knew it was right. No matter how suddenly it had come to be, she knew that she and Evan together was right.

She tossed and turned between the thin sheets, his words playing over and over in her mind, singing from her heart. The silence was deadening. The anxiety was heart wrenching. She couldn't sleep. She sat up on the edge of the sofa bed, throwing the sheets off her. Even the air-conditioning unit couldn't cool her. She knew she wouldn't sleep until she saw Evan again.

Evan was standing in the open doorway to his North Lake Shore Drive condominium as Renee stepped off the elevator and headed toward him. She smiled at the utter pleasure on his face, welcoming the instinctive spark of arousal she felt at laying sight on him.

Evan's smile showed concern at its edges as he tightened the wrap on his cottony thick, mahogany bathrobe. "Are you all right?"

"I needed to speak with you." She stood close to him, feeling the anxiety that had been growing within her for the last twenty minutes begin turning to desire. "I'm sorry I didn't call. I know it was a surprise to have your doorman ring you near midnight and tell you someone is in your lobby and wants to come up."

"I don't mind if it's you." He stepped aside, letting her in. "I got worried to death. When Mr. Cameron let me speak to you, you sounded so . . ."

"Confused?" she asked.

Renee wasn't sure what she looked like, having put herself together in a second in the dark. She'd worked out a pair of jean shorts and a satin short-sleeved button-down night top. She knew she had to see him. Had no clear idea of what she'd do when she saw him, but had to come here tonight. "You might think I'm crazy, but I'm not."

She looked around the apartment located on precious, expensive real estate.

The design was understated, neat and clean. The traditional decorations modest and warm. Instead of a wealthy bachelor pad, it reminded Renee of a middle-class, suburban home. Not what she expected from Evan Brooks, but a pleasant surprise.

"You said you needed to talk to me." Evan followed her past the opening walkway into the center of the living room.

Renee sat on the plush navy blue sofa. "Come sit down. We have to talk."

Without hesitation, Evan joined her. She felt the sexual tension between them now as intense as ever, but it didn't bother her. Nothing bothered her with Evan anymore. She wasn't going to let it confuse her, scare her. She wasn't going to fight it. "I need to apologize."

"I don't need an apology from you, Renee," Evan insisted.

"Fine," Renee agreed, taking his hand in hers. He felt warm and strong. "But I need to tell you something, so just listen."

"I'm all ears." He smiled at her authoritativeness.

"It wasn't just the circumstantial evidence that made me doubt you." Renee looked endearingly into his eyes. She was going to let the words come without even knowing what they'd be. "I hate to sound like a textbook psychology case, but all of this goes back to my parents' death."

"Listen, Renee, I can see this is painful for you." He gently caressed several strands of her hair with his hand, touching her cheek lightly. "You don't have to . . ."

"I knew there was something between us from the moment I met you," she continued, determined to tell him everything, "but I was afraid. I could see this, what we both feel now, coming, and I hung on to anything to fight it off. I was afraid to love you because I was afraid to lose you. It didn't matter whether it was because I thought you might be a murderer or just because. I thought it was too soon. I'm very insecure about this. It's something I've got to work on and I will. It hasn't been easy. My heart fought my painful past the whole way."

"I can only pray for who won," Evan said tenderly.

"My heart won hands down," Renee said, smiling at the sudden look of relief and happiness on Evan's face. "I love you, Evan. I love you with all my heart."

"I love you, too, Renee," he responded, his ever-telling eyes showing his deep emotions.

He grabbed a hold of her as if holding on for dear life. She felt a great load lift from her shoulders. It was out in the open now and everything was going to be okay. It was going to be better than okay.

When his lips finally touched hers, Renee's calm was shattered and the insanity of desire came as fast as light. The warmth of his caressing mouth reawakened the passion she'd only experienced when he'd kissed her in the past, but this time there was more. This time she knew she loved him and knew he loved her, too. This time the passion was more sudden, quick and consuming. She kissed him with a force equaling her hunger, all of her emotions coming to one cause. To be with him.

She heard him call out her name in a gasp of breath before he buried his face in her neck and kissed her there. His lips were warm and soft. Her body turned and twisted as the restlessness set in.

She felt his demanding lips touch her ear and then he whispered, his lips brushing against her skin as they moved. "Renee, tell me what you want."

He was losing control, and that powerful feeling only increased Renee's desire.

"Renee," he repeated in a passionate whisper. "You're very emotional right now. I don't want to . . ."

"You're right." She held her face just inches from his, kissing him in between each of her words. "I am emotional, but I'm clear enough to know what I'm doing and what I want. I want you and I want you now."

"I want you forever." Evan's embrace tightened selfishly. With a force, he lifted her into his arms, carrying her down the hallway and into his bedroom. He laid her on the king-size bed, covered in thick forest green and jet black bedding. Renee had never felt so consumed, so certain about what she wanted. That confidence in itself was arousing beyond words for her.

His lips recaptured hers, more demanding this time with a kiss filled with urgency. The passion was building as Renee drank in the sweetness of the kiss and let her inhibitions go. She quivered constantly, feeling new spirals of ecstasy reaching higher and higher as she felt her body melt into his.

They both hurried off what little clothes they had on, stealing kisses and touches in between. Renee bit him playfully in the back, wrapping her arms around him as he reached for the handle of his black marble drawer next to the bed. Pulling it open, he found some protection and carefully put it on. Renee couldn't stand to wait any longer.

Delicious sensations assailed her as he led trails of devouring kisses along her bare shoulders, her soft breast, her silky smooth stomach while caressing her thighs with his strong hands. He didn't stop. The second his lips left one spot as hot as lava, they started an inferno somewhere else. Savoring every moment, she felt herself weaken with a burning fire as his hand caressed her body and then moved to her most intimate place, touching her there. She knew now he could tell she was ready and had been for some time.

The kisses turned gentle again as he rose above her and returned his claiming lips to her mouth. He leaned up, looking into her eyes with a smoldering glare as he took her hands and placed them on his flat, muscled stomach. He was encouraging her to explore his body and she did, feeling every inch of him. Every groove of his warm flesh, getting to know this man in the most intimate way. She watched as his passion grew from the pleasure her touching brought him.

She took hold of his hips and pressed him down to her. She moaned softly as she felt his hardness rub against her silky thighs. Almost, she thought with a tortured head. Almost. Her hips moved to invite him, curving her body to his.

She looked into his eyes with a welcoming smile. When he entered, they both moaned in tormented pleasure. Renee bit her lower lip at the painful delight. With each thrust and kiss, she felt an overwhelming flow of sheer heat within her increase and threaten to take her over. She was engulfed by his immense strength and was falling into a web of wanton agony.

He called out her name several times, exclaiming his love for her. She returned his word as best she could, barely able to speak. Renee dug her nails into Evan's back and let out a scream. She cried his name as her entire body exploded and her insides shattered with pure throbbing sensation. There was nothing in this world but the two of them.

Only a moment later, Evan let out a tormented groan, his eyes squeezing shut. Rolling beside her, he scooped her into his arms and cradled her. He kissed her softly on her forehead and then fully, possessively on her lips. She was his. He was hers. Renee knew that as she looked into his eyes. No words were spoken. None were necessary.

TEN

Renee slowly turned her key in the lock and opened the door to Michelle's apartment. Silently, she tiptoed inside. It was early in the morning. Very early. Her plan was to sneak into bed without a sound and be fast asleep by the time Michelle, who never woke up before ten on the weekends, would know a thing had happened. Only, that plan was foiled as soon as she closed the door behind her.

"Don't even think about telling me it's none of my business," Michelle said, standing at the entrance to the hallway, leading to her room. In her cartoon pajamas, she had a mischievous smile on her face and both hands were on her hips.

"It isn't." Renee felt her face flush with heat. "What are you doing up this early?"

"I heard you rustling around last night." Michelle joined her sister on the sofa. "You gonna pull this out?"

"No," Renee said, referring to the sofabed. "This is fine. I'm exhausted."

"I'll bet!" Michelle laughed, ducking a pillow thrown at her. "Details. Details."

"Go to sleep." Renee couldn't help but smile, just thinking of making love to Evan the night before. She still felt the excitement from it all.

"Please, please!" Michelle tugged on the sheets Renee tried to gather around herself. "Just a tidbit. Look, I know what you're thinking. I'm little Michelle, but I'm not. I'm a woman. I have sex."

"Michelle!" Renee laughed, surprised to hear her say it, although she needed to get used to the fact.

"Yes." Michelle nodded. "I'm having sex and if you don't give me a little tidbit of what happened last night, I'll give you an ear full of my sex life. To start with . . ."

"Okay." Renee held out her hand to stop her. She wasn't ready for that. "A tidbit."

"A juicy tidbit," Michelle pointed out.

"Evan is an incredible man." She didn't remember any tidbit from this night that wasn't juicy. "Each kiss was magic. Each touch was from heaven. I felt like I would lose my mind with pleasure any moment. It was a night of fantasy. I can only think of words like pure passion, desire, explosion."

Renee laughed as Michelle sat there with her mouth wide open. She was still speechless as Renee kicked her shoes off and nestled on the sofa.

"Now, go back to sleep."

Without another word, Michelle did as she was told.

Renee woke up later in the best mood she could remember. As was becoming usual, her first thought was of Evan, but this time it wasn't just a kiss that made her blush. This time, she thought of their lovemaking, how he had held her afterward, how he had begged her not to leave so early

and made her promise she'd see him later that day before
he would let her out of his car.

She realized there hadn't been many encounters, but
each one had the effect of fifty. Beyond logic or reason,
she didn't doubt her love for him. She knew some would
be skeptical, but her heart told her she was one of the
lucky ones—those few who had met their match and knew
so from the first moment on. She laughed at herself,
remembering how impossible it seemed to her that
Michelle could know she was in love after only three
months.

Over breakfast, Michelle insisted on more information.
Either that or Renee had to quit smiling. Since she
couldn't, Renee gave in a bit. Michelle hung on to every
brief detail, but was especially impressed with Evan's
expression of love.

"You said it back, right?" she asked after taking a
moment to let the exciting news sink in.

"Yes, I did." Renee stuck a fork in the burnt piece of
turkey bacon Michelle had prepared for her. It cracked
into a hundred pieces.

Michelle rolled her eyes. "That is so cool! The looks,
the kiss, then making love. Do you think it's real? I mean,
do you think it'll last?"

"Yes, I do." Renee felt such relief at being able to say
that and know it was true. No doubts holding her back.

"So I'm taking it you don't think he's a murderer anymore?"

"No, I don't." Renee laughed at the question, seeing
her sister was serious. "I don't think he killed anyone. Nor
did he have anything to do with it behind the scenes."

"So now that you and Evan are, you know . . ." Michelle's
brows raised in anticipation. "This means . . ."

"I'm going to stay in Chicago a little while longer."
Renee was happy to see a smile come to her sister's face.

"I take it that's all right with you? If it isn't, I'll leave. I don't want to push myself into your life on your turf, you know."

"Oh please, girl. I love it. I'm tired of New York, but I miss you so much. I hope you decide to move here permanently."

"We'll see." Renee wasn't sure anything could keep her from Evan Brooks and being near Michelle was an added plus. She'd been concerned there would be some apprehension on her baby sister's part after hearing she wanted to stay, but was happy not to see any.

"So, do you think its your time?" Michelle asked, exaggerating the last word.

"What do you mean?"

"You said yesterday afternoon that everyone has their own time." Michelle reminded her. "I found mine with Nick. Do you think you've found yours with Evan?"

Renee spoke in a reflective tone. "I've thought about the things you said yesterday, and you had a good point."

"You mean I was right." Michelle smiled.

"I will only say you had a good point," Renee said stubbornly. "You pointed out some of my insecurities. I'm not jealous of you, Michelle. I'm very happy you're happy, and I want you to find a great guy, get married, and have ten kids. Don't ever think otherwise. On the other hand, I have found a way to love people, but only very few. I've never found a way to love, really love, a man. Even after giving myself two years to try, I couldn't do it. Then all of the sudden, I'm knocked over the head by Cupid's arrow. Yes, I guess it's my time."

"Listen," Michelle said. "I know how to exhale, okay? I know having a man isn't what makes life worth living. It does make things a little better, but I know its my family, faith, and friends that make for a fulfilling life. Mom and Dad taught me that and so did you."

"I want so badly for you to remember the way they raised us." Tears from her own memories came to Renee's eyes, she was touched by Michelle's mention. "I know you were thirteen, but even those years can fade in your memory when you get older. I hope they never do."

"I remember," Michelle said, her smile soft and wise for her young age. "I remember on my own and through you. You just have to know that you don't have to be my Mom and Dad anymore. I'm gonna be all right."

"Is this your caring way of telling me to lay off?" Renee asked.

"Just enough, though," Michelle said, laughing. "Not completely."

"Michelle." Renee sighed tenderly as she looked over this once young girl who was now a beautiful woman. "I know I nag you some and maybe I do say things that lead to comparisons and judgments, but I don't mean to, and I promise to work on it. You know I love you, and I'm so proud of you, I can hardly put it into words."

"Try sometimes, okay?" Michelle was beginning to cry. "I'm gonna do my own thing. I know you can respect that. Only, whether you like it or not, I'd like to hear you say you're proud of me for doing it. It's almost like Mom and Dad would be saying it."

"I promise." Renee reached out and hugged her. She held her as tight as she could, feeling she was finally reaching her. They were finally reaching each other. "From myself and Mom and Dad, I'm very proud of you, Michelle Rebecca Shepherd."

Both girls returned to their meals, leaving the subject of their relationship alone for now. Renee knew that Michelle understood all the problems weren't solved, but they had reached a new point of understanding and to push it right now would be a step backward. Instead, they talked more about the men in their lives. Renee was determined to forge some sort of relationship with Nick. It was obvious that Michelle really loved him and her decision had been made. Besides, he hadn't been the most horrible of late to Renee. There wasn't any way around it, so Renee stayed off the subject. Positive was what she wanted to be. Only positive.

"So," Michelle said after careful reflection. "With this . . . new development, I should be getting my raise any day now."

Renee laughed, hoping for much more out of this for herself.

If the day hadn't been going well enough, Renee logged on to her laptop after Michelle left. Jumping on the world wide web, she accessed her e-mail. It was the usual, hellos from readers.

Just as she was about to log off, the BUDDY icon flashed.

"You have a friend online," the computer said. The screen flashed Probeson@icom.com. "Would you like a conference?"

"Yes! Yes! Yes!" Renee chose the YES button. It was a great invention, that buddy list. You notify your service of the usernames of your friends, and it tells you when they're online, giving you the option of a personal chat room. Renee started typing.

"Hey, Pat! Where ya' been?"

The words appeared on the top of the left of the screen.

"Hey, girl. You know. Still checking out the city."

"Still a culture shock?"

"Always will be. You still in Chicago? So how is Michelle?"

"The same, only older, smarter, more independent, and a little crazier."

"She's getting more and more like you every day."

"How's Tony? How's the love going?"

"Never better. Cloud nine. Any nibbles for you?"

With a smile, Renee wrote. "I'm in love."

"What? Okay, I'm calm. Start from the beginning. Don't leave anything out."

Renee did as she was told, so happy to be able to to "talk" to her best friend again. Patricia interrupted with exclamation points and written "GASP," but Renee told her everything. Not just about Evan, but Kimberly Janis and Michelle.

"So," Patricia wrote. "There must be a permanent smile affixed to that pretty face of yours."

"I can't remember being this hopeful. It's like every second that passes, I feel more solid about a future with Evan."

"That's pretty good progress with Michelle, too."

"I think we've reached a new level. I think we'll finally be able to be friends now."

"Well. You'll always be sisters. That has blessings and curses automatic, but friends is good. You can work it out. When are you going back to New York?"

"Soon." Renee was in no rush to leave Chicago. She didn't like being away from Evan now, only miles apart. She couldn't stand being in another state. "I'll have to finalize everything. Put things in order. Chicago is home now."

"Michelle won't be threatened?"

"She seems happy. I'm going to keep my distance, you know. Stay off her turf."

"You'll make friends quick. Sounds like Chris Jackson has promise."

"Chris is cool. He's young." Renee had thought Alan Smith would make a good friend, but wasn't so sure, now seeing him in a new light. He seemed self-involved and fake. "Maybe you could make your way to Chi town after Tony's duty is up."

"No promise. His fam is deep in Brooklyn. Doubt it. You'll have your hands full making friends with Nick. :-)"

"Very funny. It won't be easy, but I'm committed to forming a friendship with him. As happy as I feel today, I could even come to love my future brother-in-law."

"Wow, little Michelle. Married. Can't say I'm not surprised she beat you to the altar."

"Nice thing to say."

"Seriously. It's been a long time. No, I can't remember when you talked about a guy using the words you just used for Evan."

"I've never felt this way." Renee felt sunshine beam through her.

"Double wedding?"

"Whoa girl!"

"Our kids can grow up together. Really, Renee. I've always wanted that."

Renee paused, letting the thought sink in. She liked it. No, she loved it. "You just might get your wish."

Renee tried to fill her day with thoughts of anything besides Evan, feeling like she'd go mad before she'd see him again. She thought of where she would live or even ideas for her next book, but it was no use. Her every thought returned to his beautifully smooth dark skin, soft and tender light eyes, and sexy curving full lips.

She ran errands. She stopped to pick up Chicago area apartment guides. She went to the grocery store. Renee began to feel a part of that hole that had been forming recently fill up inside of her. A new life was coming on due to so many things, and most of all, Evan Brooks. It was nothing against New York. She'd always love her native city, but it was time to move on. It was time to start new roots and be near loved ones. It was time to move to

Chicago and let go of the pain of past losses and the ~~~~ of new ones. Renee tried to ignore the thoughts of freezing winters and traffic jams. Instead, she thought of Michigan Avenue shopping, walks on the lakefront, and night games at Wrigley Field.

There were so many possibilities, she felt like a young girl out of college, ready to face the world for the first time on her own. Michelle was going to be fine. Renee felt a newfound freedom to live her own life with her happiness and well-being a priority. A lonely future didn't seem to be an inevitability now. She was entering a new stage in her life and felt something was missing. It was a life. It was a family, friends, a lover, and a support base. The future seemed everything but lonely now. As a matter of fact, it seemed swamped. Renee didn't mind that at all.

Returning home later that day, Renee was happy to be alone. Hoping that keeping herself busy would make time go by faster, she was planning to surprise Michelle with dinner. Placing her groceries on the kitchen table, she surveyed the freshly made spinach spaghetti noodles and marinara sauce she'd purchased at a store down the street. The garlic bread and salad she'd make herself after popping a few potatoes in the oven. Maybe Michelle wouldn't mind if Evan joined them.

After putting away a few other items she'd purchased that day, Renee ran for the answering machine. She vowed to herself not to bother Evan or Chris with their investigation. Last night, on the ride home, her reserve lasted a minute at most. She begged Chris to tell her something. She didn't need full details, just a brief update of what was going on. Evan had warned Chris to leave her out of it, so it took a bit of convincing. Charm won over fear, and in the end, Renee prevailed. He wouldn't tell her what they had talked about, but promised to give her a call today with an update on their progress.

The message light blinked once. She crossed her fingers and pressed the PLAY button. She waited for the sound of a now familiar voice. Her grin was wide as she heard Chris begin to speak.

"Renee, it's Chris. My meeting with Evan was productive to say the least. It turns out your info had a lot to do with this new clue. We think it might be enough to take to the police. Evan is talking to a detective friend of his right now to see what the next move should be. It's a delicate situation because it involves other cops. I'll tell you more later. When you get a second, stop by. I'm at 2414 Oakwood Avenue, apartment 34."

Dinner could wait. She headed for the door.

"I think I'll take that trip with you."

Renee screamed as she jumped and swung around.

"What are you doing here?" she asked, stepping backward, almost stumbling over a chair behind her. "How did you get in?"

"I stole your silly little sister's key and made a copy for myself."

"Why?" Renee asked. Instead of an answer, a gun emerged from behind the intruder's back. "Oh, my God!"

Nick Hamilton's laugh was cold and laced with reproachful desperation. He enjoyed the terrified expression on Renee's face. He pointed the gun at her without hesitation.

"You catching on yet, Renee?" Nick noticed she was about to yell and he raised the gun to her face. "You scream, I'll shoot you. I'll wait for Michelle and shoot her, too. Don't doubt me, girl. I'll do it."

"No." Renee's heart was in her throat as she continued to back up. Not Michelle.

"You see this?" He pointed to the tip of the pistol. "It's

called a silencer. No one will hear me kill either of you. Now quit moving back."

Renee froze in place, trying to fight the panic running through her. She couldn't believe this was happening. Nick? Yes, he did work with Kimberly, but he was Michelle's fiancé. Michelle loved Nick with all her heart and soul.

"You're a pretty smart sister." Nick leaned against the wall, holding his head up. He waved the gun casually like it could fall out of his hand any moment. "You've probably figured out in the past fifteen seconds who killed Kimberly Janis."

"Nick, how could you?" she asked through a frightened, choked voice. "Why?"

"You're surprised?" he asked with sarcasm. "I thought you'd suspect me right away. You never liked me. I could tell from the beginning. That's all right, because I never liked you either. You've got an attitude problem and you think you're too special. You're one of those women who don't recognize their place in the presence of an important man like myself."

"Why would you kill Kimberly?" Renee asked. "She was a kid. A student."

"She was a snoop and a nerve-racking, psychotic little cry baby." Nick's tone was angry and his brow formed a frown. "She was a little weird, too. You should know from the onset, I never *wanted* to kill her."

"But you did," Renee said, with anger creeping its way inside of her at the thought of what he'd done. "You pushed her off a balcony."

"She threatened me." Nick's breathing became erratic as his anger increased. "Nobody threatens me."

"I'm not threatening you, Nick," Renee said in an effort to calm him. She could see he was growing more unstable as each moment passed.

"But you are." He laughed erratically. "Your little personal investigation with that reporter wanna-be was an outright threat to me.''

"I wouldn't have done any of this if I'd known it was you," Renee lied. "I mean, for Michelle's sake. Now that I know, I'll leave it alone."

"Don't lie to me." Nick came closer, lowering the gun to his side. "Like most women, you aren't any good at it, even though you do it constantly. You expect me to believe that even if you knew I was a murderer, for your sister's sake, you'd have ignored it? Let her sleep with me, marry me?"

"Yes." Renee felt herself let out a breath with the gun out of her face. She had to get him out of here before Michelle came home. That was all that mattered now. "I already have. I don't need to be concerned with Kimberly. I never even knew her."

"You're lucky." Nick grabbed a chair and sat down. "She was a pain in the ass. So many questions. Stupid, stupid girl."

"You were stealing money from BFK weren't you?" she asked.

"I wouldn't call it stealing." His retort was quick, his tone ruthless. "I deserved that money. I have a business degree from Harvard University, an MBA from Cornell. I was an assistant controller for a Fortune 1000 company on Madison Avenue by twenty-eight. At least I was, until they fired me."

"What?" Renee asked. Nick's anger came from within, showing the depths of his disturbance. "Fired for what?"

"It doesn't matter," he snapped. "They were wrong. They smeared my name. This sexual harassment thing you women created is pure gold for you, isn't it? It's all a plot to get what belongs to men. I couldn't get a respectable job anywhere after that. I had to settle for Augusta. I'm a financial genius and I'm working for a charity heap and making pennies for salary."

"So you took the money." Renee's voice held as much sympathy as she could fake. "Money owed to you, and Kimberly found out. She was going to tell."

"It's a lot more complicated than that." Nick's mood suddenly changed to nonchalant, speaking like they were sitting together at a backyard barbecue. "My point is, everything was fine until you and that real reporter wanna-be kept going and going. Asking everyone questions. The articles in the *Times*."

"We should've left well enough alone, I know." Renee pretended to sound regretful. Meanwhile, the tension and fear welling in the pit of her stomach kept on and on. "I will now. I'll tell Chris to leave it alone, too. He'll listen to me. He's young and impressionable and sort of has a crush on me."

"Don't insult my intelligence and don't think I have that overinflated opinion of you that you seem to think everyone does. I'm sure you think every man has a crush on you." Nick pointed the gun at the answering machine. "I heard the message. Chris isn't going to let this go and now he has Evan Brooks involved. Michelle told me everything you said to her about Kimberly, but I'm sure you held back since you treat her like a child anyway."

"Please," Renee pleaded. "I don't care what you do to me, but don't hurt Michelle. She hasn't done anything to you. She loves you."

"It's amazing how things are so cyclical isn't it?" Nick waved the gun casually in the air. "I liked Michelle the moment I saw her. I knew she'd make a good wife for someone like me. A successful man always has to have an attractive background. Good for business. I'd just need her to look good at dinners, smile, and be my prize. Oh, yeah, and give me my son. I can do without any daughters. Too much trouble."

Renee contained her anger at his insults, wishing this was just a nightmare she could wake up from. Was he really going to go out like this? Spewing this woman-hating nonsense?

"Everything would've been fine, too," he continued. "Another year or so at Augusta would repair my reputation and I could move on to a real job. If you can make the cash flow, New York is very forgiving."

"What now?" Renee felt beads of sweat form on her brow. Did he think murder could be forgiven? Was he that far gone?

"Now you and I are going to see Chris." He stood up, motioning toward the door with his gun. "I'll decide what to do after that."

"Chris doesn't need to be a part of this." Renee realized he had no plan. He was irrational and he'd decided to wing it. That spelled danger for all of them. "Let me talk to him. I can convince him to let go of this. He's just a kid. I . . ."

"Shut up!" The angry face returned. "You women just don't know how to shut up. Let's go. You drive. The safety is already off on this baby, so if you scream or try to get away, I can shoot you in an instant. If you don't care about yourself, being as holier than thou as you are, remember there's always Michelle."

Renee's nerves forced her to drive Nick's red BMW convertible slowly and Nick filled that time with incessant talking, giving an unsolicited explanation of his life over the past year.

He was a genius in his own mind, destined for wealth and business success. Standing in front, he would leave everyone in the business world aghast. He would run his own company by the age of thirty-five and retire a millionaire by forty-five. Everything had been on track until an incident at a holiday party for his last company.

"I finally decided to make my move on this girl at the office." Nick's eyes darted at passing cars, but immediately returned to Renee. He kept the gun low. "She'd been clocking me for months."

Realizing his opinion of himself, Renee was inclined to believe Nick thought every woman was after him.

"She was a six on a ten scale at first." He shrugged. "But you know, what the hell? After a couple of egg nogs, any woman can become a ten. It was just a roll in the hay anyway. Turns out she was a tease. I made the move and she turned me down. I let her know who she was, what she needed someone to tell her. She turns around and accuses me of sexual harassment."

Setting off a spiral of unfair occurences, Renee was certain Nick's impression would be. "You don't have to tell me this."

"You shut up and drive." He dug the gun into her rib. "You're gonna hear this. You women need to know the aftermath of the trouble you cause. So, they asked me to leave. My name was blackballed in the industry. I was a harasser. Hiring me would mean risking a million dollar lawsuit. In these politically correct crap days, no one wanted to risk it."

Nick paused as if reflection was too painful for words. "Some people were faithful to me. Some contacts knew the real deal, and they got me this penny-pinching job at Augusta. I figure, hey, I'll wait it out a couple of years, rebuild my rep. See, I figured working at Augusta would show my community spirit. You never know when you're going to need a good rep. Look at Alan Smith. He's Mr. Good Cause."

Renee wasn't surprised by anything coming out of his mouth. She only wanted that gun out of her ribs and for him to shut up. She couldn't think with his incessant talking and she had to figure a way out of this.

"Then I'd return to make my killing in the market," Nick continued. "My schedule had been pushed forward a bit, but I just revised the master plan. Pushed it back another five years. Five at the most. Everything was going along smooth until that little ... well you know. Until Kimberly can-we-go-over-this-statement-again Janis started in on her suspicions.

"The way it went," Nick said as a proud smile formed on his lips, "was she does the draft statement, which was usually full of mistakes, calculating the finances for the organizations from which I'd skim a little off the top, make the corrections and release them to Evan. BFK was the easiest because it was growing so quick, I could take a lot and still make it look like it had grown. That little heifer kept bugging me. As if it was impossible for her to be wrong."

"But she wasn't wrong!" Renee surprised herself with her outburst. To hear him talk about the woman he murdered in cold blood as if she was the evil one made her blood boil.

Nick smiled wider, seeming to enjoy evoking her anger. "Yeah, but she's not supposed to question me! She's a damn student. *There's money missing, Nick. There's money missing, Nick.*' I saw my future flash before my eyes. I could tell she was starting to suspect me. I tried to act like I didn't have the final say, you know like that idiot boyfriend of hers or Brooks might have something to do with it. It worked for a while. She was confused. She didn't know who to go to, but she kept giving me that eye. I didn't have a choice. God, I thought murder, you know. No way, but I just couldn't risk it. She wasn't going away. I couldn't risk trying to buy her off and have that backfire only making it worse. She might spread her suspicions, now confirmed by my bribery, before I took care of her. She wasn't alive when she went over. She didn't know what hit her."

He said it as if it should be some consolation. *You killed a child!* Renee screamed from inside. She wanted to say it out loud, spit in his face.

He told her how he placed the letter near the door that night when Renee had come home from her date with Evan. He'd gone through the items in her bag, looking for papers Kimberly had e-mailed her, which explained to Renee why the bag looked so disheveled. It was an added bonus that Chris Jackson suggested Evan Brooks's involvement. Nick decided to add to those doubts with lies of his own to detract the attention from himself, since he was the one who worked closest to Kimberly. Meanwhile, he would go back and cover his own tracks so nothing could lead to him when the leads to Evan didn't pan out.

Despite this outpouring of information, Renee could tell Nick was holding something back from her. Something important about Kimberly and her death. He was holding it back on purpose, glancing at her with keen smiles. Only, she feared she wouldn't live to find out what that important something was.

"It's about time," Chris said as he opened his apartment door. "I left that message for you over three hours ago."

"Hey, Chris." Renee tried her best to smile. It was difficult with Nick standing against the wall, pointing that gun at her. He'd given his instructions and she was supposed to get them inside the apartment. That was it. She had no idea how to avoid this without it costing her her life. She still had hopes of getting out of this, but with Nick's confession, she was doubtful. "You live alone, right?"

"Uhm." Chris hesitated. "Yeah, I live alone. There's . . ."

"Good job," Nick said as he swung around, grabbing

Renee's arm just as she stepped aside. Pointing his gun to her head, Nick winked at Chris and pushed Renee into the apartment, following right behind.

"Don't try and be a hero, Chris." Nick kicked the door shut with his back heel. "This gun is loaded, equipped with a silencer and I'm actually begging for a chance to use it."

"Chris," Renee pleaded as Nick ordered her to sit down. "Please, just listen to him. Don't try anything. He killed Kimberly."

"I knew it," Chris said, his eyes squinting with anger. He took the chair that Nick's gun motioned him toward. "You bastard. You killed an innocent girl. She never did anything to you."

"No need to go over that mess again," Nick said with annoyance as he looked around the tiny living room. "They sure don't pay you reporters well enough do they? I can relate."

"At least I don't steal to make up for it." Chris leaned back in his chair, acting like he wasn't at all afraid.

His reaction bothered Renee. Couldn't he see that Nick had a gun? Why provoke him? He was aching to use it.

"So you knew?" Nick slowly paced the room. "Is that what you called Renee for?"

"I got my hands on the statements." Chris' tone was haughty and self-assured. "The real ones. Before you changed them. You forgot to check the number of donations. You left it saying seventy corporate donations of a thousand dollars *or more* for the last quarter, but the total of corporate donations only equaled seventy-two thousand dollars. Some of those *or more* checks had to be more than two thousand dollars. You got sloppy. You did the same the quarter before. Fifty-two corporate donations of a thousand or more. Fifty-five thousand dollars total. More or less, right? The final numbers were a huge leap from the quarter before.''

"You're a resourceful young brother, aren't you?" Nick turned to Chris, his anger apparently triggered by the younger man's attitude. "You should be proud of yourself."

"I am," Chris said with a smirk. "Didn't you think anyone would notice? The canceled checks are proof. Did you think we were all a bunch of idiots?"

"You are." Nick shrugged. "It amazed me how I went to work every day, surrounding by pure, unadulterated ignorance. Besides, the canceled checks and cash and money transfer receipts come back to me. Evan didn't question me. He saw the donations going up."

"You've gotten so full of yourself," Chris said, "you don't even realize how ridiculous you sound. All charitable organizations are on a first-name basis with the IRS once a year. They look for this kind of thing exactly."

"I've created administrative cost," Nick challenged. "Fake administrative and operating related expenses to qualm any questions."

"That can go only so far," Chris said, laughing like this was nothing. "You're only the finance guy. Brooks is the one with administration and expenses that could reach thousands. You don't even travel."

Noticing Nick's increasing anger, Renee said, "Chris watch yourself." She could see Nick hadn't thought this out as much as he should've and she could see he'd sooner shoot them both now than admit to that.

"Don't worry, Renee." Chris winked carelessly in her direction. "Nick is a coward. Anyone who pushes a twenty-one-year-old girl off a balcony is a stinking coward."

"You need to watch what you say." Nick stepped closer to Chris, his gun pointed directly at him. "Choose your last words carefully."

"If they're my last words, then what's the point in being careful, you spineless wimp." Chris smirked.

Nick blinked and pressed his lips. He turned to Renee. "Tell me who knows besides you two."

"So you can kill them?" Renee asked. "Yeah, right."

"Kimberly Janis knows for one." Chris's words seethed with contempt.

"Well, I won't have to worry about her now." Nick stopped talking. Raising his head to listen to a sound in the distance.

Renee heard the sirens, too. She noticed the satisfied smile on Chris's face as the wailing sound came closer. Had he seen her approaching with Nick and called the police? How could he? They had approached from the front of the apartment building and Chris's apartment faced the back. Maybe it was just a coincidence. This was the city. Sirens buzzed by every second.

"They're going somewhere else. They can't possibly know I'm here." Nick's voice reeked with doubt. "Chris. Tell me who else knows."

"Go to hell!" Chris yelled.

"Chris!" Renee screamed as she saw Nick's face tighten with anger. He stepped closer to Chris and pointed the gun directly at his head. The revolver was barely a foot away. Renee knew he had no plan, the sirens were making him nervous, Chris was upsetting him. She squeezed her eyes shut and turned away, unable to stand it.

Suddenly, she heard a yell and a gun quietly go off, sounding like a harmless dart. She screamed in terror and her whole body was paralyzed.

"Get down, Renee!"

Her eyes flew open. She recognized the voice that yelled the demand. Leaping to the ground in compliance, she turned to the action and saw the three of them struggling for the gun. Nick was in the middle, Chris on the left, and

Evan on the right. Her heart screamed as the gun was smothered with hands. It could go off and hit any of them.

"Get the gun, Chris!" Evan yelled as he finally got a stronghold of Nick's lower arms. "Renee, get out of here."

Renee jumped and darted for the door. She turned and halted a moment to see Chris grab the weapon and Evan throw Nick to the ground. Relief swept over her until she jumped again at the sound of banging against the apartment door.

"Police!" A voice said from the other side. "Open up."

Renee quickly did as she was told and stepped aside. She stood speechless as four police officers rushed in with guns in hand.

"Over here!" Evan yelled as he saw the police head for Chris because he was holding the gun. "This is him."

Chris let the gun fall from his hands onto the sofa and stepped aside as a policeman grabbed it. The other three cops went for Nick. He was screaming and cursing a dictionary's worth of profanities and threats while they securely restrained him.

When Evan stood up, he headed straight for Renee. She fell into his embrace and hugged him as tightly as she could. She let out a deep breath, never wanting to let go. She was alive. At that last moment, she'd thought she would die, leaving Michelle alone.

"Where did you come from?" she asked, still holding on.

"I was in Chris's bedroom," Evan explained. "When I heard you ring up from the lobby, I asked Chris to pretend I wasn't here. I wanted to surprise you."

"I thought you didn't want me to know what was going on. Chris said you . . ."

"I changed my mind." Finally unleashed from the tight hug, Evan looked her over to make sure she was all right. "You've put too much into this to be left out like a bystander. I was thinking of your safety. The less you knew, the less you might say to a possible murderer and the less danger you'd be in. Thinking later, I couldn't take that chance, so I told Chris he could call you after he and I put two and two together with the financial statements. We realized it was Nick who was fixing them, taking money for himself. I needed you and Michelle to stay away from him while we figured out how to get him behind bars."

"He was waiting for me at the apartment." Renee's breath matched Evan's in speed, her chest heaving. "He pulled a gun on me. It was awful."

"Did he hurt you? If he hurt you, I'll . . ."

"I'm fine." Renee allowed Evan to shield her as two officers walked by with a struggling, cursing Nick under submission.

"You think you got it," Nick spat his words at Renee, with sneering eyes. "You think you got it. You think you know everything. Stupid woman. Just like the rest."

Renee felt a chill run through her as she watched him stare her down until he was out of sight. She should have guessed. "It makes sense. Kimberly suspected fraud. Nick handled the money."

"It seemed easier to believe that a scorned girlfriend or crazy ex-boyfriend would go far enough to murder than someone at Augusta," Evan said.

"I think the obviousness of it all is what made us think it had to be someone else," Chris said as he joined the two. "Besides, with Michelle, you really didn't have a choice but to exclude him. Psychologically, I mean. That *couldn't be* aspect, you know. Still with all this, something doesn't fit."

"All that matters is that you're safe now." Evan held her in his arms again. "We'll all be fine now."

"Michelle!" Renee slapped her hand to her chest as she

remembered. "I have to tell her. This is going to kill her. Kill her."

"She loved him," Evan said. "It's going to tear her apart."

"I have to get home." Renee turned and headed for the door.

"Not so fast, ma'am." One of the two remaining officers called after her. "We need all three of you to come down to the station and give us your statements."

"Can't it wait?" Evan asked. "I'll bring her right over after she sees her sister."

"I can come now." Chris watched as one of the cops placed the gun in an evidence bag. "I can give my statement first."

"We need her more than either of you," the cop said. "The sooner we can charge him with kidnapping, in addition to attempted murder, the more impossible it'll be for him to get out on any amount of bail before we can strengthen the murder charges. We can try to get a confession when we put him in the box with her account of things."

"Fine." Renee sighed, a little surprised that pointing a gun at someone wasn't enough to ensure denial of bail. Then she remembered the cops hadn't seen any of that. They'd only seen a struggle. "He did tell me pretty much everything. The sooner we get this over with the better. I need some air."

She grabbed hold of Evan's hand as he led her out of the building. They watched together as the police placed Nick in the back seat of the squad car and drove away. Looking into his angry, disturbed eyes, Renee could only think of Kimberly Janis. She was the first of Nick's many victims.

Renee gave her statement at Chicago Police Department headquarters with Evan by her side. She told the new detective assigned to the case everything from the first e-mail she received from Kimberly to the moment the police entered Chris Jackson's apartment. It was upsetting, going over it all, but Renee wasn't concerned for herself. After all, she was out of danger and had Evan with her. It was Michelle she was worried about. How could she explain to her that the man she wanted to spend the rest of her life with was a murderer? The man she adored. She remembered how painful it had been for her as she began to care for Evan while at the same time suspecting him of murder. It would be much worse if it were a fact. If they were engaged to be married.

Saying the words came with difficulty was an understatement. Renee found the strength and repeated the story to Michelle after returning home. Evan stayed in the living room giving the women privacy in the kitchen.

"I know this is upsetting, baby." Renee wiped her own tears as she held her speechless sister's hands in her own. "Please say something. Anything."

Michelle stared at Renee with a blank look in her eyes. She said nothing, not even a trace of tears. She slid her hands from Rene's grip and stood up.

"Michelle." Renee didn't want to push, but her silence wasn't good. "You can cry, scream, curse, throw your toaster. Anything you feel like doing. Do it."

"You never liked him anyway." Michelle turned to Renee, looking down at her with an emotionless glare. She spoke with an eerie calm. "You can't be too disappointed."

"I was prepared to love anyone you wanted to love," Renee said. "I would never wish this."

"I can't believe this." The words came as a whisper from Michelle's lips as she leaned against the counter. She lowered her head toward the floor, shaking it in disbelief. "It has to be a nightmare."

"I wish it was." Renee was quickly at her side. She

wrapped her arms around her, wishing she could take some of the pain. "I'm so sorry, baby. I'm so sorry."

Michelle hesitated, but after a second, wrapped her own arms around Renee and cried heartily and without restraint. Renee held her and let her cry. She would hold her as long as she needed to. She gently stroked her long hair with one hand. *Remember how Mama made us feel better?*

"We'll get past this," she said. "We've been through worse and came out okay. No pain lasts forever. It will die down. You'll be able to deal with it, lock it in its corner and move on. We know this."

After several minutes, Michelle's sobs ceased and she lifted away.

"You're right. We do know this," she said through sniffles. "I need to be alone."

"No way." Renee shook her head. "There's no way I'm leaving you alone."

"I know you mean well and I love you for it." Michelle returned to her chair. "I'm not going to hurt myself or do anything stupid. That is unless you consider devouring a pint of chocolate chip ice cream harmful."

"I'll keep my distance," Renee promised. "I won't bother you."

"No. I want to be alone." She gave Renee an affectionately pained look. "Please. I hate to kick you out. I know you've been through a lot today, too, but I need to be alone. I have to think. You agreed to start showing my decisions more respect. Do this now."

"For how long, Michelle?" Renee asked reluctantly.

"Just tonight. I'll be fine in the morning. Please, please."

"I don't agree with this." Renee placed her hand on Michelle's shoulder. "But I'll do it on one condition."

"What?"

"You'll let me call on you once more tonight. I'll get a hotel room nearby and call you with the number."

"That's fine," Michelle said with one, quick nod.

After a long, silent hug, Renee reminded her sister that she loved her again and headed for Evan in the living room. When their eyes met, she could see his compassion for her pain and without words, he wrapped his arms around her. She found this comfort a part of what made her now. His arms. Renee finally decided to get her things and reluctantly let go.

"What are you doing?" Evan watched Renee packing.

"Michelle needs to be alone," she answered with a weak voice. "I'm not afraid of leaving her alone. I think she understands things will be okay one day. I don't like this, but its what she wants and I need to respect that."

"Where are you going?"

"There's a motel not far from here." Renee headed for the bathroom to gather some things. "I think it's within walking distance if that's necessary."

"No way." Evan followed her. "You're coming to my place."

"Evan, I can't. I have to be as close as . . ."

"Don't even try and resist." He held up a hand to halt her protest. "I'll feed you. I know you're hungry even though you don't. There's no way you're going to be alone tonight. Any more protest would be a waste of time and energy you don't even have right now."

Renee didn't bother to object. She was too tired. She didn't want to be away from Michelle, but she didn't want to be alone tonight in some unfamiliar hotel room either. So she gathered the rest of her things together and passed Evan's home number to Michelle. It hurt her to leave her baby sister, and as she saw her deep pain, she said good night. Renee begged to stay one last time, but Michelle stood her ground. She wanted to be alone, but promised to call if she changed her mind.

"Don't worry," she said, standing in the doorway. "I'm not going to lose it."

Renee left with Evan's arm wrapped tightly around her. She felt so safe nestled next to him. He had saved her life. She would never forget that.

ELEVEN

"Let me take that." Evan reached for Renee's purse. He'd already taken her bag and placed it on the floor inside the condominium.

He led her past the living room and kitchen, down a long hallway to a bedroom Renee hadn't seen the last time she was here. It was a small, carpeted room with a simple twin bed with white sheets and a black comforter at the bottom. There was a set of dresser drawers and a bare vanity table. With the exception of a painting of three dolphins jumping out of the ocean, the walls were bare. "Here's the guest room."

Renee knew the offer was out of consideration, but now that she was here, she wouldn't consider not having him next to her.

"I'm just down the hallway," he said, pointing toward his bedroom, then smiled. "I guess you know that. When you want to call Michelle, the phone is . . ."

"Evan." Renee lifted her finger and gently placed it to

his mouth. She looked into his eyes and blinked slowly, softly. "You're so sweet."

"I want you to be happy." Evan wrapped his arms around her. "I wish I could make you forget about today."

As he blinked, Renee thought, if for only a second, she saw a flicker of doubt in his eyes. Something was wrong. "What is it, Evan? Why the guest room after we've made love?"

Evan's voice hinted at apprehension. "Listening to your statement, I was just . . ."

"No, Evan." She wrapped her arms around him. "I would never have made love to you if I thought you were a murderer."

"What about seeing me at Kimberly's computer?"

"You were looking for information because you've suspected foul play all along, and Chris Jackson's article made you even more curious."

"What about me calling her friends?" Evan asked.

"Investigating." She squeezed him tighter, appreciating the timid smile on his face. That forceful, intimidating man was gone. This was the tender, vulnerable side of Evan only select few got to see. Renee knew she was one of those few now and she realized how lucky she was.

"Meeting Tamia?" He curled his fingers in her hair.

"You thought she was a friend." Renee wasn't wavering.

"What Nick said about me? What about her brother Marshall?"

"Nick is a liar," she said. "All Marshall said was that Kimberly didn't like you. You're an aggressive guy. I don't believe for a second you harassed her."

"I tried to be nice to her," he explained. "She didn't like me. I left her alone. Hell, I barely saw her."

Renee shook her head. She didn't want to talk about this anymore. "That's enough, Evan. All my questions were answered the night we made love. I swear to you."

"I have to admit myself," he said with a reassured smile, "it looked pretty bad. That day I found you in Kimberly's old office and you ran out, I saw you look at Nick and then at me. You told the detective you thought Nick was afraid of me. He was in a way. I had told him I wanted to discuss financials for a few organizations because I had a couple of problems with the numbers. You better believe he was scared, but now we know why he was really frightened. He knew I suspected him. After those lies he told you and the doubt Chris planted, I can see how you thought everything was against me. You hardly knew me."

"But I didn't have any real proof. There wasn't any excuse for me being so cold to you."

"No need for excuses." He held her away, looking her over. "No need to go back to any of that. You look so tired, baby. Why don't you take a nap and I'll fix something for both of us. I have some salmon steaks I can broil. How does that sound?"

"Terrific." Renee suddenly realized how hungry she was.

Renee napped for hours. It was past nine when she finally got up. She hoped Evan wasn't too upset to have to wait for dinner and knew he wouldn't be. She washed her face and freshened up before joining him in the dining room.

The spacious room was dark, lit only by three candles on the table. Smooth R&B played on the sleek, jet black stereo against the wall as Renee took a seat. The candles gave her glimpses of a warmly decorated room with hometown shades of brown, beige, and gold.

Evan sat waiting with a rested, welcoming smile.

"This is lovely." She hungrily eyed the broiled salmon

with fresh garden salad and a glass of red wine. "You know, we really shouldn't eat this."

"Why's that?" he asked, handing Renee a red cloth napkin.

"A lot of people don't know that, unlike most fish, salmon has a lot of fat."

"How can a fish have a lot of fat?" He gave a disbelieving grin. "Where would it come from?"

"Not trying to go too much into shop, trust me. They do." Renee dug into the food like she hadn't eaten in months. It was delicious.

"You're pretty hungry there."

"I had no idea." Renee broke a cardinal sin and spoke with her mouth full.

They were mostly silent during dinner. Renee was grateful Evan didn't want to talk about today, about anything really. She wanted to forget it all. At least for tonight.

After dinner, Evan cleaned up while Renee called Michelle. She didn't know what to make of the stable tone of her sister's voice. Was she doing better or doing worse, only hiding it?

"You can call me anytime, no matter what time it is," she told her. "I'll be right over."

Trailing the soulful jazz of Miles Davis to the living room, Renee was met with open arms by the man she loved. She accepted the embrace, cherishing every moment without hesitation.

In seconds, that embrace turned to caressing kisses on her forehead, her eyelids, her nose. Renee felt the heat returning. She felt her feet leave the ground as his lips met hers. It felt so good to her, she wanted more.

"Renee," he whispered. "I'd do anything to take away your worries, your pain. From today, from the past."

His breath was hot in her ear and Renee felt her head begin to spin. She turned to him, her face an inch from his. "Then make love to me."

She saw uncertainty slip through the desire in his eyes and said. "Yes, Evan, I'm very emotional tonight, but you won't be taking advantage of me. I love you and I need you."

He led her to the bedroom. Renee knew, at least for the rest of this night, all of her worries would be forgotten.

They lay in silence for some time, bodies still wet with sweat from their lovemaking. She rested her head gently on his chest as he wrapped a protective arm around her.

"Renee?" Evan whispered her name. "I don't think I could bear to be without you."

"You won't be without me," she assured him. "Chicago is my home now. With you and Michelle."

"I didn't plan on rushing you. I just needed to know your plans. I want you here."

"I have some things to clear up in New York, but I'm moving here." She leaned her head back, looking up at him. "You haven't rushed me. I'm ready. I'm ready to love you with all my heart."

He bent his head down and kissed her, almost with the softness of a feather on her forehead. She watched as he lay back again, closing his eyes now to sleep.

Renee woke the next morning still in Evan's arms. She lay still for a moment before gently moving away.

"I'm awake."

She was startled as she looked up at him. His eyes were wide open as he stared down at her, his smile even larger than hers.

"How long have you been awake?" she asked after kissing him gently.

"A few minutes," he answered, "I didn't want to wake you. I wanted to watch you. You're so beautiful when you sleep. You look like a child."

"That's a first," Renee said with an amused grin. "You know what time it is?"

"It's seven in the morning."

"I have to call Michelle." She quickly sat up.

"I'll hop in the shower real fast," Evan said, getting up from the bed. "It'll give you some privacy. I know you want to get back to her, so I'll make it quick."

She blushed at the sight of his muscular, naked body as he walked to the bathroom, smiling at her good fortune. She knew she'd never get used to his sex appeal. It would always make her blush.

She turned to the phone on the night stand. She loved being with Evan, their newfound love fresh and exciting, but Michelle needed her now. There would be plenty of time for Evan, and she knew he understood.

"Hello?"

"Hey, honey." Renee paid careful attention to the tone of her little sister's voice, trying to get an idea of how she was coping. "How're you?"

"I'm all right, I guess." There was a long, labored sigh. "It's all still hitting me."

"I know, honey. I'm on my way over."

"Actually, Renee," Michelle interrupted. "I'm on my way out."

"Where?"

"I'm going to see Alan Smith."

"Michelle." Renee didn't like the sound of this. "What for? You don't owe him an apology. Just because you were engaged to Nick doesn't mean you have to take any responsibility for him murdering Kimberly."

"I know that," Michelle said, like it would be obvious to anyone with half a brain. "That's exactly what Alan said. To tell you the truth, I wasn't even thinking about him. Not yet at least. He called me about a half hour ago. He wanted me to know that he was sorry it turned out to be Nick and he has no hard feelings."

"That's nice of him." Renee felt it best not to mention what she'd learned of Alan. He wanted the attention, sympathy for his image. Maybe he could be a source of temporary comfort for Michelle. "Are you really up to going out yet?"

"I really want to. We got to talking and . . . well, we decided to meet at BFK for coffee. He'll be there until noon. He said he's alone and promised no one would be there to bother me about Nick. He's really a nice guy."

"How would everyone know about this so soon?" It seemed very sudden to Renee, even though she knew news traveled fast in today's world.

"Front page of the *Sun Times*."

"Oh, Michelle. I wish I'd gotten the paper before you. You don't need to see that. I'm sorry."

"It's all right," Michelle said. "There's no mention of me anywhere. Besides, it's news and I can't expect Chris not to report it."

"That's true."

"Oh, by the way. He called for you twice this morning. I was taking a long shower, so I didn't get either call. He left two messages that it was urgent you call him back."

"Did he say what about?" Renee wasn't interested in hearing Chris relay Nick's sordid story from last night. She'd heard enough in the car with a gun to her ribs yesterday.

"He didn't say. Hey, I gotta go, but I'll be home in a few hours. We can talk then."

"I'll be there waiting for you."

Renee hung the phone up, still unhappy with Michelle up and out so soon after everything. She sounded all right, but whether or not what she heard over the phone was true was questionable. Maybe it hadn't even really hit her yet, she thought.

"Hello?"

"Hey, Chris, it's Renee. Michelle said you . . ."

"Where have you been?" His voice sounded tight and stressed. "I've been looking for you all morning."

"None of your business," she said. "It's personal. What's so urgent, anyway? Nick is still in jail, isn't he?"

"Yeah, but where's your sister. I've tried her apartment. Is she with you?"

"Not at the moment, but I just talked to her. Why?"

"Last night when I was interviewing Nick, he kept smirking and laughing like the little psycho he is. It was really starting to get to me. I knew he was holding something back. I kept asking him how Kimberly let him into her apartment if she suspected him? Why no one heard a scream? He wouldn't answer, just laughed and shrugged. Told me to figure it out. Eventually, I got sick of him and just left. Then, this morning it was nagging me again, so I went back down there."

"Chris." Renee said. "You're scaring me. What is it?"

"He didn't work alone," Chris said. "He wouldn't tell me who, but when I told him I knew he had a partner, he laughed and told me I might make a good reporter after all."

Renee remembered that same nagging feeling in the car yesterday. Nick was holding something back.

"I asked him yesterday," Chris continued, "if he placed those pills on Kimberly's nightstand."

"His aunt in New York is a manic depressive. He'd just been visiting his family before Kimberly was murdered."

"He only looked at me weird and said only, *'they were*

my pills.' Nick didn't murder Kimberly. He probably wasn't even in her apartment. He was waiting in the car downstairs.''

"For whom? Who could get into Kimberly's apartment with her already so paranoid and stressed. Who could . . .''

Renee knew that Chris had just made the same connection she had. The thought sent her into panic.

"Chris!'' Her breathing was already heavy and broken as she jumped from the bed. "Call the police. Tell them to get to BFK headquarters on Erie now!''

"I know where that is, but why there so early? Shouldn't we look from him at his home first?''

"No. He's at BFK. He's meeting Michelle there. I have to go. Hurry and call them.''

Renee quickly pressed the RESTORE button and frantically dialed the apartment. She prayed for Michelle to pick up, but there was no answer. When the machine finished its message, she yelled, "Michelle, if you're there, pick up! It's Renee. Don't go to BFK! Alan was in this whole thing with Nick. He was the one who killed Kimberly. Please listen!'' She waited a moment for Michelle to pick up, but it never happened.

She hung up the phone and hurried with her clothes, all the while yelling Evan's name. When he finally appeared, she ran to his soaked body and grabbed his arms.

"You have to help me.'' Tears were already streaming down her cheeks.

"What's wrong?'' Evan was utterly confused at her sudden erratic behavior.

"It's Michelle!'' Renee caught her breath in order to talk clearly. "Nick had help killing Kimberly. It was Alan. Chris is calling the police now.''

"What about Michelle?'' Evan started reaching for his clothes.

"She's going to BFK to see Alan. He made her think he just wanted to talk. She has no idea!"

"Let's go." Evan buttoned his jeans and grabbed his shirt without putting it on.

Renee prayed through determined tears as Evan sped down Chicago's busy streets. Morning rush hour was starting to pick up steam and traffic was getting hectic.

"We'll get there in time, Renee," he said. "She left just before us. The police might even get there before her."

"Go faster," was all Renee could say. She stared out the window, gripping the arm of her door so tightly, its design was making an indentation in her hand.

They had to make it in time, she thought. There was no other choice. She would die if she lost Michelle. She'd simply die.

"Why would he call her?" she asked in tears. "To get revenge against Nick?"

"Maybe he knew Nick was going to turn on him. Maybe he knows it's all over and he's snapping just like Nick did."

The thought made Renee's heart turn over.

Evan practically parked on the curb in front of the building. There were no police in sight as Renee jumped out of the car and ran for the door. She struggled, pushing, pulling, then kicking it to open, with no luck.

"It's locked. He must have done this on purpose, wanting her to come in from another entrance." Evan grabbed Renee by the shoulders, capturing her eyes with his own. "I know there's a back way behind the garage."

"Then let's go." She jerked away, heading for the back, but Evan held her still. "What is it? Let's go."

"I want you to stay here," Evan said firmly. "It could get dangerous. I'll get your sister."

"No, Evan." Renee was strongly defiant. "I understand what you're trying to do, but she's my sister and I have to get her. She's all the family I have left."

"Fine." He seemed to realize there was no arguing the point as they both headed for the garage. "We'll do it together. Just remember, he could have a gun like Nick."

They entered the indoor garage used by all the offices in the building including BFK. There were very few cars inside. Renee caught her breath when she saw Michelle's Pontiac. Running to it, her eyes searched desperately. She hadn't expected to see anything, but needed to look anyway. It was parked right next to a red, Mazda convertible.

"Get down." Evan came up behind her and pulled her to the ground behind the car. "I hear something."

Renee's stomach clenched as she sat waiting. Each second seemed like an hour until she also heard a sound. Lifting her head to see through the car's window, she finally saw what she'd come for.

Michelle was alive. Standing behind her, Alan Smith glanced over the garage. Renee could see she was terrified and wanted to reach for her. She wondered why she didn't run? Then she saw the answer to her question. As Alan turned to head up to the next level in the garage, a large knife was in the hand he had to Michelle's back, its serrated edge against the skin underneath her cutoff shirt. The sight made Renee whimper in pain and sear with anger. Hearing her, Alan swung around.

"Who's there?" he yelled, grabbing Michelle tighter. He nervously scanned the garage.

"Help!" Michelle screamed.

"Michelle!" Renee couldn't help herself. Evan pulled at her to restrain her, but she leaped up. The sound of her terrified baby sister was too much for her.

"Renee!" Michelle began to cry harder at seeing her. "Help me!"

Renee turned to Alan, staring with hate in her eyes. If he hurt her, she'd kill him. "Let her go."

"Can't do that." Alan waved his knife before returning it to Michelle's side. "See this? It means I'm in control."

"There's nothing you can do." Renee could feel Evan move away from her, but she wouldn't look. He was hiding behind cars and poles, sneaking his way closer to Alan. "Everyone knows. The cops are on their way."

Alan cursed out loud as his frustration showed the situation he was in was starting to cave.

"He killed Kimberly," Michelle said. "He and Nick were in it together, but he killed her."

"It's all a misunderstanding," Alan said apologetically. "It just went too far."

"We know everything, Alan." Renee looked sternly into his eyes, trying to hide her fear. She didn't care at all what Alan's explanation was, but wanted to give Evan time to do whatever it was he planned to do. "You and Nick were stealing money and Kimberly found out. But I don't understand, why murder her?"

"It was all Nick's fault." Alan seemed eager to tell his story, like it would matter. "He was stealing from all the groups. I realized a couple of months ago when I was sure my efforts had gotten more donations than reported. Nick was good at convincing you not to worry about the money. No need for me to keep track. But I did keep general track and I knew something was wrong. I asked to see all the checks, money orders, cash slips, everything. Nick got defensive, for lack of a better word. I put two and two together and threatened to tell Evan. I needed those numbers to go national! Then he offered me a part of it. With all the programs involved, it turned out to be a lot of money. So he promised to lay off of BFK a little and make up for the lower numbers by using his New York contacts to help me move the program out there. With New York support, I could take BFK out from under Augusta. I could be executive director. I didn't want to, but I guess my greed got the best of me. I was putting in my time. I did a lot for this program. I was sending it national."

"But Kimberly," Renee said. "Didn't you care about her?"

"I did." Alan's expression seemed regretful and apprehensive, but only for a moment. "I liked her a lot, but she wasn't supportive enough of me. She didn't really understand the vision I had for my future. When you get into stuff like this, you lose sight of things like love. Suddenly, all she was to me was a threat. She kept asking question after question. I thought she'd give up eventually, but Nick hates questions. I don't think she ever suspected me. She was funny that way, smart with some stuff but not with other stuff, like close stuff. I played dumb pretty well, but she was going on and on about Nick. We had no choice. She was gonna go to the police. We tried to threaten her once with a letter like we did with you, but it only made her ask more. I called her that night and she told me she was going to the reporter with whatever evidence she had. I panicked and called Nick. He was on his way back from New York. I shouldn't have done it, cause he'd been planning to get rid of her for a week or more. It was all he needed. I wanted to go after the reporter, but he said to cut it off before it got to that. No need to do two when you could do only one. I logged onto the net at home before I left for an alibi. He gave me the pills to plant. He told me what to do and I handled it."

"You didn't have to kill her!" Michelle's cries were wrapped with anger.

"I didn't want to!" Alan yelled back. "I wish there'd been another way, but Nick said there wasn't. I was confused. It had gotten past anything rational by then. My future was . . . I was just trying to keep from going to jail at that point. Kimberly didn't know it, but she was gonna ruin everything for me."

"What about Griggs?" Renee asked, wishing Evan would move faster. She couldn't see him anywhere. "How did you involve him?"

"One of the benefits of working at a boys' and girls' club is hearing what the kids see and experience." Alan was talking now like he was giving an interview. His mood was changing every minute. He seemed confident, certain now. "They see everything. I had plenty on Griggs. I hadn't thought about it until we were outside Kimberly's apartment and Nick said we needed backup. Who could help us cover? Griggs couldn't risk any more lawsuits. He worked the college area. I used my contacts to track him down. Took five minutes."

His eyes squinted as he looked from a desperate Renee to a horrified Michelle. "I knocked her out with her back turned to me. She didn't suspect a thing. She was out when I tossed her over."

Tossed her over. Like a sack of dirt. Renee wanted to scream, but she kept calm. "You started spreading rumors that she was depressed." She took a couple of steps closer. Alan was back in his confused state, looking like he was struggling to understand himself.

"I didn't have to start it," he said. "She could act a little strange sometimes. She was definitely acting strange the last week or so. Then when Nick told me you suspected Evan, we watered your doubts. At least that way, you two would be on his trail and not ours. Meanwhile, Nick said he'd work something out."

"But he didn't," Renee said. "Now look at him. He's not going to let you get away while he rots in jail."

"This is all his fault!" Alan blinked rapidly, seeming highly irritated as he let his concentration wander. "He got me into this! I was going to be everything. Just one little decision, one mistake. I let him talk me into this. I could've been a hero if I'd turned him in. None of this would've happened."

"He might have killed you," Renee said, trying to sound as sympathetic as she could, facing a man she'd like to kill. "You were trapped."

"He would've killed me." Alan nodded. "Like he's going to do now. Only this time, I'm getting back at him before he gets the chance. His little fiancée and I are going to the top of this building here. She's going over and I'm getting out of here. My goodbye present to Nick."

Michelle cringed at hearing her death spoken of so casually.

"Nick doesn't care about Michelle." Renee hated to say it in front of her sister, but saving her life was more important than sparing her feelings. "You'll do nothing to him by killing Michelle. Nothing more than having police looking for you for two murders instead of one. You can get the upper hand. Right now, everything leads to you. The cops are going to bargain with one of you for the other. You have to stop this while you can still be the one they choose."

Renee knew that Nick had all but confessed to Chris, possibly to the police. It was probably in the papers, but she was counting on Alan's state of mind to ignore that. Hoping.

Alan went on a talking rampage. He brought up other plans he could enact to get out clean and safe, changing them as soon as he realized it still wouldn't work. When he mentioned that he wished he had a gun, Renee's panic grew. She couldn't wait for Evan, although she sensed he was getting closer. Renee caught Michelle's frightened eyes with her own. She didn't need to beg for them, Michelle hadn't looked anywhere but at her sister since she'd seen her. Renee was stern, knowing Michelle was reluctant because of her fear.

"Michelle, remember PK's best?"

Her words were enough to shut Alan up for just a moment. He frowned, confused just long enough to be caught off guard as Michelle lifted her foot and kicked him between the legs. He doubled over in pain. Michelle turned and kicked him again, this time in his thighs, causing enough pain to force the knife from his hands. Evan jumped from behind the car closest to them and kicked the knife away just before Alan could reach and grab it. Evan grabbed the smaller man's arms and pulled them behind his back, pushing his entire body to the ground. Alan hit the pavement with his face and screamed in pain.

"I didn't mean to do it," Alan repeated again and again. "It got out of control. Nick pulled me in. I didn't mean to do it."

Renee was already holding Michelle, who was sobbing uncontrollably. Her knees gave out and the force of her body pulled Renee to the ground with her. Renee held her, running her fingers through her hair. She felt the blood rush from her head and return to the rest of her body with Michelle in her arms. So precious this girl was to her. More than a sister, she was like a child.

"Are you okay?" Renee asked Evan, who was holding on tight to Alan as he struggled. "Can you hold him alone?"

"I didn't mean to do it." Alan yelled. He was crying now, like a child. "I didn't mean to do it."

"I've got him," Evan said. "You get Michelle out of here."

Renee lifted her trembling sister into her arms and slowly led her out of the garage. She looked back at Evan before turning the corner for the stairs. He winked at her.

She heard the sirens as the police pulled up to the building. She winked back and headed for the entrance.

EPILOGUE

"Another toast!" Chris Jackson raised his glass of wine. "To collaboration."

Renee, Evan, and Michelle all raised their glasses in response as they sat in the dining room of Evan's condo. This was Chris's third toast.

"To collaboration," Renee said before taking a sip.

The collaboration was a book Renee had coauthored with Chris, *Living Fit and Healthy in Chicago*. Renee came up with the idea after moving into her new home four months ago. Full of interesting and occasionally inexpensive places to go to exercise and eat at restaurants that served healthy meals, the book was still in its early stages. There was a lot of work to be done, but Renee's publishing house had already agreed to purchase it and Karen was in discussions over a deal to write the same theme for books in several other metropolitan areas.

"Enough with the toasts." Evan sipped his wine with

one hand and held Renee's hand with the other. He was holding on tighter than usual. "Let's eat already."

As she studied his dark profile, Renee loved him now more than ever. The weeks after Alan and Nick's arrest, as well as that of Detective Griggs, were difficult for Michelle and Evan was understanding of Renee's need to be with her sister. She tried to spend as much time with him as possible, not wanting to neglect him or their new-found love completely. She couldn't even if she tried. Their love had grown stronger with each passing day. Not wanting to be apart, Evan joined Renee and Michelle in New York for the three weeks it took for her to finalize her life there.

Returning to Chicago, Renee and Michelle moved into a new apartment together. It was Michelle's decision to live together. They needed more room and for Michelle, it was important to start fresh, away from the many memories of Nick in the old apartment.

Youth and optimism helped Michelle heal quickly. Soon, Evan and Renee were spending every waking moment together, growing closer. Their affection and passion for each other increased steadily.

"I want to propose a toast," Renee said.

"Aw, come on." Evan sighed. "I'm starving."

"Shut up." She kissed his cheek and rubbed her hand over his bald head. He was being a little fussy tonight, but she wasn't going to pay that any mind. He'd been acting agitated all day. "I want to toast."

Everyone sat at attention.

"This is for Michelle Shepherd." Renee winked at the girl sitting across from her. "Living, loving again. Here's to new starts."

"Loving?" Chris asked with a raised brow. "What's this about loving?"

"Don't . . ." Michelle started.

"Sorry, hon." Renee shrugged. "I'm feeling gossipy today. Michelle has a new boyfriend."

"He's not a boyfriend," Michelle corrected. "He's just a guy I know. I met him at a friend's wedding. It's no big deal."

"Well," Renee said. "Here's a toast to no big deal."

"Can we eat now?" Evan asked.

"No," Michelle said, shifting excitedly in her chair. "My turn."

Evan sighed.

"To Renee," she said, sticking her tongue out at her sister's boyfriend. "For being totally cool and giving me space to make my own decisions. For helping me see that what I thought was judgment was really concern. But most of all, for becoming my friend. My best friend."

Renee felt the tears come. She was so happy with how her relationship with Michelle had changed. She'd always believed something good came from everything, no matter how bad. From their experience with Nick and Alan, they'd grown closer and were now able to relate to each other like never before.

"Listen," Evan said as he wrapped an arm around Renee. "Michelle is in love, Renee is a great sister, Chris is a hotshot investigative reporter. We're all happy. Let's eat."

Sitting in Evan's home with family and friends, Renee knew she couldn't be happier. There was only one thing nagging at her. Evan's impatience continued throughout the evening and she was curious of the cause. She waited until Chris and Michelle were in the kitchen cleaning up before asking him what was wrong.

"Wrong?" he asked, like he had no idea what she was referring to. "What could be wrong?"

"You seem a little distracted tonight." She led him to the living room sofa. "Something wrong?"

"That depends." He smiled coyly.

"Depends on what?" Renee was very intrigued by his smile. "What are you up to?"

"This," he said, reaching into his sport coat pocket.

Renee caught her breath when she saw the tiny velvet black box emerge from his hands. He'd given her jewelry before, but she knew this was more. Much more.

"Are you okay?" Evan asked in response to her reaction. "Remember to breathe. I don't want you to pass out before you answer."

"Shut up and open it!" She socked him on the arm.

Evan laughed as he opened the box and took the beautifully shimmering star-shaped diamond ring out. Renee could feel her heart beating a million times a second. She'd been looking forward to this moment for months. She knew it would come with Evan having expressed his desire to spend forever with her several times before, but its arrival was still overwhelming.

"Renee." Evan looked lovingly into her eyes. "I knew from the moment you stepped off that elevator that hot June afternoon that I'd come face to face with my match. We've been through more in five months than most people go through in a lifetime, and we've only come out stronger. So, if you're not too busy, I'd like to spend the next fifty years with you seeing how much more trouble we can get ourselves into. Then, after that's over, we can grow old together. What do you say?"

"I got nothing better to do." Renee shrugged, smiling through tears of joy and love as Evan slipped the ring on her finger.

She grabbed his face, claiming his lips with her own. Her soul laughed all over as he squeezed her in his arms, because she knew the happiness she felt now was only the beginning.